"How does this work? Bud Smith is a wild and wily bard, and his song about a songster is what the Beats might have written - if they'd had half the self-awareness and subtle humility Smith writes with." Amber Sparks, author of *May We Shed These Human Bodies*

"Bud Smith writes with the type of honesty that you would expect from a man who regularly uses a jackhammer (and shoots the shit with ex-convicts.) It's honesty that comes from knowing the downside of life intimately, while also being aware of the many pleasant surprises life can bring to your door-step— or to your bedroom." Aaron Dietz, author of *Super*

"F-250 shows literary everyman Bud Smith developing into a master storyteller full of Appetite For Destruction-era swagger and loser-illusion charm, and that's goddamn tough to beat."—Brian Alan Ellis, author of *King Shit*

"F-250 is like a nightmarish romp through an America you think you recognize, but might not want to. His characters are infectious, like the best opportunistic malignancies. Careful, you might devour F-250 in one swig. But don't. Read with finesse. Then weep." Robert Vaughan, editor of *Lost in Thought Magazine*

F-250

BUD SMITH

First Edition

Book cover photo, Mark Brunetti
Cover Design by Rae Buleri

Edited by Andrew "Ink" Feindt
Keith Baird
Mark Brunetti
Chris McEntyre

ISBN: 0996352651
EAN-13: 9780996352659

Published by Piscataway House Publications.
www.theidiommag.com

Manufactured in the United States of America

"Sometimes the love you have for somebody can fill a fifty-five gallon drum, but the love they have for you can't even fill a teacup."
— Pat Armstrong

"Stay true to the dreams of your youth."
— a fortune cookie I had yesterday

F-250

0

RIGHT BEFORE THE KID WITH THE BLOODY FACE appears, a glass smashes in the kitchen. Someone shouts. I do nothing. I barely live here. My things are still in the pickup. Seth is trashed. I'm still horribly sober.

This is my first day back. There's a purple Post-it note lying dusty on Seth's coffee table. The note is dated months earlier, when I was probably in Idaho or Utah or Arizona or on the moon. It says, simply, "Call Natalie."

Sure. That's exactly what I want to do with my life, call Natalie. But here I am, on the back deck, alone, in-between calling her and not calling her—a state of telephone limbo. I should be getting trashed with everyone else at the party at this dilapidated house.

I have a handwritten letter from long lost mom in Florida that says she's still not dead. She's feeling better all the time. "Come visit. Ha, blue water and long legged white birds, come, come." Signed: Mom. But I don't read that one anymore. I keep that one folded in my wallet. I hide that behind her photo.

Instead, I just stare at the lagoon, all green and uninviting. No blue water here. No long-legged white birds here. The sun is smothering things out. The biting flies are circling.

Inside the house, someone is fucking with the stereo and having trouble. I ignore their trouble. I ignore the yells from down the hall. I can't believe I'm gonna live here now. Somebody else staggers into the kitchen and checks an empty pizza box again.

Seth calls my name, "Lee! Get in here!" I fold the note about Natalie into a tiny paper airplane and toss it into the brackish water. It floats off. Purple. Floating. Leaving. Ducks weave between the floating bits of trash. One duck eats my purple Post-it note airplane. That duck is my favorite.

Seth sticks his head out the sliding glass door, "What you doing out here? Come on in. Gonna hit some shit."

"Not in the mood to hit any ..."

A scream claws up the side of the house. Screams always interest me. A girl. A car door slamming. I hop off the deck and trudge through the stones to look.

The kid with the bloody face falls against the screen door. His girl isn't far behind. His suit is bloody too, around the collar mostly. She's wearing a puffy black dress. I know her. Damn.

"Trish," I say. But she yells, and he falls. Comically drunk. I haven't seen Trish in ten years. He gets up. "Tim," she yells, "wait!"

He rips the screen door open, practically off the hinges, and collapses inside the house. People, strangers, stagger off the front lawn, where they are smoking cigarettes. They gawk in Trish's direction.

"Go home! Go home! Party's over!"

No-one budges. She kicks the recycling can over. Her high heel snaps. She falls to one knee.

"Go!"

I go around the back again and up on the deck. In the house, I can see the kid on the tile floor. More blood coming. Goddamn.

Everyone at the party is off the couch now and standing in the living room doorway looking into the small kitchen. I stand with them for a minute, with my mouth half open. The kid groans.

Seth staggers out of the room. "Fucking Feral, you alright?"

The kid pukes on the floor.

"Everyone out," Trish screams.

I don't move.

"Everyone!" She starts throwing things, whatever is around, things off the shelf of no value. Books. Movies. Toys. A girl narrowly dodges a trophy.

"Hey!"

People in the house scatter, pushing towards me at the back door.

"What happened?"

"Same thing that always happens, Seth," Trish says. "I'm done …"

Someone falls off the back deck, laughing. I say, "Come on, get going."

The smokers, finishing their beers, ignore me.

"Take that beer for the road," I say. "Cops are on the way. Paddy wagon. We're all going if we don't clear out."

The cops aren't coming.

I walk into the kitchen. The kid is unconscious now.

"I SAID EVERYBODY OUT," Trish screams at me. But she blinks and realizes who I am.

"Lee," she mutters.

I'm a magic trick. I've materialized out of nothing. Where have I been? What am I doing here?

"I live here now," I say.

"Oh thank god. Help me get him into the bath tub."

The tiles are slick from the kid's blood and puke but he looks heavier. Seth is terrible with blood, shrinks from it like so many people I've known in my life.

1

I DROVE A HEAVY DUTY F-250 PICKUP TRUCK. 1990. Blue. 92,000 hard miles. Loose, ineffective brakes.

There were a lot of crashes—into people, places, things, whatever was around. The truck was too heavy, I was weighed down, springs sagged, hills were too steep, roads were too slick—I couldn't control it.

The first time I crashed, it was into a woman on Route 9 in front of a gas station. The glove box flew open; Natalie's abandoned lipstick and mascara spilled on the floor. So did a mixtape she'd made with songs I used to love but couldn't play anymore.

The woman I rear-ended was at a red light in a minivan with personalized plates: CATLUVR. It was 8 a.m. The world was diabolical with black ice. My brakes did nothing.

The impact jarred her three feet into the intersection. I jumped out of my truck to see if she was okay. She cranked her window down and pegged me in the chest with a large styrofoam cup of coffee.

"Fuck off," she said.

I backed away, sticky with sugar. She dialed the police on a tiny flip phone. In the cab of the truck, I spit on my palms, rubbed my shirt, and waited.

The police showed up. I knew the one cop, Jay. We went to high school together. He had a funny mustache now.

"Did they make you grow that for the job?"

"Ah shit, look at you. Why you all wet?"

"Coffee," I said pointing at the minivan. The styrofoam cup skidded across the ice. Erratic wind.

He scratched his mustache. "Checks out." He didn't bother to ask me for any of my information. I was grateful. "Where've you been? Haven't seen you at the bars."

"California mostly," I said. "Just got back. Was gone a while."

"Well, welcome the fuck back. That lady was at a dead stop at the light?"

"Damn right."

"You sober? Never mind. Doesn't matter."

"It's 8 a.m. I'm sober."

"Sober enough to solve a Rubik's Cube? I have one in the car. Hold on, I'll get it."

"I don't drink, remember?"

"Sure. Straight edge in school. But you're not still, are you?"

I shrugged. "Yeah, guess so. Despite my environment."

"Tell me about it."

An ambulance came. Its lights flashing. A plump EMT popped the back door. Without saying a peep to the cops, CAT-LUVR climbed inside, laid herself horizontal on a stretcher, and clutched her calico cat. She was driven away —wordlessly.

We all thought that was pretty rude.

Eventually, I got a letter from her insurance company. I was being sued. Damage to the minivan. The driver's whiplash. There was even a vet bill for the poor calico cat.

Sued? Really? But what did I have anyway? No money in the bank, of course. Material possessions adding up to just a guitar, an amp, effect pedal stomp boxes, a drawer full of t-shirts, a wheelbarrow, some shovels, a couple boxes of random cassette tapes, stacks of paperback books. Nothing anyone would want.

The F-250 was a dangerous P.O.S., but I liked it. It was jacked up high over the road. Four-wheel drive. Over-sized swamp tires. Rusted out holes in the sheet metal, like gremlins were devouring it in the unguarded night. No heat. No AC. Cassette deck.

The guy who owned it before me had plastered the back bumper with rebel flag stickers. I scraped them off with razorblades and replaced them with stickers Seth gave me from the record store where he worked.

Work. I used the truck for work ... mostly. Usually, the bed of the truck was full of stone and dirt. It was awkward to control, so I hit everything with it. Whenever I got distracted and stopped concentrating on the road it was—bang: the back of somebody's car crumbling in, dirt and shovels and concrete jumping up in the bed of my F-250.

So I drove nervously.

A few weeks after I met Feral, with his face all ripped open, and barely two months of living back in New Jersey following my near escape, I was cruising in my truck towards the Atlantic Ocean, a heavy load in the bed.

I'd just finished a job building a set of concrete steps at the studio where my band was recording. It was a barter job: masonry work for studio time, so the truck was weighed down with work—rocks, sand, a few bags of leftover cement, my wheelbarrow, and shovels—but also play: my 50 watt tube amp, my guitar, cables. I was on my way to play a show. My side project, Ottermeat, was playing at Spider Bar, always a great time.

I turned off Route 37 east onto 70 towards Princeton Ave. The nectar of the world was thick and heavy, butterflies everywhere slapping against the glass. I almost had to put the windshield wipers to clear them. The cassette deck began to eat the tape. I desperately tried to eject it.

I rumbled forward, screwing with the tape. When I looked back at the road, it was too late to stop. A line of cars waited ahead at a red light that was usually a perpetually blinking yellow. I stomped on the brakes. The F-250 skidded, fish-tailed. Rubber melted on asphalt.

At impact, rocks and sand rained down. The rear end of a white Lincoln Continental caved in horribly. Its frame twisted. The tail pipe pushed up beneath the under carriage. Fluids leaked out. I felt sick.

The drawbridge was up. In all my life spent living in the area, I'd never seen the drawbridge up on Princeton Ave. Well, there it was, and there I was—another accident. A line of cars pulled up behind, blocked me in.

The door of the Continental swung open unevenly. An old man, a true geezer, stepped out and scratched his baked potato-shaped head. He wore sky-blue polyester pants, Velcro shoes, and a striped polo that accentuated his man boobs and turkey neck. This man hunched over, studied the demolition, and ran one of his leathery palms over the damage as if he could repair it by feel.

Remembering the coffee cup incident from a few years before, I stayed in my truck. The damage was b-b-b-bad. This was it for me. I was already broke. I was already getting sued by a whiplashed lady with a psychologically traumatized calico cat. They had me.

People waiting for the drawbridge got out of their vehicles too. They wanted to get a look for themselves at the show. They stretched and paced around, glancing over at us. We were high entertainment.

Then the old man with the baked potato-shaped head spun around and looked at me with soft eyes. I waved sickly, mouthed, "I'm sorry."

He smiled, waved back, offhandedly gave me a thumbs. "Forget about it. It's nothing." He got back into his Lincoln, closed the door. His bumper crashed down towards the asphalt. Nothing was done.

The worst part was to follow, we sat for ten more minutes like that, the drawbridge hanging up in the air, unseen boats possibly passing underneath. No-one knew.

I was sweating like a madman. The other people, the spectators, were all out of their vehicles, gawking and pointing. I had to sit there like a pariah basking in my careless shame.

And it was manifested so clearly. My ineptitude. I could see it right before my eyes. The rear bumper of the Lincoln hung on by a thread.

A guy walked up to my window, he was chewing gum and stunk like cologne.

"You really whacked that guy," he said.

"He said it's nothing," I said to the concerned citizen.

"S'nothing? I don't think so! You gotta call the cops."

"Zero good ever came from calling the cops," I said, glaring at him. He backed away and spit his gum out into the grass. He got into his bright yellow Geo Tracker, gripped the steering wheel with white knuckles.

We were, all of us, white knuckled, sitting still. Another five eternal minutes. Until the drawbridge descended. The light turned green. And we began to move again. Very carefully.

2

I GOT TO SPIDER BAR LATE. NARROW ALLEY. Cats leaping from overflowing garbage cans. I pulled around to the rear door plastered with hundreds of bright band stickers left there as a rite of passage.

Inside, I could hear the bartender, Gail, talking too loud.

Seth stepped out of the back door, beer in hand, a menthol cigarette hanging out of his mouth. A mess of curly brown hair. Ripped jeans. RUSH 2112 t-shirt.

"Lee!" Seth slouched, lighting his cigarette.

"Sorry I'm late," I said.

Seth shrugged. "Nobody here anyway. It's dead inside."

"I was in an accident," I said. "I caused a wreck."

"Another one? Holy smokes ..."

I walked to the back of the truck and dropped the tailgate. The jolt of the impact had ruptured a bag of cement; my amp and my guitar case were covered in dust.

"Oh shit!"

I yanked my amp out and tried to brush it off. It was no use. The dust was sucked deep into the speaker fabric. Seth tried to hand me his beer.

"Thanks, but no."

I sat down on the steps still a little shaken from the collision I'd caused. He pulled my guitar case out of the bed of the Ford and dusted it off.

"Drawbridge was up. Didn't see traffic was stopped," I said.

"Where?"

"Princeton Ave."

"There's a drawbridge on Princeton Ave.?!"

"That's what I said."

Seth grinned. I stared at my hands. Half my fingernails were black, purple, brown—blood trapped underneath the nail from being crushed by rocks, bricks, small boulders.

Masonry and playing guitar are at odds. I was nervous I was gonna break my hand one day. Then what would I do? Playing guitar, writing songs, playing shows ... that was my life.

"Come on," he said. "I need another beer."

I took his soft, pink, record store clerk hand. He yanked me to my feet. We went inside, lugging my music gear.

Spider Bar is dark, stale, ominous. A true dive. Five guys, probably from the warehouse down the block, in dirty work clothes just like mine, were leaning on the bar. They were screwing around with Gail, a former G.L.O.W. (Gorgeous Ladies of Wrestling) girl from Bayonne who's now overweight and in her mid-fifties. A wall of cigarette smoke hung in the air like a fog machine was on.

Seth's drums, a 10-piece kit, were already set up on the little stage. It gleamed in the spotlight. The only bright thing in the place. The cymbals emitted a golden hum.

All around the drums, suspended from the ceiling, were ancient Halloween decorations. Plastic skeletons. Bleeding skulls. Big, fanged, 8-legged fluorescent monsters so thick with dust that I couldn't even tell what color they used to be.

We set my gear down on the stage just as Aldo rolled through the back door. He was managing bands at the time.

"Morning, Lee." He motioned to the pool table at the center of the bar. It had to be moved to the far corner to open up room for people if they showed up to see any of the bands. The pool table was off level anyway, nobody played it.

Aldo, stocky, with a big silver beard, shaved head, Dickie pants, full sleeve tattoos. He was 58 years old, I think, unless the birthday candles I put on his last cake were wrong.

We helped him move the pool table. He was gravelly voiced and groggy. It was eight o' clock at night, but he'd just woken up. He slept in a rail car apartment above the bar. Yeah, I lived up there too for a while with him, a roommate of sorts, a stepson of sorts. Five and a half years. I knew the deal.

Aldo leaned in to give me a quick hug. I faked like I'm gonna slap him in the nuts. He grabbed my hair and put me in a headlock. "You little shit," he said. "Hey, Seth, should I break his neck?"

"FINISH HIM," Seth yelled.

"Aldo, let me go," I said. "You need new deodorant. You reek."

"Such is the cost of living: smelling bad, smelling bad things. What's new?" he asked in a louder voice that seemed directed mostly at me.

"Nada," I say.

"Nada, sure, sure. I bet."

He's a little sore that I wasn't his roommate anymore, that I was living with Seth and Feral now. But I couldn't sit at the table up there and drink with him. I didn't wanna wind up like my early dead dad and my long gone mom.

"This fucker do the dishes with you guys?" he asks Seth.

"Dishes? No. Guy's a scumbag. A savage. Filthy." Seth gave Aldo a fist bump.

"You maniacs still call the band Ottermeat?"

"Yeah," I said, we changed it so often that it was hard to keep track.

"Bringing anybody tonight to see you?"

"Hope so."

Aldo said, "First band canceled. Flaked. I'll be doing a reading. Then you guys play ... half hour or whatever. Then, Waxslut." Aldo was a poet. He was gonna read some of his stuff like he always did.

"Alright."

I sat down at the bar. Seth bought me a beer, but I didn't plan on drinking it. He's persistent. Didn't believe I'd quit drinking. It pained him greatly that I'd lasted these three months so far. I tried to give Gail a tip for the beer I won't touch. She took my dollar and slid me back four quarters. She pointed to the jukebox.

"Pick some good ones," she said.

Big lips. Blue eye shadow. A wall of a woman. Actually, that was her wrestling name, The Bayonne Wall.

Sometimes they played VHS tapes of Gail's matches back when she was on TV. Her signature move was jumping off the top turnbuckle and smashing down onto her victim of the moment—smothering her with her balloon boobs. The crowd loved it. 1984. I was just 3 years old. Now, Gail's balloon boobs were fatal blimps. On a rowdy night, everybody had to do shots off them. She required it.

I picked some songs on the box.

As the weird music starts, the worker guys from the warehouse stood up. Happy hour was over. Beer is back to full price. They couldn't stomach the songs I'd picked.

Then the bar truly was empty. I had that sour feeling in my stomach: guilt. No-one was gonna come see us play. Oh man, there's not much worse than that. Plus the club owner would give you shit, and you don't get to play again. Forget the money. You're not gonna make any money playing at these bars in this town.

Aldo sat down at the bar, leaned in to me, said low, "How's mom?"

"Haven't heard from her—still."

"Ah sonofabitch," he said. "I hope she's okay."

"The number's the same upstairs," I said, "and down here."

"True."

"Besides, who's okay in the world?"

"Goddamn you're wise." He grabbed my hair and tugged. I didn't pull away. I just smiled at my sweating beer.

"Got you one," I said and handed him the bottle.

Aldo turned and started talking to Seth. I had a hard time with my feelings towards Aldo. A part of me wanted to kill him. Another part of me was proud of him for cleaning up, for getting off drugs. The other part of me wanted to crack him in his head with a bar stool. It'd always been my suspicion that he'd been the one that got her into the shit that'd crushed her life and sent her away, far away. Who's responsible for anybody else's life though?

I got up and started setting up my amp on the stage. I had tons of guitar pedals. Fuzz. Delay. Wah. Flanger. Noise boxes for making havoc. I unzipped the guitar from its case, and the headstock came tumbling out, suspended by the nickel wound strings. It was broken. Totally snapped off.

I was in shock. I picked up the headstock like I'd be able to just stick it back on, but that's not how these things work.

Seth came over, "Oh no ..."

I cursed and kicked my pedals around as if it mattered. Seth said he's got an idea. After getting some more quarters from Gail, he goes down the rotten hallway by the bathroom and gets on the pay phone. He called Ethan.

I sat on the stage, in shock. Some college chicks came in off the street. They were from the dorm up the block, but it was cool 'cause Gail didn't check IDs. I used to drink here when I was 16, but I had a beard. I looked over at them, but they didn't pay me any mind; they were trying to order margaritas from Gail.

"We don't have that kinda stuff here."

"Oh, then ... apple martini?"

Gail pointed at the single draft beer handle.

Tension rose to a pinnacle over this decision.

Seth lurched over. Big Bird. He's got the same hair cut.

"Alright, Ethan's gonna bring his guitar for you to use."

"That fucker."

"What? He's helping you out."

"You probably had to threaten him."

"Well, kinda."

Ethan is the lead singer in our "main" band, The Bedspins. The one that was gonna make us famous. Haha, what a thing. I didn't get along with Ethan for a few reasons. I put up with him because he was a real good singer. Believe me, there was nobody better in the area. I hung a hundred thousand flyers, stapled them to telephone poles, stuck them under windshield wipers, tacked them to bulletin boards anywhere I could find a bulletin board. Well, anywhere but the college. I refuse to go there. Fuck all that noise.

I sat back down at the bar and drank a Coke. I try to talk to the college girls, but I don't make much headway.

I said, "You gonna stick around for the show?"

"No," all three said in unison.

"What if I stand on my head and drink this Coke?"

"Why would you do that?"

"My band is playing. Sucks to play for no-one."

They sipped their drinks unhappily.

"Ah fuck it, never mind. I don't know why I'm bothering."

It got worse when Aldo stood up on the stage and started speaking to us all from the microphone.

"Thanks for coming out to Spider Bar. I'm Aldo, this is my place." He waved to the girls, the only patrons. They didn't care one bit. "Okay, we got some live music for you all tonight, but first, let's do some poetry. You ladies look like poetry lovers! Buckle up. Here it comes." Aldo began to holler and roil as he read free verse in a demonic, gravelly voice to the six of us.

"Cryogenic hallucination of a paycheck and Uncle Sam riding a unicorn blowing coagulated bubbles 'cause you think you deserve your money back. Every day I'm in a world of shit, ankle deep and there's never any reason to watch TV, get your plastic injection dildo and aim your rockets up your own ass space/time traveler voodoo …"

The girls got up to leave halfway through their beers, and Aldo just kept rambling and rambling all his nonsense. He was drunk, spouting off beneath a leather pork pie hat with spittle in his beard. Half an hour I sat there listening with Seth. He didn't even wanna go outside and smoke a cig because he thought it'd be rude.

Finally, the door opened. In walked Ethan. Designer leather jacket. Spiked hair. That was a recent development. His hair used to be down past his shoulders.

Ethan had a girl with him. Italian. Dark eyes. Long hair pulled back. Maybe 20. She's not only my type, she's everybody's type.

"Bull dykes manning pleasure cannons," yelled Ando with his eyes shut, "and worrisome kids afraid of anything that's not a computer, I got your answers right here!" He grabbed his crotch and faked a long moan. That was the end of his reading. The long moan.

"Gail, baby! I need a tissue," Aldo said, bowing.

"Big crowd tonight," Ethan said spitefully. He was pissed we played on the side without him.

"Sure, yeah. Empty house," Seth said, shrugging.

Ethan didn't introduce the girl, but she was giving me the eye. So I stood up and said, "Lee," while holding out my busted up hand to her.

"Denise," she said, smiling.

Ethan warned me that I had to be real careful with his guitar, because it was a collector's item—irreplaceable. I just nod. Guys got six guitars, doesn't even play any of them. Each one cost a boatload more than my truck.

Gail gave everybody beers and handed Denise some quarters for the jukebox. Denise tried to find something to play, but she was lost.

"What's good?" Denise was looking at me.

"Any button on there. Close your eyes and push."

The headlining band streamed in. They had real equipment. There was a gaggle of people with them too. Thank God. There was ten people in the bar right before we were about to go on stage.

I was so relieved. I was happy. An audience … finally.

I took a look around, counting as we were up on the little stage: twelve people. Oh … fourteen people, counting Aldo and Gail. That's great!

I took Ethan's guitar out of the case. It was beautiful. But as I looked down, I realized, just as Seth started the count off on his sticks, that Ethan's guitar is strung upside down. He's left-handed.

"I can't play this," I said, but no-one could hear me over the drums. There's no microphone.

I tried my best to fake it through the songs, but it was pretty obvious that shit was all wonky. It was just me and Seth up there; I didn't have any place to hide. I turned all my pedals on and just made some swirling noise that circled all around the bar.

Ethan and Denise left after the first song. The headlining act went outside and stood on the street, smoking cigarettes and drinking beers away from our noise.

Aldo and Gail watched from the bar and even clapped when we were done playing. They were the king and queen of the underground and thought everything was art. I love them like the mother and father I never had.

Seth

HE WAS A SUPERNATURAL DRUMMER. That's how people knew him. He kept time and backbeat in line with the movement of tides. Passing comets. The shifting of tectonic plates beneath the surface of the magnetic earth.

Seth, to me, was the kid whose dad died when he was six. The guy who had three cats, who had a Star Wars X-wing poster hanging on his closet door, who used to sometimes buy two boxes of Lucky Charms, separate all the marshmallows from the first, add all those marshmallows to the second, and throw away the remaining cereal.

At Lagoon House, he usually fell asleep on the pink love seat—his long legs hanging off the ripped arm, stuffing spilling out and making the back of his knees itch. He was in love with flea markets, swap meets, comic book shows. He was always in corduroy pants or corduroy shorts. I figured his diapers must have been made of corduroy too. He drank beer like it was water and had a coke problem that we never talked about. He thought it was a secret.

Seth claimed to hate hippies, but every girl he ever dated was either a hippie or had just been in a tie-dye shirt when they met. Case in point: Shannon, who he couldn't stand to be around. He smoked everything: gift wrap, newspapers, whatever was lying around. He was serious and sensitive and had raised himself really.

"Mom dumped me at Aunt Kathy's and split. Nevada. Carson City, Nevada. No idea what's there. Just her."

"Well, man. At least you got a brother." I meant me.

"True that."

He also had a real brother. Mark. Yeah, Mark who worked for the government and lived in Chicago. I'd never heard of anybody who worked for the government and lived in Chicago.

"He's a spook. CIA. Like James Bond but with curlier hair, and he drives a green Volvo."

Seth counted the entire time he played drums. You couldn't lose him if you tried. He couldn't handle college though. Most people I knew were like that.

He always wanted to watch My Cousin Vinny. We had a VHS that was almost worn out. Tracking was horrible. Warped, garbled sound. He had the hots for Marisa Tomei.

He was good at Tetris, Dr. Mario, Othello. Drove a maroon 1990 Nissan Sentra that was barely big enough to fit all his drums. He played real-life Tetris with that car and those drums, stuffing in the kick drum, toms, snare, and cymbals. It was amazing to watch. If he had a full car smashed solid with his drums and you needed a ride, he'd say, "Dude, there's plenty of room for you."

Somehow you'd get in there and it was impossible but somebody else would need a ride too and Seth would say, "Oh! Come on, climb in. We'll get you in here somehow."

He was good people, but when he was too drunk or too high he changed. He became a different person. You'd forget it was a thing that could happen, but he'd be sitting across from you, usually Indian style, his head tilted back a little, looking out through the slits of his eyes, and he'd say," KISS is the best band that's ever existed." It'd turn your blood cold.

"Not this again."

"Yes," he'd grin and then bounce out of the room. When he came back, he'd have a KISS album. It could be on vinyl or cassette or CD. It didn't matter. Whatever was available to play the KISS, he'd come back with that. Guy had their music tucked in all kinds of secret spots. He traveled with it. Trunk of his car. Suitcases. Hidden under mattresses in hotel rooms.

Seth would tell me why Ace Frehley, the Spaceman or Space Ace, was the most amazing guitar player as Detroit Rock City got turned up as loud as it'd go. You'd just have to sit there and deal with it. Otherwise, he'd get mad as hell, almost fight you over it. So I'd just nod my head for a little bit and listen to Seth iterate why KISS was such an important band, if not the most important band, in the history of rock 'n' roll.

You couldn't make fun of their makeup or say their songs had no art. For your own safety, you had to pretend they're "alright."

It was only because Seth was so high or drunk. When he was sober, I don't think he'd ever put KISS on once—not even once. He'd cross the threshold with that one last slug of whiskey, that last pill, then … KISS, all KISS, for about twenty minutes. Then he'd go puke for a while. When he came back, everything was fine. You could talk about something else.

A theory I had, and one I've never proven, was that his dad, who'd died when Seth was little, had been a fan—a true fanatic. Maybe a roadie. Maybe he even died on tour with KISS. I thought that the crate of KISS records in Seth's room had come from him, this mysterious ghost father KISS fanatic, who even now was painted up in Heaven with white grease makeup and giant, knee-high, silver platform boots.

But later, I found out Seth had bought all the records at Englishtown flea market while I was away in California.

3

LAGOON HOUSE WAS TRASHED. DIRTY LAUNDRY. SPAGHETTI PLATES. Gunked-up silverware. Pizza boxes. Beer cans. Milk jugs.

We couldn't keep the place in any kind of order. Strange degenerates came over almost every night, partying with us, leaving an army of empty bottles lined along every flat surface in and around the place. It was the party house.

There were too many objects crammed into the tiny bungalow. It was a claustrophobic obstacle course. To get in the front door, I had to climb over Seth's drum kit and my amp and then snake through a maze of cardboard boxes packed with vinyl records, VHS tapes, toys, paperback books, ancient concert posters—rolled up and scotch taped.

That junk all belonged Feral. That's how he made the legal portion of his money; he was a scavenger. He sold whatever he could at the flea market on Saturday and Sunday mornings.

Feral's claim to local fame was that in 1998 he accidentally burnt down Commando Video, the local VHS rental shop. Back then, he rented a room above the store and passed out in bed with a joint. The curtain went up in flames. As the fire spread, he jumped out of the second story window and landed on the sidewalk. All those movies downstairs melted. He's walked with a limp ever since.

I walked out of my room, kicking one of the boxes out of my path. Some of the VHS tapes in it were half melted, remnants of that long ago fire. It didn't matter. Feral was still trying to sell them at the flea market.

"You got too much junk," I called through two rooms.

"Maybe," he said.

Feral was sitting on the ripped-to-shreds love seat, smoking a cigarette and watching Twin Peaks with the sound off while listening to Brian Eno's Music for Airports.

Lagoon House had a haunted, ethereal feel, as if time was stuck in heavy slime.

Feral waved, "Sup, sleepyhead?"

"I killed Laura Palmer," I said.

"Don't ruin it for me!"

I glanced at the clock on the wall. It was upside down, hands all wrong, but I could tell it was 2 p.m.

Feral still had about 100 stitches in his head from the first night I'd met him. He saw me looking and said, "They're coming out soon. Then I'll be purty again."

"Good."

"Yeah, I'll be so handsome. I'll be so suave again. I'll even let you blow me. It'll be great."

"Saying shit like that to people is how you got those stitches to begin with."

"That's some heavy-duty wisdom, man. Really."

"You'll thank me one day."

Seth was passed out on the other couch, his long legs hanging over the side. One foot had a black sock, the other foot was bare.

I checked the fridge. It made me think of Antarctica. Soulless. White. Empty. I noticed there was a box of Lucky Charms cereal on top, but the milk had gone bad. It was cottage cheese now. I poured the cereal into a red solo cup.

"Damn," I said, realizing Seth had taken all the marshmallows out and left the crappy bits of plain, tasteless cereal. In life, marshmallows are needed.

Feral laughed at something. It could have been anything or nothing. I walked into the living room and plopped down on the filthy shag rug. Dust shot up like sparks.

Feral was shirtless, belly hanging out like Buddha with the wrong answers. He was greasy. Gap-toothed. Kept rubbing his face. He's been up all night grinding his teeth and jaw, chewing on crazy straws with pastel stripes that sat in a pile on the table next to his green Martian bong. He was like a big stupid kid that couldn't get out of the 8th grade. How had be made it 32 years?

"Bad news, maing," Feral said looking up, "Johnny DiSanto came over here this morning. Pissed. Guy wanted to rumble."

"I don't blame him," said Seth with both eyes closed, "You haven't paid him rent in four months. What'd he say?"

"We gotta be out by the end of the month. Out, out," Feral said. "Up the road, off in the distance, into the sunset."

"Ahhh shit."

Seth stuck his head up, "But he said that last month too."

We nodded. It was hard to tell how serious the situation was. DiSanto, our landlord, was a state trooper who'd been kicked off the force for some kind of shady goings on. Drugs. Underage girls. More drugs.

He was Feral's high-school buddy though, so the two of them had some kind of weird link up. Total cahoots. Pills mostly. Coke. Hash. Weed ... whatever was around. DiSanto supplied, Feral sold it. I turned a blind eye.

Things were grim. Supposedly, Lagoon House was up for sale, even had an interested buyer. But the deal kept getting delayed, so we stopped paying rent.

At first, DiSanto didn't seem to care. He'd just drop by and say, in a real stern tone, "House is about to get bought. You guys better start packing." He'd kick a cardboard box full of VHS tapes and laugh. Then Feral would pack a bowl, and we'd all smoke out of the green Martian bong, put a record on to ease the tension, and pretend we were all friends.

But that morning brought a change of tone. Alarm bells were beginning to go off.

"We'll be out on our ass."

"Sleepin' in the marsh."

"They'll level this house, build a three-story Crackerjack McMansion like the one across the street," Seth said.

"Let them tear it down. Who cares?" Feral said, "We'll rent a place that's not such a dump. With a Jacuzzi."

Sure we would. I had visions of winding up on Aldo's couch again. My previous experiences had been enough. Truth is we'd probably just disband in separate directions. Seth never had money, nothing enough for rent. My attempts at getting him side cash by dragging him along to work with me had failed. He always spent it on the wrong stuff.

Seth sat up, his hair frizzy and wild.

"We're going to L.A. anyway," Seth said.

I looked down at the carpet. I don't get off on fairy tales.

Feral snickered.

Seth changed the subject, tired of fighting the disbelief of the naysayers. "Talked to my bro, Mark. My aunt died."

"Oh, sorry," Feral said.

"Yeah," Seth sighed.

"Kathy?" I asked. "Oh fuck... How?"

"Her heart."

"The one with the house in upstate New York?" Feral asked.

"Yeah," he said. "That's my favorite place in the whole world. Used to play with my bro there every summer. Now, I gotta drive up to her viewing on Wednesday. It's way up, top of New York State. The Sentra is running on empty."

Feral said, "You got gas money, bro?"

"Nahhh, that's the thing."

Feral reached under the bong into his metal cash box, took out some bills, passed a pathetic fold to Seth. At least it was something.

"Thanks, man."

"Don't sweat it," Feral said.

I scooped my wallet off the table and gave Seth some of my pathetic cash too.

"I'll pay you guys back. My brother Mark is flying in from Chicago. He's flush."

I focused in on the mess all around us. This place really did need a wrecking ball.

I'd fallen asleep early. They'd sat out in the living room until dawn, all spun out, watching TV, talking about music and which cartoon characters would give the best blow-jobs. The pros and cons to everything. The two of them could talk about everything and nothing.

It was hard to remember that they'd fought.

But most people I know back home have been in fist fights with one another at some point. If they haven't, they should.

Seth nearly broke his hand on Feral's thick skull. It still gave me a headache when I think about the haymaker he'd hit him with. See, Feral'd mistaken Seth for somebody else. (Don't ask me who. I have no idea.) Outside the diner at 2 a.m., he started laying some serious shit on him. I watched Seth come unhinged, lunge at Feral, and beat the piss out of him.

That's what happens when you say to somebody, "Your mother's a whore," and it's true. They beat your ass in the parking lot. Then they go inside and eat disco fries, their knuckles all bloody and dripping on the placemat—local businesses stained red. Hands shaking, fractured. Unable to play drums for two weeks: an eternity.

Afterwards, months later, they found common ground, lots of common ground, when the misunderstanding got cleared up after the two ran into each other at a woods party out in the sand pits underneath the water tower with the high tension power lines humming.

Feral had this house on the lagoons and needed room-mates. I, too, was on my ass after things had gone sour with Natalie. Somehow, we all wound up living together. I munched on my stale cereal unpleased with life.

"Gotta break up with Shannon," Seth said.

"Yes, you certainly do. That girl sucks."

"Agreed," I said.

"What do you think is the worst thing about her?" Seth asked.

"Hard to say."

"It might be a sum average of everything about her."

"She doesn't suck it," Seth said, "That's the big one."

"Ba dum dum," Feral said. "I'll be here all week. Try the roast beef, motherfucker."

The phone started to ring. Except the phone was actually a duck. So it didn't ring, it quacked. Seth leaned over and picked up the duck's body and spoke into the beak. It was Ethan. He was coming over. Seth slid the duck down on the receiver.

"That kid's coming here?" Feral asked skeptically.

"I got his guitar," I clarified. "He's coming to get it back."

I told him about my car crash, how the neck of my guitar got snapped, how Ethan had bailed us out for a show we were playing by lending one of his Gibson Les Pauls—like, a five thousand dollar guitar Ethan's rich-ass dad had given him.

Feral interrupted all this. "Bring me your broken guitar. I can fix it, for real."

"Nahhh," I said. "That's alright."

"How hard could it be? I just need some glue and a clamp or something."

"Glue? A clamp? Getta outta here."

"I don't think you could fix a peanut butter and jelly sand-wich," Seth said.

"I'm handy, really. I'm sure I could fix it."

"You're outta your mind," Seth said. "Fix your zipper. It's down."

Feral snorted, "For you to start sucking." He passed me

the big book of CDs, said, "Lee, make yourself useful. Pick something. I need some music. Can't listen to this motherfucking mouth breather any longer."

"I'm not a mouth breather!" Seth said.

"The fuck you're not."

I started flipping through the book. Two hundred CDs, and I couldn't find anything I wanted to put on.

"Sabbath?" I asked.

"Masters of Reality, please."

I flipped around until I found it and stuck it in the player. Track two had a nasty scratch in it and skipped, so I went right to the third track.

They began playing Grand Theft Auto on PlayStation. I took a ride to Wawa to get myself a cup of coffee and a pork roll, egg, and cheese sandwich.

Outside, I took a good look at the house. We were the last house on a dead-end street. Marsh on all sides, except the backyard, which faced a small lagoon that led narrowly out to the bay. Boats bobbed all down the line of bulkheads … except for ours.

It was a puke-green bungalow. There were stupid sharp red rocks on the lawn; you couldn't walk barefoot on it. Obscuring all the dirty windows except for mine were overgrown pine shrubs with juniper berries. Up on the roof, our weathervane, a rusted rooster who Feral had loving named "Captain Cock," spun slowly even though I couldn't feel any wind.

Yeah, tear this place down, please.

Feral's black conversion van, which sat in the driveway, was painted with red stripes and accents to resemble the A-Team mobile. It leaked oil into the earth, one drip at a time, feeding dinosaur ghosts.

Out back was a half-rotten deck that ran along the water. There were green head flies out there most of the time that'd land on your flesh, bite down.

We didn't have our tiny outboard motor boat anymore. Feral had taken Trish out one night and sunk it somewhere. No-one knew. They floated back clutching onto a Power Puff Girls boogie board.

When I got back to the house, Ethan's white BMW 5 Series was sitting in the red stones by the mailbox. Denise, his girl, was inside. She was listening to one of our demos. That was Ethan for ya. Denise didn't have any makeup on. Her hair was pulled back instead of down. She still looked impossibly good.

I walked over to her window. She turned the music down. She had on short shorts and a low-cut tank top. All her nails were painted hot pink. Her neck was tan, a gold cross hung on a chain.

"Hey," she said. "Sorry we left so quick from your show."

"No biggie," I said. "You didn't miss much."

She nodded. "I had to meet a kid for some stuff." She tapped her heavenly nose. "You live here?"

"This is my place, yeah." I pointed at my window.

"Cool," she said, smiling. "Your own place. I still crash with my parents between semesters. It's a bummer."

I invited her in the house, but she said, "Aw, thanks. I'm okay out in the car." Ethan's orders I assumed. He was good for that kinda thing. Later on, I saw Ethan tell Denise, on two or three occasions, "Babe, wait in the car."

I walked in the house. Ethan was sitting in the kitchen with the lights off, looking all serious and not-to-be-fucked-with as he drummed his fingers on our kitchen table.

Seth and Feral were still playing video games; they didn't even notice he was there. (Or noticed and didn't want to be bothered.)

"Hey, I came for my guitar," Ethan said.

"Sure." I got it from my room for him. He opened the case right away. Inspected the whole thing. Feral came out in the middle of this.

"Cut your hair I see, Ethel."

There's nothing that Ethan hates more than being called Ethel.

"Yup, that's correct," Ethan said. He didn't want to talk about something so painfully obvious as the fact that he had gotten a haircut.

"Why'd you cut it?" Feral asked. "You used to be so … metal. Hahaha. Now you look like you're in a boy band."

"Why don't you go take a shower?"

"You can take one with me if that's what you're asking. I'll wash your back for you."

"You're trash. You know that? Trash."

"Hey, man, get the fuck outta my house," Feral said.

"Was leaving anyway," Ethan said, scooping his guitar case up as he went through the screen door without even saying goodbye.

As his BMW peeled away, some of the sharp red rocks slapped against the vinyl siding.

"That kid's a pussy," Feral said.

I shrugged.

Seth said, "Maybe, but we're going to LA 'cause of him."

That was the thing. Ethan had a connection. Connections, really. We thought we could get to where we wanted to go. All we had to do was put up with his babyish bullshit for just a little while longer. Then we'd be in California.

"What's the big deal with L.A.?" Feral asked.

"I just think good things will happen there," Seth replied.

"I've been there," I said. "California is quite something to see."

"What do they have there that we don't?"

"They have Heuvos Rancheros," I said.

"What's that," Seth said.

"I'll show you when we get there."

"Heuvos Rancheros…" Feral said as he scratched his chin, stoned and transfixed. He said it again, just under his breath, as if I was talking about the city of lost gold.

4

MY ROOM WAS BUILT OUT OF THE OFF-KILTER BOOKCAS-
ES and the books inhabiting them: used paperbacks,
stacks of them, everywhere. Bookcases, bookcases,
and more bookcases. They were my only furniture. They lined
every wall. I was boxed in by gray Sheetrock that sweated reck-
lessly.

One night, I had my record player going as I lay on the bare
mattress on the floor, without a box-spring, and read In Watermelon Sugar by Richard Brautigan. There was a knock on my
window. A visitor out there in the violet tremoring night.

I peeked out through the blinds. It was Denise. I opened
the window. You'd have done the same thing. My window, specifically, was exactly the kind of window built to let a girl like
Denise in.

"Hey, saw your light on," she said all lit up in the moonlight, her eyes glowing. The diamond stud in her nose and the
six earrings in her right ear caught the light. She was a wayward
animal looking for a break from the wild life.

"Yeah, I'm up. For sure," I said.

"I'm glad." She stretched her little hands to climb in my
window. I helped boost her in.

"You coulda just came in the front door," I said after the
fact.

She laughed. "It's cooler this way. Like all stealth and shit."

I didn't have any other furniture in my room, so Denise sat
down on the rug. She was wearing painted-on jeans and a shirt

with a wolf on it—the fabric slashed away as if that wolf was trying to get at her body.

"Man, it looks like you live in a library, but that's not a bad thing ... ya know?"

"I used to go to the library all the time to try and meet girls when I was like twelve."

"Did it work?" she asked out of the side of her mouth, all slick.

"No, they were all at the mall," I admitted.

She laughed. "Yeah, ha, that's where I was, for sure. Hanging by the fountain, watching people throw in nickels and quarters, chewing gum, blowing bubbles."

I offered her a chair from the kitchen. She rocked in place on the carpet, bit her lip, said, "Nahhhh, I'm good on this hard floor. I like the floor."

"Okay."

"I like your house. My house is fucked up," she said. "My parents are always fighting. You're lucky to, like, have your own place."

I knew her dad. Everyone knew who he was. He owned a waste removal service: Santalucia Disposal. I saw the trucks all over. Santalucia. Santalucia. The family was loaded. $$$. Trucks and crews of big dudes hanging on the backs of those garbage trucks in yellow neon shirts that read Santalucia.

"You're welcome to hang here, no sweat," I said, "as long as you want."

"I miss my dorm." Denise had a habit of sucking on her own silver tongue piercing. It was distracting. "Jesus, I can't believe I'm saying that. When I was at school, I couldn't wait to get home. Now that I'm home, I can't wait for summer to be over so I can get back."

"Yeah, huh?"

"It's weird getting this freedom from your parents," she said, "and then you come back and they treat you like a little kid again. I'm not a kid at all. They have no idea."

"I bet they have more of an idea than you realize," I said.

"Man, seriously, look at all these books! You must be smart as hell."

"Oh, yeah. No." I pointed all around. "See all these? Fiction. It's all fake. There's not a single fact in any of these books. It's all make-believe."

She laughed nervously. "What-ever. I can't concentrate long enough to read anything."

I studied her. She had nautical stars on the inside of both wrists. She said that was part of the problem with her parents: they didn't like that she'd come home from Rutgers with three tattoos.

"I wanna get both my arms sleeved out," she said, nodding excitedly.

"They'd flip, right?"

She shrugged. "Hard to say. I got three that they've seen. There's more."

She said one of her guy friends worked at a tattoo parlor in New Brunswick and that she could get all the work she wanted done for free.

"He doesn't charge me jack. I pay him in trade."

"How so?"

"Oh, I got sneaky talents, kid," she stared at me, through me.

"Don't worry about your parents. They'll get used to you doing your own thing. This is just an adjustment period."

She asked me why I wasn't going to college. I told her I wouldn't know what I'd even study if I went. If I had the money.

"I work for myself," I said.

"That's dope."

"Yeah, I think it's alright. I find jobs ..."

"Doing what?"

"I got a job I'm starting soon. Gonna build a waterfall into someone's swimming pool."

"Oh, that's so sick!"

"Yeah, the job is inside the pool. You know, I just stay in the pool and build it from the inside. Just floating. Somebody hands me rocks."

"I want one! Build me one."

"Anything you want. Just show me where you want it," I said. I used to say stupid shit like that. I was just waiting for someone to break all my teeth out.

Denise kept staring at me. I felt like a creep. I was sitting there on the bed, and she was just sitting on the floor looking like she would start crawling on her hands and knees towards me at any moment.

Bad things would happen, but it'd feel good.

I've heard a rumor that repercussions are for later, maybe it's true.

"College," she led off, as an authority, "you're better off

not going. Nobody I go to school with has any clue why they're there. It's just a bunch of sluts, guys up on the sluts, parties … all kinds of bad stuff." She fished her gold crucifix from between her breasts, placed it in her mouth, started sucking. "I love it," she cooed.

"What's the attraction to Ethan?"

"It's stupid … he sang me some songs. He's got a gun. I think that's hot. Guns, really."

"He does?"

"I saw him shoot a wolf from like a hundred yards away. We were in the sandpits. It was crazy."

"There's no wolves around here. Not in Jersey."

Denise looked at me skeptically, "then what was it?"

"A dog probably," I said.

She pouted, "Ahhhh, sad. It was coming at us, fast. Scary as hell. We were stoned."

"Who knows then."

She tilted her head as "Leopard Skin Pill Box Hat" came on the player. Her mouth hung open as she motioned toward the record player. "Who's singing? Errr, well it's not really singing, but …"

"Bob Dylan," I said.

"The 'Blowing in the Wind' guy?"

"Yeah."

"My mom's Chihuahua can sing better than him."

"Yeah, but even dogs got redeeming factors."

"Right."

Denise stood up off my rug, went over to one of the bookcases by the closet.

"You read all these?"

"No. Working on it though."

"They're making me read all kindsa crap books for school. I should just tell my professors that my dad's all mobbed up. Then I wouldn't have to read anything."

"Is he?"

"What? In the mob? I dunno," she said, giving me the side-eye.

"It doesn't matter," I said darkly.

"I did like Lord of the Flies. We read that in eleventh grade. And the one with the pigs and talking horses. That was good."

"Animal Farm."

She nodded, "The Scarlet Letter was the worst thing I ever suffered through, and Moby Dick was false advertising."

We had a good laugh about that. She kept scanning through the bookshelf. I kept looking at her ass. It really was something to see. She bent down to the lower shelf, and I could see that she was wearing a purple thong.

"Hey you wanna watch a movie or something?" she asked.

"Sure. Got a ton of them out in the hallway. Some are melted though."

"Melted?"

"Yeah. We'll have to dig around for ones that aren't."

We went out into the kitchen and started going through some of Feral's cardboard boxes. A sea of VHS. I'd hold up one...

"Ever see this?"

"No. I'll watch anything though. I'm easy."

I don't even remember what movie we settled on. Feral had a small color TV out in the hallway. I scooped it up and brought it in my room. Then I stole Seth's VCR too. He was passed out in his bed with the light off but with music playing. Glacial-speed shoegaze. Walls of reverb.

We hooked everything up back in my room. Before I knew what was going on, we were both sitting on my bed, shoulder to shoulder. Denise seemed to really like the movie. She kept leaning into me more and more, and soon we were lying down and watching the tape. Then she put her hands on my chest, kissed my neck a little. I certainly wasn't stopping her.

Halfway through the movie, she had her hands on my belly. I'm getting hard and can't help it and don't care anyway.

"Oh, what's this?" she asked while grabbing my dick through my shorts, biting my ear.

On the TV, something exploded. She took her shirt off. I unclipped her bra. Her left tit had a tattoo in Old English. A scroll. "Daddy's Lil Angel."

I thought about Mr. Santalucia with a gun to the back of my head as I sucked on her nipple. It got sharp like a little rock. She stopped me, pushing my mouth away.

"Hey, you got any?"

"Any what? Condoms?"

"You know ... blow."

"Blow? You mean coke? No."

"Ah, fuck. Really?" She said, pulling back. "I thought you were into that. That's what I heard."

"You heard wrong," I said. "Sorry." Denise reached down then covered up her chest with her bra.

"I think you got me mixed up with my roommates," I said. "Either or."

Denise's attitude changed. The warmth was gone. She just kept repeating, "Really?" It was a different ballgame now that I didn't have any drugs. She said it was wrong for us to be screwing around anyway.

"I like you, so then it's a bad idea, ya know?"

I tried to kiss her, but she pulled away. She got off of my bed, went out the door, said she was real sorry. She blew me a kiss, said, "I'm so embarrassed." She'd turned awfully red.

I sighed, cursed my luck.

Denise walked down the hallway, went into Seth's room, and closed the door behind her. She woke him up with kisses on the neck, her warm tongue, her hands all over. He told me all about it later—victor informing the loser.

In the morning, when I woke up, the light streaming through the blinds horribly, I unhooked Seth's VCR and innocently stepped into his room after lightly knocking.

"Yo. Hey, buddy, you in there?"

I peeked in. The room was empty, but the bed was a mess. I went in and put the VCR back where it belonged.

Then I noticed Denise's fluorescent purple panties, rolled up in a ball on the floor.

I stared at them for a second but let them be. I closed the door. Went away.

Swamp Bear

I'D NEVER HAVE FORESEEN IT. Soon as I told Denise Santalucia I had no interest in being anywhere near a school, I
got a call from a guy at the offices of the community college. The following morning. Synchronicity.

They needed work done on a pond in the center of campus: clean it out, drain the water, ditch the muck, rebuild the
collapsing stone walls and waterfall.

As was usually the case, Feral was supposed to come to
work with me, but he was nowhere to be found. I walked out
of Lagoon House, the A-Team van gone from its usual spot.
A pool of oil on the driveway.

I was alone on this one. Seth was up north meeting his
brother Mark at Newark airport. Together, they were going to
Aunt Kathy's funeral in upstate New York. I loaded my pickup.
Wheelbarrow. Shovels. Submersible pump. Then, I headed out,
thinking about Denise and Seth.

Ethan deserved it. I couldn't exactly pinpoint why. He just
deserved it. Have you ever known somebody like that, someone who just deserved the raw end of the deal? They have a
face that looks like it was made for punching. You could clearly
visualize yourself strangling them.

That'd be a sight. The goofy fuck would turn purple from
my choke hold, hitting the panic button on the keychain clicker
of his BMW. I laughed, visualizing that while screwing with
the radio. A good part of my life was spent screwing with the
radio.

I kept scanning through the stations, I was never happy with what I heard. Nothing annoyed me more than listening to the DJs as they rattled on about nothing, played the same songs over and over again.

It was a foggy, strange morning, but the sun was threatening to come out. I drove through my hometown, drinking a large black coffee from a paper cup and squinting. I was always squinting.

I'm that guy without the common sense to buy sunglasses, just squinting through his hometown.

For the first time ever, I made a left onto College Ave. instead of going straight towards the bars, the boardwalk, the Atlantic Ocean. A row of oak trees hugged the road leading towards the grounds of the college. When the trees ended, the grounds revealed themselves as grass covered hills. I never would've guessed. The rest of town was flat, lined with scrub pine popping up out of acidic sugar sand. Somehow the community college campus was lush and green, set at random inviting elevations. Swooping. Rolling. Academic.

I couldn't believe I'd never been there.

The year after high school, I hopped in my Buick and drove across the country to see America any way I could. I'd left Natalie behind, which was fine. She was screwing around behind my back with Charlie. I had no use for either of them after that.

I experienced America by roads west and south, till I hit the Pacific Ocean. Rivers and strange little towns. Mountains growing closer. Clouds spinning around overhead like madness. The surprising appearance of wilderness as the cities peeled away behind a wall of dream.

But I came back to New Jersey because of Seth. I called him from a pay phone in Santa Monica. He wanted me to play guitar in his new band. He sounded blitzed. I got a letter from Trish where she said he was getting pretty heavy into the wrong kinda shit. On the phone, he said, "Come back, I need you, man. Play guitar in my band. We won't even do covers. I promise."

I was wasted too. I told him I'd do it.

You can't outrun where you're from, anyway. Try all you want, it's no use.

In the center of the community college campus, I found the concrete pond and parked my F-250 next to it. It was early into a wet and foggy morning, many hours before classes would begin. Every surface of this life was covered in a slimy layer of dew.

I unloaded my submersible pump, threw it in the pond, and started to drain the murky brown water down a steep hill into the woods next to the student parking lot. That lot was vacant, but it was only a matter of time. Kids were coming.

As the concrete pond drained, I thought about that. The embarrassment I'd soon endure. The kids would appear, and I'd be the main attraction at the zoo. Some of them, surely, I didn't want to see, ones I'd gone through high school with. They continued. I bailed.

I didn't drink at the bars because I didn't want to see any of them again. But there I was. The water disappeared, leaving behind a soupy sludge reeking of decay. Putrefied leaves. Dead fish. Plastic Solo cups. A deflated beach ball. Frisbee with the logo of a local bank.

I'd have to go down there and get all the trash and sludge out of the pond. I knew, too, that would be exactly when my horrible peers would find me. I'd be down in the filth, and they'd wonder what'd happened to me. I'd have no good answers either.

I scooped putrid black leaves into my rusted wheelbarrow and took the goop down the hill, almost slipping on the sharp incline. I caught myself, though, with one knee, my heart fluttering wildly, my knee cut up and bleeding.

I cursed. Spat. Rubbed my wound. That's what work was: a series of injuries I got paid for. The pain went away. I took out the shopvac wet/dry vacuum and started to suck up the remainder sludge. The sound of the vacuum echoed off every building in campus, reverberated into outer space even, alerting everyone and everything of my presence.

Deciding it was too hard to get to the bottom of the wet hill, I started dumping the sludge down the side of it instead. Nobody would be the wiser; it wasn't too visible, and it wasn't hurting anything. It was also good fertilizer for the grass.

I did that awhile longer, then went to lunch. Some strip mall nearby. Jade Temple Garden. Five-dollar chicken lo mein lunch special: egg roll, Dr. Pepper, shrimp fried rice. My fortune cookie said, "You Will Be Judged For Your Heart."

I left a five dollar bill in the metal can next to the register that showed an abused dog. Its ribs showing. I guess I related to that animal. When I came back to the college, the lots were jammed with shiny cars. Bumper stickers for all kinds of things that I couldn't relate to. The students had arrived.

Walking back slowly, I glanced in classroom windows. What was it like to sit in a college class? In a lecture? I didn't mind high school. Actually, I'd done fairly well. I just couldn't think of a single thing I wanted to study in college.

As I climbed into the scummy pond, getting more of the filthy stench and slime all over my bare legs, my neck, my face, I heard a voice.

"Hey."

I looked up. It was Natalie, my ex from way back. Long blonde hair. White dress. High cheek bones. I think I saw her working as a hostess in a restaurant by the mall recently. As soon as I walked in and saw her, I spun around on my heels and walked right back out.

"What are you doing?" she mocked.

"Eh, working," I said.

"You're filthy! Look at you!"

"Sure."

I was embarrassed. More kids came. I recognized a few faces. They all stopped, looking at me just like I was an exhibit that had come to their zoo. They seemed to really be enjoying this animal on display there in the center of their campus.

"You in school here?" Natalie asked.

"No," I said, to my shoes.

"This is my last semester. I'm going to Drexel to finish my degree."

"No school for me."

"I see how that's working out for ya," she said.

I glanced down at a pile of slimy, mucked-up leaves at my feet. Should I pick them up and peg her with them? I looked around at the kids. They seemed very interested. Did they think I was a swamp bear, that this was my natural habitat? Down here, this filthy sludge pit?

"Go away," I said, shooing her with the back of my hand.

"What?!"

She was very amused by me.

"I've got work to do." I didn't like being the butt of her attention … anyone's attention really. But Natalie took my attitude, amplified it, and shot it like a sawed-off right back in my face.

"Great idea to skip college, huh?"

She was a mother scolding her small child for spilling a cup of apple juice.

I didn't say anything. What had I done to her? She'd been the one screwing around behind my back, with my best friend at the time no less. I left her here and hit the road without explanation. That's it really. The heart of it. She was an ugly person in her heart, and she was the exact reason why I hadn't had a real relationship since. It'd been two years, and I imagined it would be a very long time before I wasted my time with attempting another one.

"Have a good day down there," she said.

"Go fuck another one of my friends."

"I will," she said, flipping me the bird. She walked towards the hill where I'd dumped all the sludge.

It was a shortcut to the student lot. She had one of those shiny cars down there. I didn't stop her. And wouldn't you know it? Natalie slipped, poor thing, and ruined that white dress of hers.

Ethan

ETHAN WAS RICH. THAT WAS THE FIRST PROBLEM I had with him. As a child, he took violin lessons in his family's conservatory overlooking the ocean. He never practiced. He faked it.

If I'd been given an opportunity, just one opportunity, you better believe I would have jumped on it. My mom couldn't stay sober enough to take me to the zoo.

Ethan probably had a pet tiger for all I know. I didn't like him, he was uptight. Couldn't take a joke for shit. Had a polo shirt in every color. Wore Ralph Lauren cologne. Had clammy, delicate hands. Wore a baby face 24/7.

He lived with his parents in a plaster mansion with a terra-cotta roof. He didn't even go on the private beach in his backyard, because, "I have an in-ground pool, and that sucker's heated, son!"

On his seventeenth birthday, his dad gave him a silver Lexus. Two years later, that was replaced by a Land Rover with heated leather seats that he never took off road even once. When I met him, he'd just been given a new white BMW 5 Series.

"That's a funny car," I said to him, at our band practice.

"Nothing funny about it," he shot back as serious and blank as the moonlight. No sense of humor about himself. It was a funny car though. Not a man's car. I wanted to key my name into it, but my name wouldn't show up anyway.

That's something I could never understand: having a fancy

white car. My truck was always splattered with mud, and constantly on the verge of collapse. That was the difference between me and Ethel. I was on the verge of destruction, and he was over-careful: cautiously drove around town rocking out to crappy frat boy rock bands. He could sing, though. I mean, he had no sense of art about him at all, but he could sing … somehow.

Ethan had framed concert posters hanging on his bedroom wall. He grew his hair long, paint by numbers long. By the time I got back from my random travels around California, Ethan and Seth had started a cover band called Shore Thang. In Jersey, you pretty much had to be in a cover band in order to make any kind of money. I wasn't down for that one bit. I thought it was the lamest thing ever. I'd rather be broke than make money playing cover songs.

Ethan was all about it. He got a job waiting tables at TGI Fridays and played there on Thursday nights twice a month: a two-hour set. Just him and his acoustic guitar. That's how he met Denise. She and her likewise underage girlfriends were sitting in a booth drinking huge, blue margaritas with beach umbrellas. Ethan had a wireless system for his electric acoustic and his head-set and started to sing personally to Denise like she was the only person in the world. "Don't Stop Believing" by Journey. "Living on a Prayer" by Bon Jovi. Denise ate all that shit right up. She blew him in the parking lot of the TGI Fridays in the back of his Land Rover.

Seth told me that story. I almost shot an entire can of coke out of my nose.

"He sang her Journey?"

"Hey, it's a good song."

"To chicks who suck cock in the TGI Fridays parking lot."

Seth was closer with Ethan, but there was a distance between me and Ethel. I thought he was a weasel who only cared about himself. I'm sure he thought I was a scumbag. That's the way it works. But he did try to be a friend to me in his own limited way.

He invited me over his house. That was right after we'd just formed the band, The Bedspins. He was only doing vocals. I was playing guitar. Seth was on drums. We'd just kicked Charlie out for fucking my girl, Natalie.

"Tomorrow, let's go shooting," Ethan offered.

I had my feet in the heated swimming pool and was listening to the sound of the ocean just past the wall.

"I got a new gun. You ever shoot a Beretta?"

"Never shot an anything," I said.

"It's fun. We'll go to the range. We can draw Charlie's face on the target. That'll make you feel better."

"Maybe."

"Got my grandpa's Luger, too. You'll dig it. He stole it off a Nazi after he shot him. Guy was getting out of his jeep to take a piss on a tree. Grandpa was up in a nearby tree, just relaxing."

I was quiet.

"And about Natalie," Ethan said.

"Yes, Natalie."

"Don't feel bad about her, man. Don't feel bad about Charlie either. He was a shitty bass player, and he's a weird dude."

"Weird, yeah."

"Couple years ago, we met some girls at the boardwalk. One in particular was way wild. Did I ever tell you this story?"

"No."

"Well, we were all way drunk. And so, end of the night, this girl wanted to come back ... come back here. And, well, me and Charlie," he laughed, "me and Charlie ran a train on her. It was kinda awkward. Especially since, get this: while I was riding the girl from behind and she was blowing Charlie, he said, 'Yeah bro, give her that hard dick!' What a weirdo. Could never look at him the same after that. Who the hell says something like that while tag-teaming a chick? Kinda glad what happened with you and him happened. Glad to kick him out of the band."

I shrugged.

"Plus, he's too serious with that office job of his. Never gonna leave that. Picture that fuck in a tour bus? Plus he's getting fat. Sweats too much on stage. Plus the whole Natalie thing. And don't get all bent out of shape about that. I would have totally banged Natalie if I could have. Natalie's a hot piece of ass. She liked me less than you, liked Charlie more than you. That's all," he said.

"If you'd have touched her, I'd have set your BMW on fire."

"Wow. As if. Relax. Law of the jungle, right? Kill or be killed. You're too touchy," he said, sitting up. "I'm gonna make myself a vodka and cranberry, you want one?"

"No, I'm leaving."

"Don't be sore."

"Well."

"Besides," Ethan said, "if you set my car on fire, my dad will just get me another one."

Apartment

GAIL SANG IN THE SHOWER, OPERATIC but with made-up words. Bombastic. Her own joyful language. Aldo sat on the tin chair at the tiny yellow table wedged between the lone window and the door to the kitchen. He was half squinting but his eyes were clear.

"How's things?"

"Problem at the house," I said.

I unzipped the leather pouch with the meter and the needles.

"You can always come back here if you need to," he said.

"I appreciate that."

The room down the hall had been home when mom and him were together—before she split down to Florida. Aldo forced me to finish high school as part of a promise he made to her. Gail was in my room now. I wasn't going back, not to that couch by the kitchen table where he sat all night drinking and talking to himself.

"Okay. Now, seriously, watch how I do this," I said. I had to take some blood from him for the test.

"Can't kid, I'll pass out."

"Watch."

Aldo looked out the window as I started to take his blood, but he wouldn't look.

"Just a little bit. Come on, man. Didn't you tell me once that you stabbed someone?"

"I did. But I didn't look at the goddamn b—"

"Blood," I said. "B-l-o-o-d. Get over it."

The meter beeped.

"See, look at this. More insulin. Told you," I said.

"More? Goddamn, been eating better. They'll turn me into a rabbit. Fucking rabbit food. Eating the goddamn lawn. Munch munch munch. Eat the lawn, or we'll take a foot. One or the other. If they take a foot, I won't dance as good. If I can't eat anymore hamburgers, I'd rather do a swan dive into a wood chipper. Lee, who would love me if I couldn't dance?"

"You can't dance. Me, I can dance. I'm like a wave on the dance floor. Forget dancing, forget poetry, forget drinking, forget blabbing to me about your bullshit. See this needle? You've got to learn to do this yourself."

I flicked the side of the needle, dislodging suspended air bubbles.

He sighed. "I can't be taught."

The shower shut off through the paper-thin wall.

"I'm leaving. Soon."

"These kids are like California, California, California. They say it like it's fucking the lost island of Atlantis. Have your cronies read Grapes of Wrath," he said. "You'll go looking for oranges to pick and there's too many fuckers there picking all the oranges."

"Enough negativity. Even though I agree with you."

"You agree with me! Fucking A! Besides, you just got back, you're not leaving Jersey. It's just not in your stars."

"Fuck the stars," I said.

"Oh, I'd like to."

Gail kept singing ... started coughing. The coughs were as big as her. I got a little more worried.

"Way she goes on like that, I barely sleep," Aldo said.

"Never seen you sleep."

My memories of living there consisted of Aldo reading at the table, lips always moving, or playing solitaire, cards flapping down and lips moving. The a.m. radio babble or classical music in-between static. Gail wasn't around yet. I forget the last bartender's name.

Now, times were different; listless Gail needed help too. She had the room I used to have. Keep it, Gail. She was snoring in the bed down the hall, where I used to snore. Keep the bed, Gail. If I came back, I'd be tossing and turning on the couch. Fuck no. A nameless alley cat used to walk across my body randomly in the sweaty night.

Things are different. Cat's gone. Radio's broke. Aldo's deck of cards was missing the ace of spades. I like where I am now. Think I'll stay.

Aldo shakes, but doesn't know it yet. Slight.

"Went over there the other day," Aldo said. "Ya know, the Mayweather. Read to a new blind guy. Terry. Terry is in the middle of a terrible book, a courtroom drama. I wish I had more time. I'd read him a good book."

There's a rotating circle of volunteers that read to patients at the Mayweather. Each volunteers about an hour a day.

"Takes all my will power not to make stuff up. People need each other," he said. "All throughout."

At Christmas, Aldo does the Santa Claus routine at the Mayweather. The suit, the only nice clothes he has, is hanging up in the closet. The fake beard is in a plastic bag. I volunteer my time too.

"I won't be here forever to do this. Gotta toughen you up, old man."

"Leaving, I know. I know."

I put the insulin needle in. I dropped the dropper. The fluid slid in.

"I did all that when I was your age. Touring. Three weeks in the van west. Home a month. Two weeks in the van south. Home two months. A month north. It's how I lost this tooth. Started to lose my hair in St. Paul, where I first noticed. VFW bathroom mirror. Music saves a man's soul. Soothes the savage beast. Gets ya laid. Even the ones as ugly as me."

Gail came out in a pink towel, humming. She went down the hall, into the room where Aldo's mother lived before her fall down the stairs. Before the new wheelchair. She's in the Mayweather now, too. Gail doesn't like needles either. Had a junk problem in her youth. Said, "It's a miracle I'm alive."

I put the test meter and the insulin needles away. I zipped up the leather pouch. Aldo looked at me again. The color came back to his face.

"Not so bad," he says.

Gail coughs, louder, down the hall.

"You'll outlive everybody," he says.

"Oh fuck."

"No, it's true. She's not doing so well. Listen to that rattle. Cancer probably."

"Nobody has cancer."

There was a poster of Gail from her wrestling days on the

wall above the radiator. It was warped from the moisture.

"And I'm not doing so well, either. You'll be the one," he said, "my only family."

"I'm not your only family."

But I was.

"If something happens to me—let's say, the doctors want to keep me going, hooked up to a machine, breathing for me or whatever. You gotta tell them no."

"So grim, man. All the time. Grim. Either drunk or grim."

He pulled a napkin out of the holder and wrote on it in neat block letters:

DO NOT RESUSCITATE
ALDO KACZMAREK
5/15/2003

Then he signed it.

"Don't care if I get burnt or buried," he said. "But I don't want to keep living if I decline much more than I already have. I used to be able to pick a washing machine up over my head."

"What good did that serve?"

"Do not resuscitate."

I crumpled up the napkin and tossed it out the window. "You fucker."

"You little shit."

Gail came out of her room dressed but wet-haired. "What are you two conspiring about?"

"Nothing," I said, standing up. "Gotta go."

Aldo rubbed the silver stubble on his red scalp. He shrugged like a child. A jack-o-lantern smile.

I said to Gail, "Sorry to be running so soon."

"It's fine, doll."

Aldo said, "See you next Tuesday, Lee Casey."

"Going across the street," Gail announced.

"Wine and smokes," Aldo said. "Please."

Out on the street, I picked up the napkin rolled into a little ball. Unrolled it. Pressed it flat in my palm. For a time I kept the note in my wallet with a letter my mom had sent me. But both those things got destroyed by the ocean on a beautiful day.

5

"YUP, I FUCKED HER." Seth's first words as the screen door
smacked shut behind him. He struggled to climb over
Feral's obstacle course of vinyl and VHS boxes.

Her. Denise. "It was good," Seth said, nodding. "That
chick is nuts." Nuts. A Compliment.

He'd just walked in Lagoon House following a six-hour car
trip from upstate New York. I hadn't seen him for three days. I
knew he hadn't slept much, but he looked no worse for wear—
wired even. He was returning from Aunt Kathy's funeral up
past Tull Lake. Mount Mercy. I'm surprised his little shit box
Nissan Sentra made it.

I stood in our kitchen looking at all the dishes in the sink.
If I was gonna make some ramen, I'd have to wash some. I was
making calculations. A pot. A spoon. A glass for some water.
A few black flies were circling. I felt ill. Seth threw his army
backpack on his bed. I wondered if his suit was all folded up in
there. I didn't own a suitcase either.

He came back out. Wild eyed. Bounce in his step.

"Denise Santalucia," he said. "Denise Santalucia."

I nodded. Didn't even ask anything stupid like, "Are you
gonna tell Ethan?" I knew there was no point. I'd been with
Denise the same night too. The only reason I didn't get laid
was because I didn't have coke. Seth did.

After a long ride back to Jersey, I expected Seth to sit down
or collapse on the couch or straight up just go to bed. Instead
he said, "Let's go out."

Alright. That's all he had to say to me. It'd been a long day for me too, working out in the sun, dragging boulders from the quarry to a house on a hill. But I wanted to go out. See the bright lights. Watch the world shift all around me as I sank into drunkenness or better.

I found my silver Nikes, washed my face, dug out a clean t-shirt. My beard was getting too long. I was starting to look like a Neanderthal. I frowned in the mirror.

"I need a haircut."

Since my troubles with Natalie, I'd grown my beard, hiding. I was hoping to find some chicks at the boardwalk who didn't mind a Neanderthal hiding behind a beard.

We drove the F-250 away from the lagoons and the marshes that lined the bay and cut across town. Strip malls. Dunkin Donuts. Fried Paradise. Mattress Mayhem. I took a shortcut through the development where we used to live as kids: small houses and town cops sitting in parking lots beside blinking neon signs—watching, waiting, hoping. I took the back way out of the development and past the Mayweather, past the high school where I first met Seth in seventh grade.

The guidance counselor there actually introduced us, in his office, right before summer. I'd been in a fight with somebody and Seth was new—transferred in halfway through the year. He was quiet and withdrawn. Hadn't made any friends yet. His mom had died, and his aunt couldn't afford to keep sending him to a private Catholic school anymore. The guidance counselor knew that my mom was gone too, but in a different way, and he thought Seth and me could be friends ... both of us being motherless and all that.

Turns out it was true. We hung out most days that summer. He had a drum set, and I'd sit there and watch him play. At first, he was trying to teach me how to play drums, but it didn't stick; I have no rhythm. One day, a band forgot a guitar in Spider Bar after their set, and Aldo gave it to me after it wasn't claimed for a while. I mowed lawns and saved up for a little ratty amplifier. We started playing in Seth's bedroom while Aunt Kathy read her mystery novels on the couch downstairs—earplugs jammed in deep.

Seth dug through my cassettes but couldn't find anything he wanted to put on. He flung them into the glove box one by one.

"Boo! Hiss! Lame tapes, man."

"Lame? Get bent. There's nothing lame there," I said. "Besides, fucker, what you consider lame is taken with a grain of salt."

"Why?"

As if it was a great mystery what I meant.

"KISS," I said. "A KISS fan can't be completely trusted."

"Don't be afraid of the crap you don't know. Don't be quick to judge."

"I know enough."

"Says you. Sometimes something can be so bad it's good. Not ironically either. It can be so bad it's great."

I turned onto route 9, finally, leaving the pine trees behind. Headlights pointed on the highway.

"Hey, tomorrow morning, you should come with me somewhere," I said.

"Well this sounds ominous. Did I get you pregnant? Do you need an abortion?"

"Yes, yes. That's it exactly. It's a job I'm bidding on: a waterfall into a swimming pool. You should come with me. We could both talk to the home owners."

"Sure, I'll come keep you company."

"If we get it, we'd do the job together and split the cash."

"Ah, this again."

"Come on, you lazy sonofabitch."

"Lazy, ha. That's a riot. Yeah, I'm lazy. I just don't want to dig around in the goddamn dirt. That's hard work. I like working in the record store. I like giving drum lessons. I don't like anything at all about cement and shovels and sunburn."

"We could do this as a business. And it's a good idea too … if the band thing doesn't work out. Even if the band thing does work out."

"If? You're out of your mind. You know what the biggest cause of failure is in the world?"

"This ought to be good. No, what's the biggest cause of failure in the world?"

"Having a back-up plan."

"Screw you. Having a plan B isn't a bad thing. Fuck, I might even have plan C and D and E and F. You don't?"

"No, I'm serious. A person can't commit fully if they know that if they fail they can go with the back-up plan."

I didn't say anything.

"All in or nothing," he said.

On the side of the highway, we passed a drunk stumbling up the shoulder. He was either on his way to the porn shop or

Dinosaur Liquor right next door.

"Did that guy have a plan B?"

"That was probably his problem," Seth said. "He was going to law school and it didn't work out, because his plan B was to be a wino who pisses himself every night walking back and forth to Dinosaur Liquor for a fifth of swill."

"Damn, you got it all figured out."

He laughed.

My idea at the time was to eventually get bigger and bigger jobs. I wanted to steal my friend Dale from the rock quarry. He was a great heavy machine operator. I wanted to steal Steph from the quarry too. She was their bookkeeper, knew a lot about bidding on material, and was great to look at. We weren't on good terms at the moment. We'd gone on some dates, and it hadn't worked out because of me. But I liked her. I could talk to her. Even if it was just endless insults, we could talk. That's how it was with most people I knew—we'd just sit around and insult each other.

This dream business. Working at rich people's houses. Getting paid to sweat and get good suntans. Me and Seth would own the business, and Steph and Dale would work for us. Maybe I could even get Trish a job. It's not like she was in love with her cash register at the Dollar Store or anything.

Seth pointed at a strip mall. "Muchacho, pull in there."

It was the OTB, off track betting. The lot was nearly full. I'd never been there before. Always just cruised past.

"What are we doing here?"

"Kentucky Derby," he said. "Man, you live under a rock."

We parked in the back, fought our way inside. Mullets and jean jackets. Creeps that looked like they had knives on them (if not worse).

Inching forward in line for the window to place our bets, Seth said, "Be good if I scored a little here, ya know, for studio time." He elbowed me in the gut.

"Thought you were fine with Ethel paying for all of it," I said. "Now you're guilty because you banged his girl."

"She's got a supernatural pussy. I mean it. And ... she called me when I was gone."

"Denise called you? How? You don't have a phone."

"My brother, Mark ... I called her from his phone."

"She called back?" I laughed. Now, I knew a few more things about his older brother Mark: he had a cellphone and he could drink more alcohol than anyone on earth—it didn't affect him. Seth was a little bit like that, but not truly immortal like Mark.

We studied the racing forms. I didn't know what to make of it. Horses with strange names like Limehouse, Imperialist, Smarty Jones, Song of the Sword, Tapit, Castledale.

"My money's on Song of the Sword," I said.

Seth cracked up, "I'm going with Smarty Jones."

I dug around in my wallet and found five bucks I wouldn't mind throwing away. Seth gave the mummified woman at the window his bet: forty bucks down on Smarty Jones.

"Mark gave me a tip about that horse. I take Mark's tips, ya know?"

"Why'd you let me bet Song of the Sword then, you putz?"

He snickered, "Come on, let's find a spot at the bar."

It was tight over there. On one side of the OTB was a trailer park. On the other side was a retirement community. The place was like a hot white light in the dark attracting insects. It hummed with strange energy. Girls who looked like they'd been on the streets their whole life sat with chattering teeth glaring into the Jumbotrons, TVs bigger than their whole lives. Guys in trucker hats rocked on stools, glanced at the tickets in their hands, and hoped beyond hope to 'hit' so they could make the mortgage, or rent, or buy back their stereo out of hock … whatever their plight was. This place was a hotbed of tension. No-one was drinking for fun.

I looked all around and began to worry. Was I gonna wind up like them one day? Without a leg to stand on. Clutching at straws. I wasn't in college like I was supposed to be. I wasn't doing anything to advance my career. I was in a band that was going nowhere.

Seth wanted to do shots of Jägermeister.

"You kidding me," I said. "Jägermeister?"

"Come on! Hit it."

"Fuck that. You can have mine."

And he did. He threw back both shots. That was the problem with Seth: he never wanted to go to the good places—where the girls were. He was happy drinking at the VFW, at the dive next to Fried Paradise, at Spider Bar, and the perfect example: at OTB. Seth ordered a beer. He didn't bother me anymore to drink with him. He knew I still wouldn't.

When our bass player, Charlie, went and snagged Natalie, he said to me, "Charlie's got herpes, honest to God. Severe stuff."

That made everything better, somehow.

We were staring at the Jumbotrons too. We couldn't look away. It was just too bright. The horses were beginning to trot around and get warmed up. It wouldn't be long now before the race went off.

I scanned the place with worry. What would happen when all those desperate people lost? I mean, they were used to losing by now. So it was no big deal. They'd been doing it their whole lives, right? But somebody was bound to snap. It always happened. As Seth rattled in my ear about Denise and how tight and slippery and yadda yadda she was, I disconnected from his voice. I overlooked the OTB, playing a little game: find the one that would lose their shit and go hog wild when their horse didn't come in.

"I broke up with Shannon," he said.

"Oh, I thought you broke up with her a while ago. I can't keep track."

"Nah, we patched things up. But I told her last night, before I came down here, I said, 'We're through.'"

"Ahhh," I pointed, "look. See that?" It was a rail-skinny man from the trailer park, bleached hair all fluffed out and haywire, faded jean jacket, and skintight, stonewashed denim pants. He was on his hands and knees, praying—actually praying—to the Jumbotron. The horses were at the gate. Tears streamed down the man's leathery cheeks. I noticed his shoes were gone.

"Whoa," Seth said, taking a draw from his beer. We were in awe of our surroundings.

The gun went off. The gates sprung open. The horses burst onto the muddy track. Colors flew everywhere: banners, outfits, streams of paper. Nostrils. Whips. Jockeys bouncing up and down. Everyone out of their seats, yelling "GO _____," "GO _____," "PLEASE GOD, LET _____ WIN! I'LL DO ANYTHING!! ANYTHING!!"

Actually heard this one too: "PLEASE SATAN, DARK LORD, GRANT ME THIS DEMONIC WISH! ALLOW _____ TO FINISH FIRST!"

I couldn't believe the fire that suddenly lit up this dreary, smoke-filled place. People were on their feet, filled with a life I didn't think they could possess. The horses thundered forward, hooves pumping, spittle flying. A quarter mile in 2 minutes! You'd think that the people in the OTB were running the race themselves given the fury they were whipped into.

I leaned on a carpeted column. I couldn't relate to any of it. What else was new? I'm usually floating around somewhere in my own head—even in the middle of a party. It's a problem; I'm never quite "there." I'd make the worst Buddhist. I've never lived in the moment. Not once.

Seth punched my shoulder.

His horse was winning. Smarty Jones by a nose! Smarty Jones by two strides! Smarty Jones crossing the line by 2 ¾ lengths to win!

He grabbed me, squeezed me, squeezed me and bear hugged me up into the air. I felt one of my ribs crack. We fell over on the ground, and as soon as we hit, he was up on his feet—running towards the mummified woman in that pay out window while waving his ticket over his head.

I got dizzy, looking around at people as they ripped their tickets and threw them into the air. Confetti. They angrily sucked back the rest of their drinks, gathered their purses, racing forms, car keys. Pissed, pissed, pissed. So very pissed.

At the bar, I realized I was broker than I thought. Shit. I looked down into the empty folds of my wallet and worried about work. Finding another job. Would I have to deliver office furniture again?

Seth came back and sat and drank.

Within ten minutes, OTB was cleared out. Only the winners remained. A handful of us.

"Twenty three hundred bucks," Seth said low into my ear.

"Get outta here."

"Most money I've ever had in my life at one time. It barely fits into my wallet."

"Let's get going then."

He bought himself another beer, and as we left, he had two fresh road sodas in his hands. I clipped the curb pulling onto the highway. We laughed as we headed east towards the blinking lights of Seaside Heights, the boardwalk.

As I drove, Seth said, "I think my jinx is lifted."

"What jinx?"

"Exactly, man. What jinx?! We'll be in California soon. Sunset Strip. Shows lined up for us. It'll be sick."

"You think?"

"I know," Seth said. He took the money out and whipped me on the side of the head with it. "Here, I owe you two hundred. Take it."

"'Bout time. Holy hell."

We drove in silence over the Seaside bridge. The Ferris wheel loomed ahead. Its green lights twinkled. Our windows were down, and the cassette deck was so loud it was ruining my speakers.

I parked at a meter but didn't put any quarters in. Then we walked down the boardwalk, bar to bar to bar.

The night took on a neon quality. Two thousand dollars in his pocket, Seth bought everybody beers. Then shots. Friends everywhere. We kicked around the boardwalk until nearly dawn. Around two a.m., I started to feel less like a friend and more like a babysitter, but I didn't care. I led Seth as he stumbled from place to place. We ate pizza and talked to any girl who was standing around and seemed to be in possession of a pulse.

When the bars closed, we piled back into the F-250 and made the trip back towards Lagoon House. We took back roads and were careful to avoid all the lots and nooks where the local police liked to wait (even though I was stone sober).

The marsh stunk as we got nearer Lagoon House. The water was too low. The mud and rotting cattails reeked. Seth claimed he couldn't even smell it anymore. He'd lived back there a year now. I'd only been there two months.

"Another month or two, you won't smell it either."

"You think the house will last that long?"

"You sure you're not drunk?" He began to hiccup.

"I can punch you in the stomach if you want, that might help your hiccups."

"Won't be the first time I puked on you."

I parked the truck. As we walked around the side of the house. I wanted to go hang on the back deck; there was a full moon, low and good heavy. I wasn't ready for bed even though it was 3 a.m.

When I got to the deck, it was gone. It'd been demoed out. We'd been warned by DiSanto this was gonna happen.

"Shiiiiiiiiit," Seth said.

Well this was it—they were starting to demolish our house. Feral lid (slid?) open the door. Thankfully, it was still there.

"Can you believe those fucks?! They leveled the whole thing in like an hour flat!"

"You didn't try to stop them?"

"What was I gonna do? There were four guys, and they had hammers. I wasn't gonna battle four guys with hammers."

I climbed up into the sliding glass door. Seth fell onto the shag rug.

Feral looked down at Seth. "Have some self-respect, young rocker. You need a beer."

Denise

I T WAS RAINING. Man, was it raining. Wind gusts slapped red rocks violently against the vinyl siding. Lagoon House shook. The world as I could feel it flinched in unequal jolts as the bay lapped against the bulkhead, rising ominously across the marshes.

Denise Santalucia materialized from that storm, tapping on the door in the middle of that havoc like a field mouse. I barely heard her knock over the lull of the stereo.

I opened the door trepidatiously, the way somebody would open a gate to let in a lion.

"Hey," she said, stepping in to get out of the downpour. She'd parked a few blocks away so that her car wouldn't be in the driveway in case Ethan came looking for her.

"Seth here?"

She had a way about her now, like she just couldn't help herself. I like that in a person—however it presents itself. Her long hair was soaked, and the water rolled off as she wrung her hair out onto the floor.

"You need an umbrella."

She shook her head, her hair flew everywhere.

"I need more than that."

I looked for a towel, but we didn't have that kind of thing in our house.

"Sorry about the other night," she said with softness in her voice. Her eyes were warm, genuine. "I guess that was pretty weird, huh?"

"Don't worry about it," I said. "Weird is good."

Denise set her purse, the color of a yellow highlighter, on our table, and pulled out her cellphone and a paperback romance novel. The cover featured a shirtless pirate guy clinging to a red-haired siren.

"Look, you got me reading again."

"Always a good thing."

I thought about her on my bed without sheets, the way she'd stared at my bookcases, shirtless.

She touched my arm then pointed to his room.

"Seth here?"

I nodded. She left me, opened his door without knocking, vanished inside. I heard their low voices in there. Talking. Murmuring. Laughing. The rain came down harder. I turned the stereo up.

The lights flickered. Held.

I was goofing around on a busted-up acoustic guitar in the living room. It was missing three random strings. I was just making some noise, taking my mind off things.

When the door opened again, Feral tumbled in with Trish. They were soaked, hollering and laughing their heads off. Trish cradled a 30-pack of PBR like it was a baby calf. Feral pulled off his soaked, Bad Religion t-shirt and said, "Holy mother of the god I don't believe in, it's raining like the world is ending."

Trish, in her tie-dyed dress and white girl dreadlocks, set the baby calf down, gave me a big, wet hug. She's heavy and always hugs real good. I hadn't seen her for a while. The three of us sat around the living room for a while. The beers never even made it into the fridge. We just kept popping them out of the cardboard box. Ducks in a row—knock 'em all down.

"I'm glad it's raining like this," Feral said. "They'd be knocking down the house if it was a nice day."

"What," Trish said.

We gave her the lowdown about the house getting demolished. She just sat there with her jaw dropped, asking us what we were gonna do. It was funny, and it was sad, but we didn't have any kind of explanation.

"Somebody's phone is ringing," Trish said.

It was coming from the kitchen. She went out there brought Denise's phone and handed it to me, thinking it was mine. When I took it, my fears were confirmed: Ethan was calling. I set the phone down onto Seth's bongo drum next to the coffee table and tried to get the two of them to talk about something. But the mood was tense, and we kept getting interrupted by the phone; Ethan kept calling. Left voicemails too. The phone kept ringing. Ding-dinging.

Trish shook her head then looked into her beer can. She wasn't friends with Ethan, but she was too good a person. Loose lips sink ships. We were doomed. Our band was doomed.

Who was gonna sing the songs when he quit the fucking band over this?

The door to Seth's room opened. Denise came out. She was wearing Seth's RUSH shirt, nothing underneath.

"That my phone?" Denise asked. She walked into the living room, her bare legs sticking out from under the over-sized t-shirt.

I wondered if she was naked for a split second and then felt stupid: of course she was.

She flipped her phone open and looked at the screen, deeply concerned, as she sucked on her lower lip. Seth walked into the living room in his boxer shorts and a wife beater. I wanted to tell the both of them to put on some goddamn clothes.

"What's up?" Seth asked groggily.

"He keeps calling," she said, pointing at her phone.

Seth's eyebrows raised. He motioned for Trish to hand him a PBR. Feral was looking at Denise's tan thighs. I was too.

"What am I supposed..." The phone started to buzz and ring in Denise's hand. She panicked and hit the red button. The phone went straight to voicemail.

"Well, gig's up," Feral said. "Now he knows straight-up that you're ignoring his calls."

"It is what it is," Denise said. She plopped herself down on the couch next to me and looked back and forth between everybody. "Come on, shit happens."

Feral said, "Amen."

We put the TV on. Trish and Denise were going through cardboard boxes trying to dig up the VHS for Overboard with Goldie Hawn and Kurt Russell because they both just decided that it had to be watched. Our lives depended on it. Seth got up and walked down the hallway to help, crouching down next to Denise, rubbing her shoulders.

The wind picked up even more and the lightning set in. Thunder followed horribly. The lights flickered, went off. "Welcome to the haunted bungalow of doom."

"Spooky now," Feral said. "Beware the wolf man, little girls." He started howling.

I dug up some candles and lit them in a circle as if we were about to sacrifice a virgin. I was out in the kitchen looking for matches in the drawer when the house phone started to quack.

It was Ethan.

Feral answered in the living room, on the second phone. (the Sports Illustrated football), "Yeah ... yeah, Ethel. Whatever. Yeah, we're here." Then he hung up the phone.

My heart fell into my stomach.

"Why'd you tell him that," I said, walking out to the candlelit altar.

Feral just looked at me dumbly. I wasn't aware of just how obliterated he was. That was the thing with Feral. He was often stealth-wrecked. You never could tell till it was too late.

Seth and Trish and Denise came back in holding Overboard. "I think it's a little melted from the great fire of 1997."

"He's coming over here," I said.

"No! Fuck!"

Everybody looked like they'd just seen a ghost and weren't sure how to react. Any second, Ethel was gonna show up in his white BMW and he was gonna find naked Denise in Seth's Rush 2112 t-shirt and he was gonna lose his shit. He was going to kick us out of the band, and that would be that. We were in the middle of recording an album to pitch to a label in Seattle.

Denise ran back into Seth's room, gathered her things, which were really just her soaking wet, pink dress and her flip-flops. She stood in the hallway, looking frightened.

"Hide me!" she said.

"Hide you?" Trish said. "Damn."

Feral got up and pulled the cord for the attic. "Get up there."

"No," Denise shouted; lightning struck again. "I'm not going up there alone."

Trish grabbed an armful of PBRs and said, "Come on, darling, I'll hide out with you."

No sooner did they get up in the attic and we shut the door behind them, Ethan's headlights appeared in the rain-soaked windows. He parked behind my F-250 and came to the door.

"Holy shit."

The three of us ran to the living room and sat down, all nonchalant, in front of the candles. Ethan pounded on the door. Rattled the whole house.

"COME IN! UNLESS YER THE POLICE," Feral hollered.

Ethan stormed into the living room. His eyes were adjusting slowly to our new light. He saw it was just the three of us.

"What's up," I said flatly. "You look all twisted up."

"Was just looking for Denise. Thought she might be here."

"Nah," Seth said. "She alright?"

"Yeah, she's fine," Ethan said. "She keeps trying to get a
hold of me today and I keep missing her. She's driving me
nuts."

We invited him to sit down and have a beer, pointing
out that we had a lot of them. He was weird and evasive and
said that he couldn't hang around. He had to get rolling along.
Feral, laying it on thick, said, "Have a beer with us, you pussy."

"Dude, I'm cool." Ethan said, "I'm not gonna drink and
drive."

"Oh true," Seth laughed.

Ethel spun around on the heels of his motorcycle boots,
slipped out the front door. As he pulled away, the lights came
back on, and my first vision was Denise's highlighter-yellow
purse sitting on the kitchen table. Her romance novel sat there
too. Ethan wouldn't have missed that, no sir.

"Is it safe to come down?" Denise called from above.

I got up and pulled the cord, unrolled the attic stairs, and
took her hand as she carefully descended the stairs.

"Safe as it can be," I said.

6

IT WAS LATE. SETH CLICKED AROUND AIMLESSLY ON THE COMPUTER. He was trying to mix the drum tracks—digital colored blocks: orange, purple, blue, green—as they flickered on a white screen. Our eyeballs were burnt out.

It was tedious work. He'd adjust something, a knob or a fader, hit play, and thirty seconds of noise would explode into the small room. He'd slam the space bar to stop everything, shake his head. Seth wasn't so sure of what he was doing, became more annoyed as the nights in front of the studio computer labored on. I was no help.

We were at Mike's studio in the basement of his house on Noon Ave. Gear, rack upon rack of it, surrounded us. Who knew what any of it did? Black egg crate foam insulation covered every square inch of the walls and ceiling. Dust burned up on hot surfaces; the place smelled like an electrical fire. Seth sat before a massive 32-track mixing board, which loomed like an altar with tubes glowing orange, humming, fans spinning on and off to cool components, red and white lights strobing, in sync with ... something.

Other objects cluttered up the place, adding to our already heightened hysteria: a heavy console as big as a pinball machine with two-inch magnetic tape, a tangle of black cords with red jackets running out in every direction connecting into compressors and reverb units, and god knows what all these square analog units, with their bazillion knobs and switches did. I felt like I was inside a Sherman tank and about to be killed by my own senses.

I sat on a pink love seat with tropical flowers underneath one window, and Mike was stretched out on the other sofa, with his Gilligan hat covering his eyes, his bearded face, his gaping mouth. He'd begun to snore around 9 p.m. It was funny then. By ten, it irritated us both.

Seth spun around in the computer chair.

"We gotta wake him. I'm lost. I can't figure out what's going wrong."

I shook my head. As much as I wanted to wake the guy up, I couldn't bring myself to do it. He was working a day job at the rail yard; he got up at 4 a.m. and drove an hour to work, worked a ten-hour shift, and then, when he got home, had to deal with punks like us who thought their album was more important than anything else in the world.

"Nahh, maybe that's it for tonight, ya know?"

He didn't want to hear that. Our project was almost done, and we'd worked so hard on it.

I mean, first you write the songs in your bedroom or wherever, and then you show them to a close friend. They say cool, so you start jamming in a cold garage—your fingers freezing while crowded around a kerosene heater and hating life. You rehearse for months like that. Then you find a bass player. The bass player knows a singer. Now you've got a band. You show the singer the songs, and he says, "That totally sucks, I can't sing over that." Back to square one. New songs come, they're dumbed down. A different style. Lyrics get slapped on top of them haphazardly. The singer wants to call the band The Bedspins.

I nearly quit, but girls started to show up to the rehearsals. They liked the music. They liked the crap lyrics that the rich snob kid sung over them. They thought he was cute. Those girls danced and kissed our necks in dimly lit rooms. We played shows. More shows. A little bit of money came in. Then, Ethel dropped the bomb—his sister is connected to a record label, and she's insinuated that, if time and money was invested into a really stellar demo, the band would have at least a shot at getting heard by the label. Okay!

"So here we are, and where is he?" Seth looked at the clock, scowling.

Ethel should have been at the studio hours ago, but he never showed up. It didn't surprise me. He hadn't been very involved in the process. There was always some lame excuse for why he couldn't be there.

It'd mostly been me and Seth. We tracked the drums first for the Bedspins. Everybody played together, but the amps were isolated in separate rooms. We played communally in the drum kit room and listened to the mix through headphones. After that, it was bass. I tracked the bass, while Studio Mike punched me in for overdubs. After that, I spent a Saturday doing multiple tracks of guitar. When it was Ethan's turn to come in and do the vocals, he kept delaying things.

"I'm not happy with my lyrics, I'm gonna work them out a little bit. I don't think they're sexy enough."

"Sexy enough? What does that even mean?"

He was fronting the money for the project, because me and Seth were broke and he had the connection. But things just kept dragging on and on. He kept delaying coming in and recording his final vocal track. Finally he said, "Just mix everything down with the original vocals and I'll come in and re-record everything when I finish my lyrics."

Months went by. Seth and me kept going to the studio and messing around. When we'd taken things as far as we could, Seth wanted to record the original songs that we'd written around the kerosene heater while freezing our nuts off in Aunt Kathy's garage. Mike flipped out when he heard those songs, the one's Ethan hated.

"Why aren't you guys playing these songs with Ethan?"

Nothing had to be said; Mike got it.

I did a bunch of odd jobs for Studio Mike. I tore down his front steps with Seth and Feral in exchange for some recording time. I tore up his back yard, graded it, put down a small brick patio in an area that used to flood. I raked his leaves, and cut down a dead tree, chopped it up with a chainsaw, and even got to use all that wood for a big party out in the woods that Studio Mike came to. He was a good guy, loved beer, and seemed to really like Ottermeat. It was complicated music: bizarre time changes and unexpected shifts in feel.

"We'll record that music," Studio Mike said, sitting around the bonfire underneath the water tower, a beer in his hand, his Gilligan hat crooked. "It'll be sick, let me play synth and make noises. It'll be sick."

"Sure," I said with a grin.

So that's where we were then. A month after the party. In the studio. Our side project all tracked out. Seth just finishing up the last of the mixing. The album was a stark contrast to our other one with Ethan. Ottermeat was raw, weird, wild, complicated music bursting apart in every direction. Drums going crazy. Guitars freaking out. No vocals, just walls of strange Moog synth and sounds manipulated by cut up two-inch tape.

Mike snored like the world was ending.

"I can't take it any longer," Seth said. "Wake that fucker up."

Mike's snores had reached a crescendo, and any moment, Seth was gonna start smashing the mixing board. I leaned over and lifted the Gilligan hat off Mike's eyes. Immediately, he sat up like I was a ghoul that was going to eat his face. He drew back his hand ready to punch me.

"Whoa," I exclaimed, rolling away onto the carpet as Mike's fist came flying at me.

"What what what what? What what!" Mike sprang to life.

Seth busted out laughing. My heart thumping in my chest. Mike would have knocked me out had his aim been better. He sat up, figured out who we were and what was going on, and said, "I punched my wife right in the face once ... accidentally of course. She'd done what you just did."

"Now you're divorced," Seth said.

"Ha! Yeah, now I'm divorced," Mike said, scratching his beard like a maniac and grinning. "Bye bye, Mary Lou," he said. His face dissolved into a frown. "All it takes is one good accidental sock to the jaw. Fuck." Mike looked at the clock. "You guys are still here?"

"Yup," Seth said, pointing at the screen. "I'm stuck on something."

"What're you stuck on?" Impatiently, Mike went to the computer and hit the space key. The music sprang up. It was jarring and heaved around like a rabid animal. Every time I heard it, it made me smile. Seth was a force of nature on the drums. "Owww, that sounds like shit."

I couldn't tell, I'm deaf in one ear and can't even hear in stereo. My world is in mono.

Mike forcefully removed Seth from the chair and practically tossed him away. That guy's strength is deceptive. He's small but solid as hell. Mike sat down at the console and started to move some knobs around. When he hit the space bar again, and the music came back on, Seth's head was nodding and so was Mike.

"Look, see that!"

"That's it," Seth screamed. "That's the mix!"

They high-fived. I was just going by what they said. I couldn't tell if it sounded better or not. I just went along with it.

"Done!"

"Done? That's it?" I asked.

I sat up on the couch, feeling like I was getting sprung outta jail. That's what recording an album is like: doing time in county.

Mike started bouncing the whole project down from his hard drive to CD. It was almost midnight, and he had to get up for work in four hours. He said, cool as a cucumber, "We need some beers to celebrate." He fished some out of the fridge in his garage, came back, and handed us one can each. I popped mine and faked a sip and set it on the table.

Then, with his feet up, he picked up the manila envelope that Ethan had brought over. It was pre-addressed to his contact at the label, his sister, the lawyer.

"Now all we gotta do is get that prima donna to come here and finish his vocals. Then we can send your tape off into the void."

Studio Mike

STUDIO MIKE HAD HEAVY EYELIDS and looked like he was
in a biker gang except he didn't have a single tattoo. He'd
been married to a very pretty blonde named Mary Lou.
He'd had an Indian motorcycle and a golden retriever. But
all that was gone. Sometimes I'd find a dog toy. There was a
framed photograph of the motorcycle in the downstairs bathroom. But that was it. When I met him, he was living in the
shell of a two-story house that used to be a home. All he had
was the recording studio.

The house was haunted. The studio never made a profit.
He'd take the money he made off of recording random local
bands and dump it right back into his recording studio. He up-
graded equipment constantly. Half the time, there'd be some
big cardboard box he'd be cutting open.

"See this, this is the sickest tube compressor on the market."

"Oh? What's it do?" I'd ask as he tore away the bubble
wrap and exposed another rack-mountable steel box with a
face that lit up, dials, gauges, and a needle that'd jump around
and measure something.

"This powers the mic, makes kick drums sound big and
monstrous ... just sick."

"Oh. We just got done recording the drums," Seth would
say, hurt.

"Damn..." Mike would take off his Gilligan hat and scratch
his head by his long black ponytail. "Yeah, that's pretty rude of

me. You guys wanna re-record the drums?"

When we would re-record the drum tracks, another cardboard box would appear.

"What's that?"

"Oh, this is the sickest mic..." He'd look at us embarrassed. "It's awesome for snare drums, so ... shit. Let's re-re-record the drums."

His wife left. His hobby used to be his motorcycle, their annual trip down to Sturgis. His ATV. He used to have a boat that he went out fishing on. When she left him, all that stuff got sold, and she got half the money. He took the other half and invested in studio equipment that was as long gone as his wife was. Sometimes he would get a glassy look in his eyes after a few beers and say, "I wonder where my Fender reverb tank wound up? That thing was cherry."

He'd point at his digital rack mount and say, "I thought digital was the way to go. I was mistaken."

The next time I'd come to the studio, the rack mount reverb unit would be gone and there would be a massive Fender reverb tank the size of a small television. "See that," he'd beam with pride. "That sucker is even better than the first one I had."

Mike was a little punchy. He had a lazy eye. He explained that it was better that his wife had left and taken the motorcycle and particularly his ATV, because he'd crashed it into a pine tree out in the sand pits and nearly split his head open.

"I was a different person then. I used to drink way too much. Now I'm glad I have the studio to keep me occupied."

We'd hear footsteps above us in the house sometimes. No-one was there, but we swore we heard them. Mike said his house was haunted. He claimed he saw ghosts sometimes.

"They're hot, too. Big tits," he'd say as he snickered, dozing off on the couch with tropical flowers and exposed springs.

Another cardboard box appeared at the door.

"What's that?"

"Nothing," he said, leaving it sealed. "Let's pretend we're the happiest and most fulfilled we can ever get."

7

THE ROCK QUARRY WAS DEAD. THAT MADE ME HAPPY. After I pulled the F-250 onto the scale to get an 'empty,' I peered through the glare on the glass of the weigh trailer at the silhouette of Steph. She waved me on with an exaggerated motion as if landing a jet. I parked the truck, went into her trailer.

Steph was sitting behind the register. Wayfarers with orange lenses held her hair back out of her shadowy eyes.

"How you doing?" I asked, leaning on the counter. I wasn't really looking for an answer, just saying what you're supposed to say.

"What're you getting," she said with disinterest.

Steph was impatient. She was through with all my bullshit. She looked down at the counter and jotted down some inconsequential numbers. She was still mad at me. It was a real inconvenience that I had to come there two or three times a week, real inconvenient that she never wanted to be bothered by me again. We had history.

"I need Dale on the machine," I said.

"They all say that," she said. "Show some originality."

This was a new development; she was cracking a joke. Good. It'd been long enough.

"Moss Rock?" she asked.

"Yeah."

It was my usual routine, buying boulders to build walls or waterfalls. In this case, the job at hand was a rock wall at an estate on the ocean not far from Ethan's place. I cracked my knuckles. Steph stopped slouching.

She glared at me, "You gotta shave. You look like shit."

"Maybe," I said. "Suits me fine for right now."

For somebody who was only five foot one, she seemed fifty feet tall at that moment.

She didn't smile at me. I was used to it. I left the weigh house trailer. The door slammed behind me on its own. I drove my truck through the quarry, stirring dry caked dust as I passed the many assorted pallets of flagstone wrapped in chicken wire. I passed between the jack pine, that hung low with heavy cones, and crossed over the copper-colored creek, stained that way by cedar trees and spanned by a small stainless steel bridge, I came into the open pit where the mountainous piles of stone were: blue chip, honey beige, Delaware river stone, the same sharp red rocks from the Lagoon House yard. The sky opened up in there, blue and expansive. Clouds zipped by as if riding a conveyer belt. The space was circular, and the outer fringes were lined by a thick wall of pine and cedar. Past the loose pebbles piles, but contained by the pines, were slabs of heavier rock broken off of mountains that existed far away from the flat, wet coastline of New Jersey.

I found Dale asleep in the 5-ton, rusted-out Kubota bull-dozer. The bucket was almost big enough to drive my truck into.

I woke him up by laying on the horn.

"There you are," Dale said, grinning. He wore a cut off white t-shirt, from the junkyard where he and I worked brief-ly many moons before, and a backwards Yankees cap. Once he saw me, he reached instantly for a joint and started to fish around for the harder to find commodity, his lighter.

He looked at me for help.

"I don't smoke," I said, meaning I would but that I couldn't help him light up. He cursed me, sliding the joint behind his ear. He knew from past experience that the cigarette lighter in my truck was shot.

"I need 2 tons of moss rock." I pointed at the pile in the corner. It was hunks of mountain snapped off. Moss, lichens, and roots all stuck to it.

"Bro, not so quick. I'm on break."

"It's 8 a.m."

"I wanna hear what happened between you and Steph."

"Oh come on, let it go."

"She hates your guts," he said.

"There was a little misunderstanding. So we stopped seeing each other."

"Like what?" he asked, spinning his hat forward. "Spill it. She won't give me the time of day 'cause of something between you two. I've got the bad luck of being your friend. What is it?"

"Well," I said, "really it's ancient history, and it's none of your business."

He laughed. Just then, another truck came over the little metal bridge. He waved it over. The guy looked like a hick farmer. He wanted a load of river pebbles, the kind that are abundant and free anywhere there are mountains and a river. Ha. But we paid fifty dollars a ton in Jersey. Dale pointed at me.

"He's first, but you got a light?"

The farmer guy passed a nickel zippo, and Dale lit the joint. The guy took the lighter back and drove the rack body back by the bridge. There he waited.

Dale took a hit, exhaled. "What'd you do to that pretty little thing to make her so jaded?"

"Steph? I saw her online when she was seventeen—her profile, ya know. I waited till her eighteenth birthday to message her. I was 22."

"Sure, you waited. An absolute gentleman. So you took her out?" He passed me the joint.

"Yeah, a few times. We got into it right away too."

"She's a slut?" he asked, perplexed. "Doesn't seem it."

"I don't know," I said. "No, she's not a slut. Not by a long stretch. She was real into me. We used to screw around in her room, and she still had stuffed animals on her bed from when she was a little girl. It was kinda sick."

"Bet it was. So what's the problem? Why does she spit whenever your name comes up?"

"She spits when my name comes up? For real?"

Dale put his cap backwards again. I was almost ready to take his cap and stomp it into the dust of the quarry.

The guy sitting by the bridge honked the horn lightly. Dale looked over at me.

"Running out of time. Yer 'bout to lose your spot."

"She was a pretty wild girl."

"Yeah, huh?"

"One time, I was getting her from behind and tried to put it in her ass, but she freaked out and wouldn't have anything of it."

"Rightfully so," Dale said flatly.

"I pressed the issue," I said.

"Pressed the issue," he laughed.

"I said, 'That's okay. I understand why you don't want to do it. That kinda thing is an adult thing, ya know.' I said, 'When you get mature and you grow up one day, you'll find out that you really like it.'"

"Get outta here."

"She turned and looked at me. Gave me the dirtiest look. Then she leaned down, defeated, and said, 'Alright, go ahead.'"

"Well, that is fucked up," he said, driving the machine away.

"Where you going?"

"Lee, you're an asshole. I can't help you. No one can!"

He dumped the fork lift attachment, came back over the bridge with the bucket, gave the rack body three heavy scoops of stone, and sent it off on its way back to Steph in the weigh house trailer.

When Dale came back with the forks on the massive yellow machine, I was standing on the pile of moss rock like it was the mountain itself.

"You should let her take you out," he said. "Let her fuck you in the ass. Only fair."

"Oh Jesus."

He spit too, laughed.

"We're all jerkoffs when we're 21," I said.

"Some of us more than others. You win!"

"Oh fuck off."

"Back to business, what do you want?"

I spun around in a circle pointing at everything. He lunged forward with the machine at the pile and almost knocked me over. "Enough of that crap you wacko."

He backed up and I hopped off a boulder as it slid away. I started to show him the specific pieces of rock I wanted, because I liked the way they looked. That's how this worked. I pointed them out, and Dale did his best to fish the exact boulders out of the pile.

I'd tap on one, and he'd lunge in with the machine and flip a ton of boulders up in the air, causing an avalanche and dust to fly everywhere. Then he'd bring the boulders to the side of my Ford and dump them in.

When my truck started to sag a certain way, I could tell that it was enough stone. I waved Dale off.

I went to his window, thanked him, Shook his hand, and gave him a five buck tip.

"It's an adult thing ..." he said, smirking.

"Sure."

I went back into the weigh house trailer. Steph told me I had 2 1/4 tons. I nodded. It was plenty. I'd have extra. I signed the paperwork and passed her the cash.

I said, "I'm sorry."

"About what?"

"You know," I said. "By the way, I think that kid has the hots for you."

"Dale? Gimme a break," she said.

I shrugged. "He's really alright. One of the few. Give him a chance."

"We'll see. Hey, almost forgot," Steph said, "the other day a lady came in, wanting some work done. I recommended you for some unexplainable reason."

"No you didn't. Really?"

"Yeah, really. I'm not a total asshole," she said. "I could be, but why?" She stapled the woman's information to my receipt: a name, an address, a telephone number.

"Call."

"I will. Thank you." I waved and started to leave.

"Hey," she called as I walked towards the door, "You want a soda? I saved you the last one."

"What flavor?"

"Grape."

"Sure," I said. She passed it gently across the counter.

I left the quarry. As I pulled out into the road, the truck was sluggish and unresponsive. The springs screamed out; I turned the radio up.

I was feeling good.

Maybe I'd ask Steph out again.

I popped the soda. It sprayed everywhere, exploded all over me. I had to toss the damned thing out the window.

Then I was soaked and sticky and sitting in a parking lot. The yellow paper receipt from the quarry had a special message from Steph written on the back:

"Enjoy your bath, motherfucker."

The dot above the 'j' was a heart.

8

THE JOB WAS AT A LARGE CEDAR-SHAKE ESTATE with a long, winding pebble driveway flanked by colorful gardens and lush green trees. I parked the truck as close as I could get it.

I was still soaked from the exploding soda. Stickier. The yard was full of bees thanks to all the gardens. They'd find me. I saw a dip in the ocean in my future.

I hopped out and looked at the white columns of the house in awe and in shame for what I, myself, had. The place was really something else. I'd never have a place that nice.

The house had an expansive footprint; it just kept going: four-car garage, separate guest house, exotic woodwork around everything, including the back deck with its infinity in-ground pool. There was a private beach too. All the residences around there had them.

I didn't bother knocking on the door or anything; I'd already got as much money from the homeowners as I was gonna get until the job was done. Plus, they'd said they'd be gone for three weeks. Some European business. They were Scandinavian.

I had two tons of moss rock to carry, by hand, up a small set of wooden steps, through a tall back gate, and past the infinity pool and its mahogany deck. The homeowners wanted a stone wall built to separate their entertainment area from the dunes and dune grass that were getting closer and closer every year.

I took my shirt off and threw it on the bench seat. I left the truck running, adjusted the radio so it was loud enough to be heard but wouldn't blow out my speakers when the commercials came on.

I was anxious to get started. The weather report said it'd hit 95 degrees by lunch. The humidity would be at jungle level. I was hoping to be done offloading the material by then.

I pulled the boulders out of the bed of the truck. They were heavy and had sharp, jagged edges, which made them awkward to carry. I struggled up the side steps while lugging one and saw my error when I got to the gate. It pulled open, didn't push. A large barberry bush scraped my arms as I set the boulder down, opened the gate, and anchored it open with a small marble statue of a deer.

I picked the boulder back up, I lugged it to the far corner of the deck and tossed it down into the dune. I huffed, leaning over, out of breath. I wiped a bead of sweat off my brow, as an upper window opened and an old woman with bleached hair stuck her head out.

I waved. "How's it going?"

"Be careful of the deck. It's very expensive. Don't you dare nick it up."

She just kept staring at me. I kept staring up at her.

I laughed, "That's it?"

"What," she called out. Her mouth opened like she was going to speak, and then she closed it again along with her window.

"Hold on, lady!"

She looked at me again, just another shirtless moron.

"What?"

"What happens if I smash one of these boulders into the deck like I've just scored a touchdown?"

She slammed the window closed. I never saw her again. That's the thing about working on those big houses. People were always warning you about things. Those people probably didn't even live there. That woman, she was a housekeeper or something. She was probably dusting up there. Folding linen. Rotating ties on a tie-rack.

I went back to my truck, lugging boulder after boulder into the back yard and setting them where they all belonged. Within an hour and a half, I was completely drenched in sweat.

The infinity pool loomed before me like a fantasy.

I thought about it as I crouched down and drank water out

of the garden-hose spigot. It was pathetic. I'd always remember to bring beer to the job (when I was in the mood for it) but never remembered to bring drinking water.

The sweat peeled off me. My head was soaked. The sun getting hot, and the air became more humid. I took my shoes off and stuck my feet into the pool.

Behind me, I heard the back door open. "Great," I thought, "I'm about to get in trouble for having my fucking feet in the swimming pool." I turned my head, round two with the old blonde housekeeper.

I was surprised by what I saw. A girl in a string bikini walked barefoot across the deck. Pale. Long, brilliant blonde hair and heart-shaped sunglasses. Her breasts pointed up, indicating the rumored location of heaven. Mouth parted ever so slightly. Towel with neon tetra on it tucked under her arm, but she wasn't coming into this swimming pool. She walked past in a flash, down the wooden steps towards the private beach.

I stood up and watched her leave.

The ocean. She was going down into the surf. Of course she was.

I unloaded the rest of the boulders, cutting my hands— little droplets of blood, dirt, scratches from the pine trees as I passed and they tried to wrap me up. The smell of Juniper and salt water. Birds screamed in branches without rhythm. It took about another hour and a half, but then, when I was done with the work, I shut my truck off and made my way down the steps to the private beach.

The girl was lying on her stomach, reading a book, kicking her feet lazily. She was spread out on the towel, sometimes drumming the white sand with her palms. The sun was too strong this early in the season. She was burning but didn't know it yet. The top of her bikini was gone, lying at her side. There were no tan lines yet anyway. It was too early—just late spring. As I got closer, I could see her bikini bottom was covered in small cherries. I studied her ass as if it was a cypher that would unravel every code in the universe, making the great mystery of life nothing more complex than a Sunday morning comic strip. I was only close enough for a second, however, as I fought across the sand toward the surf, which broke violently as if it was a challenge looking to swallow me up too. She didn't look up from the book.

In front of the girl, halfway towards the waterline, was a pit that had been freshly dug into the sand. It was full of fresh dry wood: a bonfire for later.

I went down, waded out into the cold surf in my camouflage shorts and just floated out there—watching her from just inside the foam spray of the breakers, as she watched me.

She never came down the sand. I never bothered her. We didn't talk. We just looked at each other, like two animals in separate but adjoining cages at a vacant zoo—feeding time somewhere long off.

The water was rough, cold, violent—the aftermath of the storm that'd sent Denise up into the attic to hide. But the water felt good. I bobbed up and down, looking at the rows of houses. The ridges of their roofs. For such a hot day, it was surprising that none of the rich people from those houses were in the water. I swam out farther.

The sun reflected and cooked all who were uninitiated.

When I looked at the girl, she was sitting up, staring out at me in the water. Her breasts fully exposed. I bobbed there, treading water, watching. She just kept staring out at me. It was surreal. Something wasn't quite right with her. I could tell right then.

A wave came and smacked me on the back. It knocked me under. Never turn your back on the ocean. When I came back to the surface, the girl was putting her top back on. She'd gathered her book, her beach towel, all of it. She went back up the steps, into the shade and security of the house.

White Bird

L AGOON HOUSE WAS EMPTY. I took a shower and sat on the couch. The sun was setting over the marsh. A big white bird, a Florida bird, the kind that shouldn't be here, was walking through the mud. I whistled at it out the window, and it looked over at me but just kept walking away, vanishing into the maze of the reeds.

The evening had no direction. I picked up the phone and looked at the numbers, considering a few I could dial, but ultimately dialed no-one. I closed my eyes, almost nodding out. But I was hungry. And I didn't want to be alone, in an empty house, trashed, demolition looming, and refusing to clean.

"To the boardwalk," I decided. Muscle memory. Fail-safe. Going through the motions. Pizza. A slow walk to see who's walking around. Someone's always around.

I grabbed my keys, but when I looked for my wallet, I couldn't find it. A quick search revealed it was nowhere in the house. Nowhere in the truck either. But I knew where it was. My wallet was lying on a flagstone next to the boulder wall.

That afternoon, when I'd gone down into the ocean, after that girl, I'd had it in my back pocket. I'd left my wallet on the stone to dry out and forgotten it.

"Guess I'll be going back," I said to no-one. "Right now."

Bonfire

BIG MOONLIGHT. I parked beside the mailbox on the street and walked silently up the crushed seashell driveway, through the gardens loopy with whistling night birds sipping from fountains bathed in lunar light—darting from flower to higher perch as I passed.

The night was warm but windy. Like the spirits of the dead were out in the ether. Branches and small animals moved all around. An electric, doomed charge was in the nectar-heavy air. The world that I knew had been overtaken by honey suckle and shadow.

The estate's windows were black, but when I got around to the back deck, I saw a flicker of light coming up over the dunes. The dune grass and cattails waved in the breeze kicking in from the endless ocean. A bonfire was going on down there. Just like I figured. It was that kind of night.

I found my wallet and my shirt next to the wall, right where I left them. Down on the beach, I heard laughter and voices.

I stood on the edge of the steps, looking down at the bonfire. The girl from earlier was wrapped in a bright blanket, bands of vivid color. A few young, stuffed-up college guys sat around her in a circle. Three of them; no-one important. Close cut haircuts. Hooded sweatshirts for colleges I'd heard of but couldn't point to on a physical map. Khaki shorts. Visitors. Tourists. They made uncomfortable small talk.

The girl looked over. My guess was that she could feel me looking at her. It's funny how that happens.

"Hey, who's up there?"

I stepped out of the shadows, and then she got a good look at me.

"Oh, you. The swimmer. Come on down here, swimmer."

I walked over, and sat across from her. The guys got quiet. This was war. She looked up, and the fire reflected in her eyes shone like headlights on a parked car revealed in the trees.

While looking at me, one of the guys—square-jawed, pointy nosed—said, "Excuse me." I introduced myself. He didn't say his name. He had the kind of nose I'd love to break. The girl leaned over, held her hand out, shook mine.

"K Neon," she said. "I was hoping you'd come back."

The guys remained quiet but with their feathers all puffed up. I kept talking to K, ignoring them. She had an edge to her voice. The guys were messing around with a bottle of wine.

"I can't believe you don't have a corkscrew," one said.

"Well, I don't just carry around stuff like that."

"Give me that bottle," I said. "I'll open it for you."

"You'll just break it and get glass all in the wine."

"Pass the bottle over here. I'll show you," I said like a father talking to insolent children.

The pointy nose kid reluctantly passed the wine bottle. I took my knife out of my pocket.

"Oh, look at this … he's gonna hack it out.»

"You'll get cork in the wine! That's just as bad."

"Shut the fuck up," I said. I stuck the tip of the blade into the cork. I spun the knife, twisting and pulling, moving the cork out of the neck of the bottle by walking it up. The cork popped out. I passed the bottle immediately to K Neon. She took a big gulp.

The college guys weren't interested in the wine now. I took a mouthful. I'll drink a little wine sometimes, on a special occasion … like this. How bad can it be for a person? It's holy blood. I passed it back to K. We looked at the three of them, the fire glimmering in our eyes.

The kids had a strange useless fear about them.

The bonfire was getting low. I threw more driftwood on it, even though the guys warned, "It's getting late and the cops come over after 10 p.m."

"I'm from here," I said. "I'm not worried about the cops in the town where I live."

"What does that even mean?" one of them said while walking away. They were done with K Neon. It was obvious she wasn't interested. Up the beach, they kicked sand.

Sure, go away. Leave us. We have much to discuss.

K told me she was going to Brown University, majoring in nothing. The house belonged to her rich aunt. K kept laughing, talking about drained bottles of wine that were buried in the beach sand, her aunt's sailboat, and someone named Brent.

"I met those guys at a party. Strange how you can meet so many un-fun people at a party."

"They're everywhere," I said. "Shame on them."

"They disinterest me, and disinterest is a weapon I'm highly skilled with."

"Oh wow, shut up."

She started to say something else, but then we were all over each other. Wrapped up. Breath on breath. Very much involved in stopping all the words ever from coming out each other's mouths. Our tongues actively fought back all conversation. Our bodies collided together, a magnet for sand. Her hair fell in waves across my face as the wind pulled sparks from the fire at us. The driftwood exploded, showers of embers occasionally burning my back, her neck, our ankles—it didn't matter.

I'll never forget: we rolled over, and she let out a cry. Her sweatshirt had caught fire. I'd thrown it too close to the embers. We covered it in sand, and, laughing, lay back down. I recall throwing her clothes off piece by piece, trying to get each item to land in the fire. For some reason, that was my goal within the goal.

I heard a noise behind me and looked up. It was a cop. K covered herself with the colorful blanket.

"Someone called and complained," the young cop said. He looked familiar but I couldn't figure out from where.

"You'll have to put out that fire," he said.

"But it's keeping me warm," K pouted.

"I hear ya. Not my rules though. I just work here."

I zipped my shorts up, and the cop ignored the fact that we were drinking on the beach.

"I know where I know you from," he said.

As it turned out, I knew his sister, Victoria, and had been over the family's house a time or two back in sophomore year. He didn't write me a ticket and left on a good note, which was fine by me. I can watch cops walking away from me for any length of time.

I threw sand onto the embers. She kicked her bare feet to help and laughed and laughed until she stubbed a toe. Then we were in the sand again. She kissed her foot, in pain amongst the noise of the moon, the tide, the fading engine of the ATV carrying that cop away, the creak of the wooden fence on the dunes, the cattails slapping against it.

My head was feeling good, not minding the alcohol. After all, it was just a little bit, the first time in years, but with this girl, I could've drunk wine all night, all tomorrow, all the days of all the week, weeks, forevers. I didn't care if I went crazy and ran off to Florida and disappeared afterwards. That'd be fine. The noise of my human heart slowed as my brain fogged up and she leaned over and said, "Pour some of that wine on my toe."

And I did.

Helping her walk, both of us pretending that she was badly hurt—crippled by some war, she led me off the private beach, up the steps, past the swimming pool, and into the estate.

We closed the bank vault doors and engaged the security system. She released her grip on me as we stood inside, on that marble floor, with a look in her eyes like an excuse was about to be given.

I said, "You wanna see how to open a bottle of wine with a shoelace?"

"Yes, please."

K NEON

KHAD EYEBROWS, but they were so fair I could only see them in certain light. "The curse of the Norwegians," she said, "no eyebrows." Her family descended from Eric the Red. We sat in the empty estate, and she showed me an ancient leather-bound encyclopedia of Norse legends and lore. She would open up to random pages, hold the book next to her cheek, and say, "Doesn't that look just like me?"

"Without the Viking helmet, of course."

"I have the Viking helmet. I'll put it on if you want," she said, kissing me through the air—the perfect combination of drunk and high.

"I'm afraid I'd laugh, and I'm afraid you'd kill me."

"Why?"

"You don't get laughed at, do you? Ever?"

"Not that I recall."

"Ah fuck. Put the Viking helmet on. It'll be good."

She went down the hallway and came back wearing it. She didn't look funny at all.

"Damn," I said.

She placed it on my head.

"It's not a crown," she said. "Don't turn into a punk about it."

I looked in the mirror, adjusting the thing.

"You can have it," she said. "if it fits your melon head."

"Thanks." She slipped the not-crown on my head.

"Works."

The days were swallowed up by K Neon; no work got done. Sun up. Sun down. No progress. I vanished from the earth as if exiled to her lair.

"This is Ogygia," she said, meaning the house was to me as that island was to Odysessus. When she poured more wine into my glass, it was the color of crushed cherries or blood.

"And you're Calypso?"

"Worse," K said. "I don't believe in God, so Zeus has got nothing on me."

K was slinky, catlike. She didn't move, she floated. Everything, every surface, was a catwalk. She reminded me of Nico. She reminded me of Twiggy. I'm unoriginal like that; not to say that K Neon was unoriginal. I suppose she reminded me of all skinny beautiful blondes that had fallen out of some tree like it'd just been shaken by better men than me. These classically beautiful girls, like fruit, and me—with my ripped up hands, surprised as hell to have found one so randomly and inexplicably on the ground.

Or the beach.

Mostly, K Neon and me hung down in the depths of the vacant place—electronic music echoing off the marble and the glass and the exotic wood that everything was made of. Money. To be in a place so thick with money. It was crushing me as I thought about my meager room back at Lagoon House. The nicest things I owned there: some hardcover books I'd bought used that just happened to be first editions, my mattress on the floor, my guitar with its snapped neck.

The house, if you could call it a house, was made even more lonely by a maze of empty rooms. We split our time equally in each room.

"I shut off the security cameras," she said. "It'd be embarrassing—a hundred hours of me on all-fours."

"I'd buy that tape."

"They wouldn't appreciate it as much as you would."

"What if I'm a thief?"

"Steal whatever you want," she said. "I don't live here. I'm just visiting. They trust me not to do anything screwed up. Their mistake."

We tried all of the beds and all of the other places too. Everything was too nice. We fucked on all of it. I kept waiting to be told the house had been designed by Frank Lloyd Wright. It felt like a possibility.

K liked to hang out nude. I didn't really care either way.

I mean, once you see someone naked for more than a minute and a half, you just become used to it. She would make breakfast, fried eggs and toast, with her clothes off. She'd walk through the entire house, from end to end, and I'd hear the soft pad of her feet. "I wish I could be nude all the time. In class mostly. I think it would help my studies a lot. Test taking. I think I'd be getting a 4.0 if my pussy was out."

She touched herself lightly. I got hard ... again. It was a running cycle with us.

"I don't think it would help your classmates any."

"I'm concerned only about me. Not them. I'm already getting a 4.0. My IQ is 136."

"Bravo," I said, clapping.

Her breasts were small but looked like weapons of mass destruction. Sharp nipples pointed up and out. Her ass was not human. It appeared to have been stolen from a classic statue. Something from the Louvre. She liked to shake it at me, which was fine with me. It was not every day that fine art just wanted to shake at me.

The expansive living room upstairs could easily swallow up the dumpy Lagoon House. I sat in my boxers on the leather couch, looking out the window at the Atlantic Ocean and feeling kinda starstruck in a way.

"This is my problem with them," K said, pointing at a walnut desk. "They're stupid."

I knew right away what she meant. It had bothered me too.

"The desk is facing the wrong way," I said.

"It's right in front of a window overlooking the fucking ocean, and these idiots have it facing away. 'Cause, Jesus Christ, this living room is soooo interesting!"

I considered the grand piano and the spiral staircase leading up. Still, I agreed.

"Let's move it. Spin it," I said.

She liked that idea. We went into it right away, rotating the desk around so that it faced the ocean (as it should). Then she cleared all of the stuff off of the top of the desk, sat on the top of it herself. "What do you think?"

I didn't have to say anything to that question, and she didn't need an answer. That's not what I was there for. At least that's the impression I got. Maybe I'm underrating myself. I kissed from her knees down and then back up to the inside of her thighs, where it counted.

"Oh, that's it," she said with her legs wrapped around my

neck, pulling me farther in.

There were piles of fashion magazines in the downstairs bathroom. They were on a rack of shelves next to the space-age toilet, the automatic towel drying rack, the luxury tub with whirling jets, and a TV built into the marble wall. I sat in the whirlpool tub looking through the magazines, while K Neon kissed my neck and fooled around with me under the surface of the warm, swirling water.

"Here's another one of your descendants," I said, holding the fashion magazine up to compare the two: K and a blonde runway model—rail skinny, lips parted, eyes painted coal black, head tilted. "You've got more freckles," I said.

"But a better mouth."

"A much better mouth," I said. She was slightly deranged. Her head disappeared under the hot, swirling water, and her lips closed around my dick. She slowly started to suck.

She was down there so long that I thought she was gonna drown. When she came up, she came up laughing. Hair plastered to her face, gasping for air.

"I need a scuba tank!"

"You don't have one somewhere in this house?"

"I don't know ... so many closets. I can hold my breath for three minutes. Let me show you."

There was an element of dark genius to her, and, to be honest, I had no clue what she really meant when she talked most of the time. K was one of those people who talked in layers, in questions—questions that aren't meant to be answered. I did my best to keep up with her in conversation by just saying funny shit and being opaque, even playing dumb. I was certain that, at any moment, she'd find out I was a moron, and our little game of house on the ocean would come to an end.

She'd been places. Paris. London. Barcelona. As a little girl, she was a competitive horse rider.

"An equestrienne," she said, splashing the water. "But I didn't do very well. Some gates are just toooo high, and I didn't like pushing the animals."

K Neon had been out on a sailboat, spent many nights at sea, looking up at the stars.

"One night we'll lay out and I'll tell you the history of the cosmos."

"Ah, go to hell," I said.

She splashed me again.

"Accurately," she said, "it was more of a yacht than a sailboat."

She was out of my league for sure, and I often felt like she was just tolerating me.

"When are they coming back?" I asked.

"Who?"

"The people in this house … your family?"

She laughed, darkly, and lowered her eyes.

"Don't call them my family. That's just so sadly inaccurate."

"I don't have much of a family either."

"You live alone?"

"With people."

"People?"

"I'm in a band. I live with the drummer. And another guy."

She led me out of the tub, as if I really needed to be led anywhere, and dried me off with a warm towel that probably cost more than my weekly paycheck.

"We can't be dripping wet all over the place," she said. "Slick surfaces. It's one thing I won't tolerate in this house. I'll freak. I mean it. Danger, danger, boy. That's how my mom broke her neck. She doesn't walk anymore."

"Where doesn't she walk?"

"Where? She doesn't walk everywhere. Anywhere. She's in a chair."

"Where's the chair?"

"Zurich."

"Don't know where mine is," I said. "Florida last I heard."

"That's nice. Florida can be nice."

I didn't get into how not nice the part of Florida that my mom "lived in" was. K didn't talk anymore about the wheelchair. We probably looked like two sea urchins, covered in spikes for self-defense, standing by a bath tub and trying to change the subject to something, anything that hurt less.

"Let's go do something."

K Neon took my hand. We walked down the marble hallway and through another set of doors. She adjusted the lights, many of them, with a movement of her wrist. There was a large bed. A room with windows that opened up on the gardens. K stood next to me at the window and rattled off names of the flowers.

"Foxglove, mullein, bearberry, wild lupine, blue salvia, morning glory, hibiscus."

K pointed to a bird sipping nectar from one of the flowers, the name of which I had already forgotten.

"That's a magnolia warbler."

I turned away from the garden window, looking at the wall. There was a large painting of a Japanese woman with blue lips in a kimono. I leaned in and looked closely.

"That's expensive. They're collectors," K said, pointing up at the ceiling.

An empty house. The empty people. The missing persons. "Cool shit."

She shrugged, faked a yawn, and took me over to the bed.

"I'm more interested in what's alive," she said.

She started to work her magic, but stopped abruptly, pulled back.

"Hold on ... we need..."

"What? What do we need?" I said, wishing she hadn't stopped.

"Music!"

She was gone for a moment, but when she came back, she had a small, white device in her hands. It was the size of a bar of soap. She plugged a cord into the jack and started to click away.

"What's that?"

"An iPod, duh. It's got all my music on it. I threw the CDs out. Useless now."

"You're insane," I said. "Useless?!"

"I feel like I'm about to show fire to a caveman."

"Okay," I said eagerly, "show me what you got."

K Neon hit play, and a machine gun of bass hits exploded out of the speakers all around us. She rose to her feet and began to move around the room, turning and extending and coming towards me in sync with everything and nothing. She danced around the room, feet never touching the Persian rug. She lowered herself onto me, and the music threatened to level the house, the ocean, the sky, and even me.

It was a good day.

9

I RESURFACED INTO LIGHT, DESCENDING SLATE STEPS. My sneakers crushed the seashells. I felt like I'd dwelled in the darkness for eons. K Neon had kept me occupied for days.

My intention for this new day was to get some work done on the boulder wall along the dunes, but it was raining again.

I left K in the master bedroom, still naked and just starting the New York Times crossword puzzle. I'd be no help to her with that anyway; she was brilliant on her own. She seemed fine with me leaving. Barely looked up. Just filled in blocks of the puzzle in with a green, ball-point pen.

Outside, the sky was gray, and I had no clue what was happening with the forecast; the radio didn't make it clear. It was triple shot Thursday, so they just kept playing Rolling Stones songs I'd already heard too many times: "Brown Sugar," "Satisfaction," "Tumbling Dice." There was no room for the weather forecast with all that triple-shotting.

I drove away from the ocean, headed inland. To stay on errand, I ducked into a concrete supply yard and got one ton of screened white sand, six bags of crushed white limestone powder, and twelve bags of Portland cement. The sand was loose. It got dumped into my truck by Bernie on the front end loader. The cement came in 75-pound paper sacks. I wrapped them well with clear plastic and duct taped them shut so they wouldn't get wet and ruined.

I was hungry. K Neon didn't eat very much. I was starving, actually. That's all that was on my mind as I cut through town in the rain. Eggs. Bacon. Eggs and bacon dancing together. Eggs pushing the bacon on the ground. Both of them rolling around on the floor, grinding, groping, and me with a fork, swooping in and eating them both while they were distracted.

Near the river, the elevation dropped sharply. I made a left. Even though I'd driven down that hill a thousand times in my life, I was horrified to find how different the hill felt that morning. My truck had no traction due to the weight in the bed.

At the bottom of the hill, a maroon Buick LeSabre sat at the light. The cross street was deserted. The car could have made the right on red, but instead it just sat there with its turn signal on … waiting for some reason.

I stepped on the brakes. The F-250 lunged forward, vibrating as the brake pads rubbed ineffectively on the rotors. My vehicle began to skid—gliding over the wet road beneath it. Madly, I stomped down harder. The truck shuddered, the gap closing. The rear of the LeSabre grew. The bumper was a solid line of dancing rainbow Grateful Dead bears stickers. I closed my eyes and gripped the vibrating wheel.

A violent shockwave. I bit my tongue.

The LeSabre was knocked into the intersection. Thankfully, no cars were coming. We spun out in opposite directions and quickly came to a short rest. A metal shovel shot out of the bed of my truck and landed in a bush in front of an office complex.

Out of the LaSabre bounced a woman. Mid-fifties. Gray turtleneck sweater. A mop of curly, salt and pepper hair. A small trickle of blood below her brow. I cringed. She didn't appear to be seriously injured, and was, for some reason, walking over to my window in a hurry.

"Hey! Are you okay?" she asked. She had a thick Irish accent. It further disoriented me.

"Me," I stammered.

"Yeah, you," she nodded. Then the Irish lady motioned towards the parking lot. She wanted to get off the road. Sure. That was wise.

We moved the vehicles. We were standing out in the light rain. It misted on our foreheads, making us furrow our brows as if we were in pain from it. We stood there and glared at our ticking, hissing machines as if they were unruly pets who'd just misbehaved with each other and had to be separated. The Irish lady was understanding about the whole thing. A little too understanding. I didn't know how to take it.

"I'd like to handle this outside of insurance, but I'd need to have the money quickly," she said, "for repairs."

"Absolutely," I agreed. Cash. We'd do it cash. As soon as possible.

"My brother is in collision," she said coolly.

"So are you," I thought.

She bent down and rubbed her open palm on the crunched devastation as if receiving a transmission directly from the LeSabre itself.

"Five hundred," she said. "Seem fair?"

"No, it seems low," I said, ashamed again of my driving. "I can give you seven hundred."

"Sweet, but unnecessary," she said definitively.

She wanted to see my license. I handed it to her.

"Lee," she said, looking at my face and the photo on the ID. "I'll give this back to you when you bring the money."

She put my license in the back pocket of her jeans.

"Jesus."

"Don't bring Him into this," she said. "You come by tonight. Yeah, 7:30. My husband is out of town, and I need to have the car fixed before he gets back."

She opened up the LeSabre and fished around inside, came back with a tube of lipstick. Metallic. Silver.

"Halloween," she said to explain and then wrote her address on the hood of my F-250:

Mary Beth
118 Mermaid Ave.

"The Tin Man," I thought.

I said I knew where it was, and that I'd come by. It was just a few miles from the Lagoon House.

"Seven-thirty," she said again as she waved and climbed into her car, pulling out of the lot. "Come alone!"

I jumped in my truck and started to pull away. A girl with an umbrella tapped on my window.

"Yeah?"

She pointed at my shovel sticking in a bush with red berries. I thanked her and threw the shovel into the bed of the pickup, while she smoked a cigarette beneath her umbrella, eyeing me.

As I left the lot, I noticed that the office belonged to a lawyer. I imagined him in one of the upper windows, looking down at the rainy street, at the scene of the collision, and hoping we'd need him.

But we wouldn't.

People like us don't use lawyers unless we're forced.

Feral

HERE THE FUCK DID YOU GET THAT MOTHERFUCKING SWEET VIKING HELMET?" Feral said.

"A girl."

I set the helmet on the coffee table.

He was on the couch, shirtless and playing Grand Theft Auto.

"Your stitches are finally out."

"Trish yanked them."

"She's good like that."

"Yeah, oh, mos def. She's the best when she's not bitching me out. The best."

She'd mentioned the problems with Feral to me, so it didn't surprise me when he said, "She must be getting born again for Christ or something. Getting all Holy Roller. Get this: she wants me to go over to the Mayweather. She says I've got a problem. Me. Imagine that! Me, with a problem. I should get her a giant Bible with her name on it."

"What kind of problem did she say you have?"

"It's a long list," he said. "Mostly, I think she wants to marry a Boy Scout. I said, 'Trish, you ever been fucked by a Boy Scout?'"

He paused the game, set the controller down, and opened his mouth to say something else but froze up. I almost started telling him about everything, about K Neon and the house on the ocean and the two days of crazy sex and the Irish lady I'd just slammed into with my truck ... but I didn't bother. His eyes were narrow slits. He was sideways on pills again.

I ate a few slices of pizza, left over from what they'd ordered the previous night, and sat by myself in the kitchen.

"Seth keeps bringing Denise over. She's a real cool girl, real chill." He keeps saying, "Real chill. Which is good, 'cause her and Trish seem to get along real good. Best butt buddies."

"Yeah," I said. "I like Denise too."

"They're off now getting tattoos," Feral said, all wide eyed and entertained by the idea.

"Seth is too?"

"Yeah! Denise said she'd buy him a tat if he went with her. She's real chill, ya know? She didn't wanna go alone. 'In case things got weird," she said. Know where she's getting inked?"

"Her pussy."

"Her pussy! Exactly! Oh man, if this was a game show, you woulda just won a washing machine or something."

"Seth getting the KISS logo?"

"Yeah," Feral said, busting a gut, "on his pussy."

Mary Beth

A<small>T SEVEN-THIRTY,</small> I went to see the Irish Lady. The Tin Man silver lipstick on my hood said her name was Mary Beth. There was a line of cars parked in front of her little yellow house: 118 Mermaid Ave. A swan mailbox. Chipped and faded paint. Cars in the driveway too. I was both troubled and relieved to see the other cars. It felt wrong going to this woman's house, like something was gonna go down that I wouldn't be happy to take part in. ("My husband's outta town," I kept hearing her say).

The LeSabre wasn't there. I double-checked the address on the hood. It was the one.

It reminded me of the house where I grew up and Seth and I played. Cramped. Crowded. Tons of junk packed onto the tiny crabgrass lawn.

I went through a chain-link fence, past an army of bird baths and garden gnomes. I knocked lightly on the door, my other hand clutching the envelope of money.

The door opened right away. Mary Beth. She'd changed her outfit. Now she was in a black shirt covered with sequins. Her hair had been straightened, and she wore earrings that dangled. A necklace with a large octagonal emerald hung down, swaying.

"Oh, you! Good," she said. "Come in, come in, come in."

I stepped inside her house. It smelled like one of those candles that people think smell like the beach. She touched my back, patting it like we were old friends, as she guided me further in. We walked down a small hallway with benches, crowded with umbrellas and wet shoes, that opened on a packed-tight kitchen full of music and food and many odd-faced people.

I was at a large family dinner. There were maybe fifteen of them, all sitting on various tables that were set up as hubs around a large wooden table with a flank steak on one plate and corned beef on another. Bowls of cabbage, potatoes, steamed broccoli, and carrots. Rows of 3-liter store brand soda: black cherry, cream, and orange.

There was music: the oldies station. Aretha Franklin belting out, "At last, my love has come along ..." A baby cried. A woman was scolding a pre-teen girl in a red, fluffy dress. Colorful balloons hung over everyone's heads and against a deactivated ceiling fan.

Mary Beth pointed at the table and said, "Have a seat. I saved you a spot."

Everyone was looking at me, like: "Who the hell is this weirdo?" I told her I was okay, and kept trying to pass her the envelope full of money. She kept slapping my hand away, saying, "Sit down, sit down, sit down!" She wasn't the only one who thought I was being rude. A woman, severely wrinkled and all crunched over, demanded, "SIT, BOY! SIT!"

I took a seat, an uncomfortable wooden chair without a cushion. The fat envelope of cash sat next to my plate. The people at the table kept glancing at it, perplexed. It was beyond awkward.

A bearded man, who was sitting beside me, extended his beefy hand.

"Rudy," he said. "Who are you?"

"Just a friend," I said for some reason.

"He crashed into me at a red light today," Mary Beth said.

The table of people grumbled. "Where?" asked a lady with thick-framed glasses who looked like she could be Mary Beth's sister.

"Oh, down over there by Dr. Dean's. Downtown. By the boat basin."

"I'm sorry," I said.

"What're you sorry for, you didn't make it rain, did you?"

"How'd the accident happen?" Rudy said.

I shrugged. Turned red.

"You were speeding," Rudy said.

"I ... I—"

"It was wet out. Pouring," Mary Beth explained.

"You must drive more careful in the rain," the wrinkled woman offered as advice, "especially near children."

A little boy had materialized at her knee, gripping it and looking up at me curiously.

"I'm sorry," I said again to everyone.

Mary Beth nodded, waved me off.

"Silly, it was an accident."

She dished out a massive amount of food onto my plate: meat, boiled potatoes, cabbage. She set the plate down and passed me the mustard and soda bread. Everyone watched me. No-one else had been served yet.

I couldn't recall the last time I sat a table like this and had a meal with a family. It's something I'd never done. My mother and me never ate like this. It was usually eating ramen noodle or fast food, quickly, at a small table or a motel room bed. It was no better when we moved in with Aldo, although sometimes he'd make a pot of spaghetti. We ate off TV trays in the living room, never enjoying our food. Seth invited me to eat at his aunt's house about fifty times, but I never went.

And here I was, with a big plate of food and many eyes on me.

The family leaned in. Holding their breath. They were very concerned about me and the plate of food. I could feel them all collectively suck their breaths in and curl their toes.

What would I do?

I put the fork to my mouth and took the tiniest bite of cabbage. The tension immediately lifted. I heard an audible sigh. Everybody started getting plates of food, standing almost in unison. A glass of wine appeared before me.

"This is his birthday," the wrinkled woman said.

"Who?" I asked, confused.

"Come out here, Jackie, so the bad driver man can sing you your special happy birthday song."

The small child was evidently hiding under the table. I froze.

"Jackieeeee," she sang like it was its own little song, "come on out! He wants to sing you your birthday song!"

Just then the door opened, and Trish walked in. I couldn't believe what I was seeing. Her dreads were fuzzy.

She looked at Mary Beth and she said, "Sorry I'm late mom. Frickin' Dollar Store. They act like we're saving lives in there."

"Well the value is great and a lot of people are struggling

..." Rudy said, sipping his wine.

Trish looked over at Rudy and saw me sitting at the table. She was bewildered. I thought about her climbing up into the attic with Denise on that stormy afternoon.

Trish looked slowly around the room at the faces of her family members, perhaps expecting to see other strange, unexplainable faces. Satan. Jerry Garcia. Dr. Strangelove.

"Lee?" She was blinking and stunned.

I gave a little wave.

"What are you doing here?"

The little kid, Jackie, jumped out from under the table and yelled "HE'S HERE TO SINNNNGGG ME MY HAPPY BURFDAY SONG!"

10

ETHAN WANTED A REHEARSAL. We hadn't played any of our set in quite a while, and he'd booked us a show in New York City. It was a big deal to us.

I left K Neon's house. She wanted to come watch us rehearse, but I knew it wasn't a good idea. Ethan freaked out about that kinda thing. He didn't like people watching him sing unless he was on stage. I found that silly and childish.

Ethan's parents' ocean-side manor was lit up with soft orange lights in every window. I drove down the long pebble driveway and couldn't help but feel a little bad for Ethan. Unlike K Neon's vacant manor just up the road, where freedom was abundant, this place was always occupied by parents that kept a hawk-like eye on Ethan's movements.

He'd had a pretty crappy childhood despite all the money. His dad, Claude, was overbearing.

"He used to make me play the violin when I was seven, eight, nine years old ... I hated it," Ethan told me once, drunk. "So I stopped practicing. He'd come home and say, 'You haven't been playing your violin, I can tell.' I said, 'I have, dad.' He'd take off his belt and ask me again if I'd been practicing. I told him, 'Yes, yes, yes! I swear!' Then my dad would point at the violin case. There was a small feather sitting on it. He said, 'I put that there a week ago!'"

"Now you can kick his ass," I told Ethan.

"I don't think so. His attempts at bonding with me usually involved a trip to the gun range. Automatic weapons."

"Yeah, you don't fight somebody like that," I advised. Ethan didn't laugh. But then again, when did he? "Well, I never shot a gun before. What's it like?"

"For you? You'd break your nose."

I parked my truck and sat. Thought about the tropical bird they kept in the house. It was a very pretty bird. It must've been one of that bird's feathers that was placed on the violin case. I smirked. If K was here, she could take a look at that tropical bird and identify it.

Ethan and the bird were both pets. When you're somebody's pet, you don't get to live your own life. Them's the rules.

Behind the large bay doors, Claude had a massive, detached garage that was set up as a BMW speed shop. Claude didn't do any of the work himself and didn't race the cars. He just liked to have the place. He used to hire a guy named Gunny, who was a real ace mechanic, but something happened with the car shop and with Gunny. The shop was empty since then. That was fine for us, because we were able to rehearse there. I went to the door and punched in the code. After the door opened, I clicked on the lights. It was expansive. Three antique cars—a Jaguar, a Model T, and an Aston Martin—were parked along the back wall.

Seth pulled up in his Sentra and asked, "Where's Ethel?"

I shrugged. We started carrying his drum set into the shop. There was a small rubber-backed rug that we unrolled for his kick drum (so it wouldn't slide around on the painted concrete floor). I had just set my amp up in the usual spot and flicked on the PA system when Ethan walked in. He stood in the doorway, glaring at us.

"Oh, here it goes," I thought.

"We've got a problem," he said ominously.

"Problem, yes," I confirmed.

"Realized something today. Wanted to hear it from you two. Wanted to hear you say it."

Neither Seth or me said anything, for over a minute. Ethan just continued to glare.

Finally, Seth said, "Alright, gig is up. You know about me and Denise."

"Yeah," Ethan said.

I watched his bottom lip tremble. He looked on the verge of tears.

"It just happened," Seth said, "and continues to happen. What am I supposed to do?"

"I should've seen this coming. You're both scumbags."

I suppose there was no denying that.

"Both of you are out of the band. We're done."

Fair enough. Seth was screwing his girl. I was an accomplice in all of it. Seth started to pack his cymbals away, and I put my cheap backup pawnshop guitar in its case.

"You're leaving all that," he said to me, pointing at my amp, guitar, and pedal board. Then he pointed at Seth's drums.

"Those too. They're mine now."

"The fuck they are," Seth shot back.

"You owe me twenty-six hundred dollars," Ethan said. "I know you losers don't have the money. I'm keeping your shit."

Seth started to laugh.

"Yeah, that's a good one."

"Call me a loser again," Seth said. "You won't like what happens."

Ethan stood his ground in the doorway. He said, "I'm serious. I want all that cash. You give it to me, and you can have your toys back."

It was unreal. He really thought that we would just be like, "'sall cool, Ethel! Go ahead, keep our stuff.'"

"I hope you've got a gun, 'cause you'll need one," Seth said.

"In the house," Ethan replied coldly.

"That's Claude's gun. That's Claude's money," I said.

"I liked her," Ethan said.

"She's a good girl," Seth said. "Liked doesn't matter."

"You can't play drums for shit," Ethan hissed. Pointing at me, he continued, "And you're a joke. Your songs suck. It was a waste of my time having anything to do with you."

"Hey, I fucked Denise too," I said.

"She's a whore. You're all trash," Ethan, hurt, snarled.

Seth had one of his Zildjian cymbals in his hand. He smashed it into Ethan's chest. The alloy rang out after being knocked to the floor. Seth was around his drums, quick, like a German Shepherd coming around the side of a house. Right on Ethan. Knocked him on his ass.

They were on the ground. Seth knocked that kid hard in his stomach. Ethan's knee came up, catching Seth in his lip.

"You motherfucker!" Seth's lip was bloody.

Ethan scrambled to his feet and then out the door, heaving, sucking air. I heard him slam his car door, start his BMW, and peel off down the driveway.

I looked at Seth.

"You're bleeding."

"You're next," he said.

"I'm next ... fuck off. I didn't really bang her. She climbed in my window. It was close, but it didn't happen."

"When?"

"The first night you were with her."

"Get outta here," he spit blood on the floor.

"She was in my room first," I admitted.

"But nothing happened?"

"Nothing major," I said.

"Good enough. Keep it that way."

Nothing else was said about it after that. We packed up our equipment quickly. As we left the garage, drops of blood kept smacking on the floor. It felt like at any moment the cops were gonna show up and drag us off.

"I'll talk to you tomorrow," I said to Seth.

"Right." We drove in opposite directions on Route 35. He was going to Lagoon House and Denise. I was going back to K.

The night felt dire. Raw. Worrisome.

Ethan was gonna shoot Seth in the head. At least that's what I kept thinking. Seth would be asleep on my couch. The gunshot would wake Feral up ... maybe.

K was up on the balcony in the backyard when I got there, drinking Tanqueray and bitter lemon and painting her toenails. I stood down on the mahogany deck, looking at the moss rock boulders strewn around the edges of the dune.

"I better get to work tomorrow."

She laughed. Her voice carried nicely. It flew around like a gull sailing across the moon.

"It's strange seeing you in a dress."

"Thought I'd dress up for you," she said. "Come up here. I'm lonely."

K leaned on the metal railing and smiled.

She had the lights of the kidney-shaped pool on. That illumination made everything seem foggy, otherworldly. I went through the house and came out onto the balcony with her. After sitting in a patio chair, I got ready to tell her about everything that had gone down. But I didn't get a chance. K stood up from her chair, came to my lap, leaned across, and kissed me deep.

"I like you ... too much," she said, pulling on the back of my shirt. "I'm excited, but worried."

"Yeah? Why are you worried?"

"I have a girlfriend. This isn't cool, what we've been do-ing."

"No?"

"It's serious, me and June."

"Yeah?"

"We're exclusive with each other. It'd break her heart, what me and you've been getting into. And she's coming. That's the worst part. She'll be here tomorrow morning. She's on a bus … coming here," she said.

"Your girlfriend, on a Greyhound bus."

"A real sweetheart. A southern girl. She's never been with a guy—so she claims. And I'm nervous," she added, "because I want something to happen, and I'm not sure it'll go okay."

"Want do you want to happen?"

K Neon ran her fingers through my hair and said, "I want to watch you fuck her."

JUNE DOOM

JUNE DOOM PULLED INTO THE STATION AT NOON. I sat in the F-250 with K Neon, watching the silver bus glide in. My hand was on K's knee. She tapped the dashboard nervously.

"I hope she's on this bus."

"Why wouldn't she be?"

"We had a fight," K said, "just before I left school."

The bus settled low to the ground hydraulically. The doors opened.

"About what?"

"She wanted me to stop seeing somebody. A boy."

I nodded.

"I said that I would, but here you are … a new boy."

"I'm not a boy."

"Your only saving grace."

The first of the passengers started to trickle out of the Greyhound.

"Which one is she?"

K sighed, "Oh you'll know her when you see her."

I watched a string of passengers exit the bus, shuffling off in random directions into the bus depot and its rows of waiting cars packed in the lot. Most of the people were waiting for the connecting bus to Atlantic City. They were going down there to feed their hopes and dreams into video poker machines, slot machines, the open hands of baccarat dealers in white shirts and black vests who smiled like angels of death.

An old woman struggled with an assortment of bags.

A man in a tan suit held a large wrapped gift with a balloon scotch taped to it. A girl with a cat in a travel case. A black lady held her son's hand, pointing up at a plane in the sky dragging a vinyl banner towards the beach. The banner was for Tooth Town. It featured a drawing of a fine set of white teeth under red lips that smiled at the world below.

A girl—tall, doe-eyed, dyed red hair—came through the doors of the bus. She wore a dress covered in constellations and star charts. One hand clutched a suitcase, the other gripped sky-blue skateboard sneakers slung over her shoulder. She glanced around, looking for K. Cool. Calm. Barefoot on hot asphalt. Not frightened by the broken glass strewn across the surfaces of the world.

"That's her," I said.

"Duh, dummy." K leaned over on the bench seat and honked the horn. June looked up, smiled at us in the beat up truck, and walked over. She stopped at my door.

"And, so who are you?"

"He's the driver," K said.

"Yup," I agreed, "the driver. I'm gonna take you all over. High, low, up into the sky. Down into the valleys, through the secret tunnels beneath the asylum. Even to the boardwalk."

"Sounds fun."

I said who I really was. She said who she really was. We shook hands politely. She got in the passenger side and kissed K. We drove nowhere, just forward.

"Where you wanna go?" I asked.

"I don't know. Never been here."

K lifted June's dress and exposed her pale thighs.

"Hey, what gives?" June was pissed.

"I was hoping you had your bikini on underneath. We could go to the beach."

"No," June said. "No beach, please."

"What's your problem?"

"Been on a bus for four hours. Can I just get a minute?"

"Take all the minutes you want," K said.

Were they gonna fight like this the whole time?

"I've got a full tank of gas. I can just circle New Jersey. We'll do laps: from here to the southern tip, then up through the farms…"

"Farms? Just stop."

"Called the Garden State for a reason," I said.

"The toxic waste state," K added.

"Hey, you're here. Can't be all that bad. I'll drive you through the pine barrens, then up into the mountains…"

"There's no mountains in New Jersey," K said.

"Any real genius knows that there certainly are," I said. "I'll show you. Big rock peak cliffs. All the way up there. Castles in the clouds. And then, after the mountains, I'll take you both to the city. Blinding lights. Singing. Dancing. Etcetera."

"Let's just go to the ocean," K said.

June said, "I think I'd rather get a beer."

I nodded, pleased. I aimed the truck in the direction of beer.

11

T HE FERRIS WHEEL WAS STUCK. Mashed or severed gears. Some girl screamed, wild and desperate, imprisoned at the top. Her voice was shrill, contained hot panic—as if sentenced to public death for a crime she didn't understand. Not quite a child, not quite an adult, she hovered on the fringes of the void.

A wax paper soda cup flew down to the boardwalk planks; ice spread everywhere. There was nothing that could be done. People stood outside Midway Pizza were staring up, excited.

The moon was full, and the roller-coaster flashed by—a mechanical snake creating thunder.

One thing was certain. You could spot the tourists. They came there for the spectacle. On Friday afternoons in the summer they packed the turnpike and parkway, coming south from NYC, Staten Island, Bayonne, Elizabeth, Newark ... bennies. The girl up on the Ferris wheel was one of them, a visitor, and she was the greatest spectacle of all.

The wind came down the boardwalk with the smell of zeppole: fried dough and confectioners' sugar. There was the off-kilter music of the carousel. Electric lights. Electric motors. Flying horses. Fairground organs.

Grits of sand whipped against all rough edges, making everything smooth. The crowd stared up at the screaming girl.

I put my hand in the back pocket of K Neon's cutoff jean shorts and tugged. It was no use. Sensory overload. She was wide-eyed wonder—transfixed as she looked up.

"Let's go," I commanded. "I'll show you something."

My voice broke the spell from the girl's sky screams, brought both my girls back to me.

I was there with two beautiful college girls, like I'd just won the lottery. As a result, my feathers were all puffed up like some champion peacock let out on a Saturday parade. I kept myself from floating off up over the Ferris wheel, victim of an over-inflated ego, by reminding myself, continuously, that this kind of thing wasn't a normal occurrence. I should treat it like a delicate gift that could be ruined as offhandedly as it had arrived.

K Neon, the blonde of proper-bred blood and money, dressed in a candy stripe, nautical tank top; tight jean shorts; and flip-flops. June, a native of Savannah, Georgia, who, like me, had nothing. She didn't even have a bra on. She wore a necklace of hundreds of shards of black obsidian. Ripped jean shorts. Fugazi T-shirt, painted on and faded to near pink.

June was in love with K, and K liked June. Both of them thought I was alright, but I got the impression that was just because they had no clue where I was coming from, what I was thinking, what I wanted. They didn't know if I was for real or just some weirdo that would dissipate when the wind normalized.

I took whatever opportunity presented itself to show them the depth of my oddness and the way I belonged nowhere and everywhere at the same time. They took the hint and removed all posturing, although a nervous tension throbbed beneath like a nest of baby rabbits under a patch of lawn. These two girls were squirming, pulsing with the possibility of conflict, collision: self-destruction as means of re-envisioning.

They liked to drink. I remember that. They'd drink anything you put in the vicinity of their full, wet, welcoming lips. They both preferred straws, thinking it was cute (for some reason) to drink everything through a straw … even beer. I took great joy in feeding them both drinks. June sucked back Gin Gimlets. K Neon liked straight vodka.

K had become a tad quieter and more restrained with the appearance of June off the bus. June seemed excited to see the boardwalk and showed me joy and warmth and politeness. Each time I brought her a drink she said, "Thank you kindly."

"It's nothing. You're visiting. I'm just trying to make sure you have fun. Don't want yet another person to have something bad to say about me or New Jersey."

"You're off to a good start then."

She wouldn't look me in the eye. There was a distance between us. I didn't make her blush, not even once. K smiled,
looking at her girl.

"You look best when you're all pink."

Neither one of them had seen and been doused in the true
filth of the boardwalk, although they both seemed eager for an
introduction. The line of bars in a strip flashed neon. Stuffed
animals more outsized than even the most runaway bloated
dream, hung suspended, waiting.

"One Win Choice," the barker yelled as we passed. "Step
up! Play whatever game you want. No-one loses."

I took them to a stand called Frog Bog. Five bucks for a
bucket of rubber frogs. Players put the frogs, one at a time, on
a catapult and smashed the catapult with a mallet to send the
frogs soaring into the air. The object was to land the frogs on a
lily pad that rotated mechanically in swirling water.

I thought about my cock. Wasn't it just like the rubber frog,
soaring into the unknown? Weren't these girls lily pads, rotating around me?

My frogs splashed into the water, vanished. June was luck-
ier. She won a massive Rastafarian banana with a Jamaican flag
bandana wrapped around its neck, sunglasses, and a joint hanging out of its mouth.

"Your first banana," K exclaimed. "Congratulations!"

At the arcade, we played Mr. and Ms. Pacman and could
not decide which was better.

I said, "My friend says Ms. Pacman is better, of course."

"Why?"

"More cherries."

K looked at me knowingly. "He's right," she said.

Then they watched, hanging off of each other for sup-
port, while I chased ghosts around the electric maze, carefully
rationing my power pills and disappearing off screen to hide
and reappear as if reborn on the other side. Duck and weave
and live forever.

When I was finished, caught in a corner by the pink-sheet-
ed digital undead, I dumped a new quarter into the slot, slid
away from the machine, and guided June up to the joystick
by placing my hand on the small of her back. It was our first
touch. The colorful carpet, with its Arabian Night design,
caused static electricity to pop. Both of us jumped.

June gave me the side eye, her long, braided hair swaying.

K pushed me playfully into June.

"You two are getting along as well as I'd hoped."

"Enough with that, please," June said.

K backed off. It was only time I'd ever seen her do that. Things were headed in a particular direction. Two of us knew it, and one was unsure.

I treated the girls to fifty-cent drafts at the Sawmill and pointed at the bouncer, Boyd.

"See that tiger-tank-sized human over there?"

"Yeah," K said.

"He broke my nose last summer."

"Still looks pretty good," June said, playfully tapping the tip.

And just like whenever there are fifty-cent drafts being served anywhere, a fight broke out. A little man with spiked hair lunged at a meathead, a block of human muscle. The stool flipped over, and both of them rolled on the floor. Spit, shouts ... the bar erupted in havoc and horrible voices.

There was a secret weapon though: Boyd—two hundred and seventy five pounds of sheer doomsday. He rumbled through the crowd in his canary yellow SECURITY shirt. Getting in there somehow, Boyd split the red-faced, veiny-necked men.

"You'll have to leave. The both of you. NOW," Boyd shouted.

I thought about the time I'd seen Charlie at the bar after the whole incident with Natalie. I was drunk. Charlie was drunk. The standard. We got into some shit. Boyd grabbed me by the nape of my neck and pulled me out onto the boardwalk, telling me, "Be cool."

At the time, I wasn't so easily receptive to instruction. I charged back into the bar. Boyd reeled me in by my shirt— broke my left hand and my nose too. Ahhh, the days.

You get what you deserve though. You can't blame anyone else for the things you do. Desire makes us wild, opening up sacred wildflowers sopping wet with dew. Even if you're intentions are to rip off the petals one by one and swallow them, you can't hope to resist for very long. It's in your nature.

The fighters were removed from the barroom. The particles and ions settled. The air compressor kicked on. Much needed cool air flooded through the ducts. I looked at K, she was sweating, glistening. June Doom was bone dry. Georgia is a different world. She chewed her lower lip, as if it was gum.

No-one questioned what that fight had been about. It was

about war.

K smoked an American Spirit Light on the bench outside some shop with black light mushroom posters, concert t-shirts, and incense. It had some stupid name, Rockin' Robin's or something. Locals called it something stupider: Bong Depot. June wanted to go to another little booth to have their fortune read by Madame Woo-the Dead.

"I don't think so," K said coldly. She turned her face and exhaled smoke, the wind tugging it a thousand miles out over the unknown ocean.

"Why not?" June was hurt.

"Not my thing. I don't believe in it."

To me, K looked frightened. Not her thing? More like terrified.

June, impatient and giddy, took my hand and brought me instead.

Madame Woo-the Dead's boardwalk booth was decorated to resemble the inside of a gypsy tent. Mystical. Bones and stars on strings. Chants playing from a tape deck hidden behind a curtain. Sage burned. The smoke drifted up into the air propelled by a small, battery-powered fan.

Madame Woo-the Dead, herself, was dressed in a loose satin robe. Violet. Her eyes were painted green, the color of the unknown ocean. She was not Chinese. She was not some sort of gypsy. She seemed French Canadian by the way she spoke.

Still, we hung on every syllable she uttered. We were seated on unpadded steel folding chairs across from the mystic. Madame Woo-the Dead took both of our right hands and scrutinized them, the palms especially.

"There's someone else," she said. "But, the two of you will one day get married."

June started to laugh. "Married?"

A memory consumed me. K Neon and I lay in bed, still panting, our hearts fluttering from exertion. She said, "I don't think June has ever been with a boy. I think she might still be a virgin ... in that way."

June Doom pinched her own leg.

Madame Woo-the dead shifted in her chair. Her robes went swoosh. Then she nodded, repeating, "Married, yes. It's a certainty."

"Is anything certain?" asked June.

"Love is," Madam Woo-the Dead said.

I paid the three dollars. We left.

K was gone from the bench. We found her standing on the fringes of the crowd of spectators looking up at the Ferris wheel.

There was talk of the fire department coming with a cherry picker, one of those machines that could extend up forever. It'd pull the people out of the sky one by one and reintroduce them to the ground where they belonged.

That girl was still screaming up there. Her horror-stricken voice was strained to the verge of hoarseness. It'd been some time, but her desperation had not lessened. She wasn't getting any more comfortable with her isolation. She hadn't figured out isolation can be a gift.

Someone in the crowd said, "You know whether or not the thunderstorm's coming?"

"They said …"

"Think they'll cancel the fireforks?"

I tuned out the girl's calls for help. It all became a silent hum to me. It was almost that time of night. My eyes went to June. I looked at her tight, ripped cutoffs and wondered how she'd taste and smell if we could somehow get alone.

12

THE CRUSHED SEASHELL DRIVEWAY WAS PACKED solid with cars. Everyone was blocked in, and they were in no condition to leave anyway. Walking up, the gardens were bright, pulsing with nectar-heavy flora throbbing beneath a full yellow moon. K was throwing a party in the ocean manor. "My family will be back any day. Make it count!" was the theme.

She was a party person, a rave girl, and would look for any excuse to throw one. Your band broke up? Let's throw a party. You'll be homeless any day now? Let's throw a party. You're lost, directionless, motherless, and fatherless and looking for some scraps for fun in the wild? Let's throw a party.

Music poured from the upper windows. Strobe lights flickered vividly with the music that seemed to float, stutter, and pulse like life itself.

The house was locked tight; no-one was allowed in there except June, K, and me. Everywhere you looked, the kids were wrecked—laughing and shouting on the slate steps, leaning on the white columns, standing in the brick path that led through the fence; rocking and rolling in white plastic chairs, or sitting on my boulder wall: animated, yelling, smoking, drinking strange serums from red solo cups. Life: full and blur buzzed with slanted beauty on a Saturday night.

It felt that good to be that close to the ocean. We could all feel it and were responding accordingly. The dune grass swayed. In the distance, if you squinted on the horizon, the Ferris wheel could be seen spinning again.

It was close to midnight. Things shifted into a drunken fog. I leaned over the railing, looking at the kids crowded around the kidney shaped pool below.

Feral and Trish were swimming in the pool, drunk and looking like they were gonna drown. They were all pilled up. So was K. So were a lot of the guests.

Some kid I didn't know, dressed in backwards red Yankees cap, was heckling Feral savagely, saying, "I feel like I'm at the Philadelphia zoo watching the polar bears swim."

"Careful, bro," Feral called, his arms flailing in the water ineffectively.

"Why?" the kid asked with a smirk.

"Bears bite heads off."

"I got a head for you to bite," the kid said, grabbing his own nuts through his board shorts. The kid was a typical Jersey douchebag.

I yelled down, "Hey, Feral—you're gonna fucking drown, man. Get over to the shallow end."

Dale appeared through the gate with Steph at his side. I waved, but they didn't seem to notice me in my perch.

Feral laughed, swallowing more water as he drifted over to the kiddie side. Trish swam to him, and they embraced next to the pool light, obscuring it, sending shadows across the water, altering the light for the whole backyard.

I looked down at all of the people from my chair, not sure who half of them were. June was across from me. She had a gin gimlet in her hand. She kept half smiling, half grimacing.

"What's the matter?"

"Oh, I don't know," she said. "I'm just not feeling so good."

"Well, you're at a party," I said.

"Just because you're at a party doesn't mean you have to be the party." She was full of wisdom beyond her years.

I pointed to her drink, "Give it time."

"Like, where's K, right now?" June asked. "I never see her when there's a party, and there's always a party. That bums me out."

"She surrounds herself with people."

"Exactly. There's always got to be someone else," June said, "always."

"But you'd rather be alone."

"I'm not so sure," June said. "You seem like good enough company." June looked at me sideways. "You should let me cut your hair."

"Why would I do that?"

"Don't be an asshole. I'd shave you too."

"Shave me? Shave yourself."

She laughed. "I'm good with a straight razor. My foster mom raised rabbits. I skinned them. Made stuff out of the fur."

"That's weird as hell, but it makes me like you more."

"In school, I used to cut hair. All I'd do is hang up a little sign by the soda machine, and they'd come to my dorm or call me to go to theirs."

"Beats working at Taco Bell," I said. "Fuck it, cut my hair."

"That's how I met K."

"Cutting her hair?"

"I went to her apartment and didn't leave for three days."

"Déjà vu," I said, but June didn't hear.

The sliding glass door opened behind us. K Neon stuck her face out and said, "Look who I found."

Seth and Denise were right behind her.

"Look at this house," Seth said. "Unbelievable."

"Yeah, something else," I said, shaking his hand.

Seth had grown up like me, without any money and living in a small ranch house without much to his name. Actually, he'd had it worse than me. He didn't have a mom or dad. He lived with his aunt at the end of our dead-end street. But at least he used to have the lake house on Mount Mercy to escape to every summer with his older brother. I used to hear plenty of stories about how nice it was there, but I never got to go myself.

K let everyone onto the balcony. Then, as June Doom opened her mouth to say something sweet to her, K closed the sliding glass door—vanishing into the house without saying goodbye.

"What's that cunt's problem?" Denise screamed, referring to K.

Denise looked like she was already wasted. Seth didn't look much better. Droopy eyelids. Quivering jaws. On the verge of nosebleeds.

She repeated herself, "Seriously, what's that cunt's problem?"

I ignored the question. June didn't say anything either.

"She gives me one more dirty look, I'm gonna break her teeth right out of her bitchy little mouth."

"Hey, cool down," I said. "There are no problems here."

Denise was on edge, but Seth offset it by saying, "Look, a jacuzzi. Wanna go in?" He looked at me then looked at June. "Can we go in?"

"You should," June said. "Yeah. Go ahead."

That's all Denise had to hear. She started pulling her dress over her head. In a moment, she was inside the hot tub wearing just the same purple bra and thong that I'd seen on Seth's floor.

The three of us sat in the chairs, having a pretty adult conversation and drinking our adult beverages, while Denise bounced around in the hot tub, singing songs to herself and saying, in a high whine, "I'm lonely. Someone come in here and play with me."

I laughed and looked at Seth.

"She's wasted. She gonna make it?"

He made the sign of the cross.

We moved our chairs closer to the hot tub so that maybe Denise would quiet down a little bit. Down below, a kick drum throbbed. A synth wailed. Someone splashed down in the pool. June seemed to be coming out of her quiet funk, even began joking around with Denise.

"I like your tattoos," she said.

"I wanna be the Illustrated Woman!"

"You have the body for it."

"Well, thank you! Not so bad yourself," Denise said, her arms behind her head and Daddy's Little Girl in Old English lettering poking out of the top of her bra.

"What'd K say to piss you off?"

"Oh, the blonde bitch? She was just being a little pain in my ass because me and my guy walked in the front door and she didn't like it. She was making a big deal about 'nobody being allowed in the house.' It's not that nice of a house. You should see where I live."

"Her dad's in the mafia," I told June. "Be careful. Denise already has a hit out on K. You'll be next."

I pantomimed shooting June in the head at close range. She pantomimed falling over dead. Seth took out a smoke and lit up. June asked if we wanted anything to drink.

"I have a nice bottle of gin."

Seth said, "Bring the bottle, please."

"Your wish is not only my command, but also my plea-sure," said June.

"Vous es le meilleur."

Alone now with him, everything around us got quiet, except for Denise, who was still singing her songs and splashing around. The noise of the party was still raging on, but all that seemed to fade. It was just me and Seth, leaning on the balcony, when he looked at me and said, "We've got to go to L.A."

"Yeah, I said, we do." I didn't really believe it though. I just said it because he needed to hear it.

"We'll get a little ratty house out there, and we'll play shows all up and down the Sunset Strip."

I didn't even know what that entailed. I just nodded my head. Seth was obliterated. I didn't have the heart to get into it now. Ethan was gone. If we'd had a chance at all of going to California, it would have been riding on his coattails. His coin.

"There's just so many things I wanna do with my life, and I can't do any of them here," he said.

"And you think you'll be able to do them there?"

"I hope so. I feel like I'm dying here. You don't?"

"Maybe, but is that real?"

He hugged me. "Come on, bro. I need you to help me get outta here."

"Alright, alright," I said.

He let go, slouched on the column, and looked at me sideways. "Feral's already got the van," he said. "You teach him how to play bass, and we'll drive cross country in the A-Team van. Party in every city on the way. It'll be good."

"Sure," I said, although I'd already tried to show Feral how to play bass many times and it just never stuck.

"I've got to get outta here," he repeated. "Denise is coming too though."

"We'll go. I just have to finish this job," I said, pointing down at the boulder wall. "Almost done here. Then I got one more quick one. We'll take that money. We'll go try California."

I'd been there. I knew there weren't any answers in California that you couldn't find in New Jersey. I didn't have the heart to confess that to Seth. Not then. So I just left it at, "For sure. We'll go."

He smiled, relieved. His jaw quivered. I'd never seen him so trashed.

June came back out holding three gin gimlets with little wedges of lime in them. She passed them to us. Seth threw his back in one gulp. June looked away uncomfortably.

I said, "Hey Seth, have you ever told June Doom how KISS is the best band ever in the history..."

"Fuck you, man," Seth said, "I'm going in the hot tub."

He pulled down his pants and climbed in the hot tub bare-assed.

"Jesus! How drunk are you?" I laughed.

"Oh! Worse than you'd ever wanna know."

Denise howled with shrill laughter. Then, abruptly, she said, "Ethan's a pussy. He can't sing, and he can't get it up."

"I wanted to go to L.A.," Seth said.

"So go to L.A.," Denise said, kissing his neck. "I'll come with you. We'll steal one of my dad's garbage trucks."

She really was a riot, that girl.

"You'd do that for me, girl? You'd boost me a trash truck?"

"I love you, fucker."

"Well, I love you too, even though—"

"What?"

"You're Italian."

"Oh," she laughed. "You…" She kissed him. "Shit. I gotta pee," Denise said.

June pointed into the house. "There's a bathroom at the end of the hall."

Denise thanked her and got out of the tub. Walked into the house dripping wet.

June sighed, "Shit, she shoulda dried off."

It wasn't two minutes before K Neon came back out onto the balcony. "Who was in the house all wet?! It's soaked!"

She looked at Seth in the hot tub with his arms stretched out behind him.

"Wasn't me," he said.

"K, be cool," June pleaded.

K wasn't gonna hear that. She started mouthing off about Denise. "That little slut... That little ho."

Right away, Denise was in the doorway.

"Shut up, you blonde bitch," Denise said, shoving K hard.

I got out of my chair. Seth sank down into the water. June flinched. K turned around to face Denise, and—wham—got an open hand slap to the face. K fell over, shocked.

"You want some more?"

I pulled Denise back into the house. She kept squirming away. Seth jumped out of the jacuzzi, scooping up his corduroy shorts. He followed behind me and Denise in the house, tracking more water. I took them out to the front porch and said, "Denise, sorry, but you gotta leave."

Seth was cool about it. Denise was still yelling and mouthing off about K.

"We're outta here in a week!"

I walked them all the way out to the road, where Seth's Nissan was parked, but when we got to his car, I said, "I'm good to drive. Let me take you home in my truck."

"No way, man," Seth said, "I'm fine. I mean, I'm not, but you'll crash anyway. I've never crashed into anything—no matter how fucked up I've been."

"Just get in," I said as I opened the door to my truck and shoved him onto the bench seat. Denise was screaming with laughter as she helped me shove Seth in the cab. After that, we cruised across town without anyone putting up a fight. They'd get the car in the morning. But Denise had more to say.

"Those girls are assholes."

"They're not assholes," I said.

"No, they totally are."

"Okay, maybe one of them is an asshole. But June is fine."

"You're a little biased, because they're sucking your pole," Seth said.

"Trish said they're cunts too," Denise said.

"Well how the hell would she know that? She's barely even talked to either K or June."

"I can spot a bitch a mile away. I've got an eagle eye for cunty bitches, boy. They're everywhere on my campus. I could climb the bell tower and look down and identify them all if I wanted."

"You're too funny."

"These chicks are no good."

"Dead wrong," I said.

"I'll punch them both in the mouth if they say one more thing to me," Denise said.

"You're not punching anybody," Seth said.

"Oh? Just fucking watch me!"

"How you gonna do that if I got both your hands…"

He grabbed Denise and pinned her against the door, leaning in, kissing her. She tried to dodge him but couldn't.

"Lee! Get this freak off me!"

But she was laughing. Seth was bumping into me, making the truck go all over the road, bumping into the goddamned steering wheel. I crossed over the bridge and cut through the development to Lagoon House.

"So, are they like, both your girlfriend, or what?"

"Who knows? I certainly don't. They don't know."

"I just think it's messed up, and I don't want to see you

get hurt," she said, leaning over Seth. "You're a good guy. And when people screw around, it always ends up in some kind of big confrontation, ya know? Just be careful."

I dropped them off. Seth said he'd just have Denise drive him to get his car in the morning. All was well. They stumbled into the house, and I drove off.

Most of the cars were still there at the party. On my way walking back up the seashell driveway, I found Feral covering something up with a drop cloth in the back of his van. He seemed real surprised to see me.

"Where you been?"

"Drove fucking Seth and Denise back."

"What the hell happened with them?" he asked.

"Ahhh, a fight."

"No shit? I missed it. Damn."

"There'll be more," I said. He closed the van doors, and we walked back towards the house.

More people were showing up. It was one of those kinds of parties. People were being sucked in magnetically. When I turned back and looked at the house, there was a bunch of people standing on the porch who were looking at me while they drank out of red solo cups.

"What?"

No-one said anything.

I went back up on the balcony. June was hugging K, who kept touching her face and then looking at her hand as if expecting to see blood ... but there wasn't any.

"You alright?" I asked.

"I can't believe that maniac."

"Sorry about that," I said. "Honestly, I can't believe them. This type of thing never happens." A lie.

June hugged her girl and kissed her forehead.

"You'll be OK, babe," she said.

"Oh, I've been hit worse," K said, "and the reaction is always the same."

"What?" I asked.

"It turns me on," she said.

June let go of K.

Down below, I heard someone vomit. Unrelated: I heard the police coming through the gate, a scanner radio getting louder, and saw a flashlight swoop up.

The party was over.

Trish

I WOKE UP ON THE COUCH. MY NECK FELT ALMOST BROKEN. I kept looking up at a giant clock, its pendulum swinging over the mantle. June and K were in the master bedroom. I'd fallen asleep out there like a castaway. I got off the couch and looked out the window. The swimming pool was full of floating red solo cups, as if that's what the pool was put there for: a holding tank for red plastic cups.

A voice surprised me. Trish was sitting down there on a chair by the rock wall. She was wearing a flowing, bright, tie-dyed dress as she alternated puffing a cigarette and sipping the last gulp from a jug of orange juice. She was looking down at her feet as she sang "Sweet Child O' Mine" to herself—just the first verse.

"She's got a smile and it seems to me, reminds me of childhood memories, where everything was as fresh as the bright blue sky."

I opened the window and leaned out. I realized I was hanging out of the same window that the housekeeper had yelled at me out of that first day, when I was just starting to build the wall down there.

"Hey, Trish."

She looked up, surprised. "I forgot where I was, man."

"I understand."

"Been down here all night," she said, rubbing her eyes. "I forgot there was anybody else in the world kinda, especially up in that house."

"Understand completely," I said. "I'm coming down."

I walked through the house, each step echoing out on the lonely marble. Out back, the air was warmer than I'd expected it to be. Summer was setting in.

She looked up and waved weakly.

"Oww. I hid when the cops came. I was real high. I'm not now. I think I came down. The sun hurts."

"Oh, I know," I said.

"I hid underneath the deck," she said. "It was kinda funny listening to everybody scramble."

I'd known Trish ever since I was a boy. We went to grammar school together. In the second grade, I got it in my little kid brain that I wanted to throw a Halloween party at my mom's house. She was sober then. A brief window when things were normal. Dad was gone. There was no Aldo yet. Mom said I could invite 25 kids. I went to school the next day and started handing out invitations to the cool kids. I was so excited. I was gonna have a badass Halloween party, impress them all with my goblin act. I got down to my last invitation, and Trish kept bugging me for one. She was the weird, chubby girl who sat next to me and smelled like cold Chinese food. Sure, she let me use her crayons, but she wasn't pretty and she wasn't cool. Trish kept pushing and pushing and pushing, and even though I wanted to give my last invitation to Allison Lewis, I gave it to Trish. When it came time for the party, we had cobwebs up all over the house, we had a big cauldron to bob for apples, we had spider rings and cupcakes with ghosts and Frankenstein's monster on them. None of the other 24 kids showed up.

Just Trish.

We've been friends ever since.

In the backyard, I looked at her profile, her red puffy cheeks, and her squinty eyes with the low brows. I studied her little nose, which was a little crooked. It'd been fractured when Trish was ten. She tried to jump as high as she could off the playground swings.

She had a good heart. Trish was the toughest and funniest girl that I knew. Trish didn't take crap from people. Trish cared. Trish worked at the Dollar Store but was going to community college; she was gonna be a nurse. Feral wasn't good enough for her.

I pictured Trish, nine years old again, dressed in a witch costume as we played in the leaf pile in my backyard. She was trying to cheer me up because nobody came to the party. I remember she dug around in the leaves until she found a weird bug and gave it to me.

"What is that?"

"It's a wooly bear."

I had on rubber wolf man hands. She placed the super-hairy, brown and black caterpillar in my synthetic rubber paws, and I looked down at it as it curled into a tight ball.

"Thank you," I said.

"It's just a bug," she said. "World's full of 'em."

"Still, I like it."

Now it was all these years later, and I sat down next to her on the cement by K's family's pool.

"Bright as hell out here," I said.

"It sure is. I've been up all night," she said.

"Doing what?"

"Thinking," she said. "... and watching the moon set and the stars get fainter. Then the craziest thing happened."

"Dawn. Gets me every time."

"When are you guys leaving for your big California tour?"

"I don't know if we are. They seem to think we'll go. I have my doubts. And how could I go anyway?"

"You just go, that's all. That's how anybody does anything."

"What about Aldo?" I said.

"What about him? He's a grown-ass man."

"He's sick."

"Yes, he is. I know him well. Know all about his sickness."

"He has to check his blood every night. I've got to stay here and keep an eye on him. And I don't know..."

"I'll do it," she said.

"He's stubborn though. He won't let you."

"Then I'll whack him in the face with a frying pan, and when he's unconscious, I'll check his blood. I'll do it. Just shut up. Just shut up and stop making excuses not to go."

"I'm not making excuses."

"You make a lot more excuses than you realize."

"The fuck I do," I said.

"I just think you have a bunch of potential. Is that gay to say out loud like that? You probably should have never come back here. You'd already gotten away. I was pretty damn jealous."

"I don't mind it here. It's nice. The ocean's just over there.

That's nice."

"Sure, nice. So nice. It's nice if your family is loaded, like these girls you're screwing around with."

"You don't like them either? Denise says she's gonna give them black eyes."

"It's none of my business."

"Kinda true."

"I've been in plenty of dead-end relationships. Maybe I'm an expert at it. My job. Feral. School. Feral. My job. My cash register job at fucking Dollar Store. Living with my goddamn mom still. Ughhh. And did I mention Feral?"

"You did, three times."

"Just don't waste your time on people that don't love you the right way. That sound fair?"

"Like a battle plan," I said.

"Where is Feral?"

Trish pointed over by the storage shed where the pool stuff was usually stashed. I didn't understand why she was pointing at it, but then I noticed all the pool stuff was spread all over the deck.

"Feral's in there," she said. "He just passed out a little bit ago. I should wake him up and dump his ass."

I nodded. I was looking at the boulder wall, the big hunks of moss boulder scattered along the last twenty-five feet of the dune wall. I'd have to finish it today. I needed to get paid. I looked back at the ocean house as if it was a guard on a watch tower. I'd screwed around long enough. The guards would be home tomorrow.

"Come on," I said.

"Where're we going?"

"Coffee," I said, leading her out of the backyard and towards my pickup.

We went and got pork roll, egg, and cheese breakfast sandwiches; cigarettes and another jug of OJ for her; and coffee for everyone. As we drove back, we joked around about me totaling her mom's car.

The maroon Le Sabre. The Tin Man lipstick. Little Jackie's birthday party. Corned beef and cabbage. The art of sliding in the rain.

When we got back to the house, I pulled the tarp off the cement and took a good look. I'd have enough to finish the job. Just a couple hours of work.

Trish wanted to help. I said sure

"What can I do?"

"You can hand me scoops of cement when I need it."

I made up some cement in the wheelbarrow and went to town. It was quick work. Really, it felt like it was building itself in a way. Sometimes that happens with manual labor. Especially when it's creative. It's like making a sculpture. Sure, there is a psychical element to it, but it's also a lot like painting a picture. You lose yourself in it.

I slapped boulder after boulder down into the cement. Trish kept passing me scoops. Before noon, I was done. A lot quicker than I anticipated.

"It looks beautiful," she said.

"Yeah?"

"For real. So nice. I hope I have a house someday. Then you and me can build some stone walls there."

"Of course," I said.

There was a low, guttural groan from the pool shed. The door kicked open. A pool float went flying out. There was Feral, all sweaty. Hair plastered to his head. Shirtless. Swaying.

"Ahhhhh," he moaned.

"You look like you were being cooked alive, man."

"It's like an oven in there!"

I started spraying him with the garden hose. He just smiled at me.

"I like that," he said.

I soaked him for a good minute and a half before he said, "Alright, alright. That's enough!"

"Why didn't you sleep in your van?" I asked. That was his trademark: sleeping in the van when he got blitzed.

"Nevermind," he said gruffly.

Trish and Feral said they were hungry, and I was done with my work. So I loaded my wheelbarrow and shovels in the truck, and we drove separately to Jade Garden Temple, a Chinese buffet. I was down to my last hundred bucks, but I bought them both lunch. Figured I was going to get paid the next day from the mysterious Scandinavians anyway.

Feral was quiet and didn't really want to talk. Trish and me kept joking around.

I said, "Hey Trish, maybe I'll take you with me to L.A. This grump over here wouldn't even notice."

She started to pretend to choke him.

"I couldn't abandon my savage! I'd miss him."

He knocked her hands away.

"L.A.? Still talking about that?"

"No, it's a go," I said. "Just getting the money together. Two weeks tops."

Feral grinned, "I got something top secret going on."

"I'm sure you do," said Trish from the corner of her mouth. She was smirking at me across the table as she ate noodles.

"Big money," Feral said.

"What?"

Motioning with his fingers, Feral zipped his mouth and threw away the key.

"That's lame," I said. "Locks don't even work with zippers."

"If it works out, you won't think I'm lame at all."

Just before we sat up from the table, I decided to fix Denise and Seth their own take-out styrofoam clamshells full of food. I figured they were still passed out at Lagoon House. It was a safe bet. I felt bad about what happened the previous night.

Through town, we rolled together. When we got to Lagoon House, Seth's car wasn't there and neither was Denise's. The driveway was completely empty, but the front door was wide open.

I went inside. The stereo was on. KISS Alive II. Blasting. The TV was on too, but muted. I went down the hallway and opened Seth's door. He was on his bed. I flicked the light on.

"Yo, you awake? Got you Chinese food."

He didn't say anything.

"It's late, man. Even for you. Rise and motherfucking shine."

He didn't say anything.

I went back out into the kitchen, shut the stereo off, and sat down at the table. Trish and Feral walked in, the door slamming behind them. Its hydraulic piston was weak and needed to be replaced. It didn't matter. The house was about to get torn down.

Feral went into Seth's room and started hollering and making fun of him.

"Can't party anymore, can you? Weak skills, amigo."

Then I heard Feral curse. He came out of the room, looking like he'd just been punched in the stomach.

He motioned back towards Seth's room and then ran to throw up in our sink—full of dishes. Trish was in the bathroom. I heard her whistling "Sweet Child O' Mine" as she

brushed her teeth.
I looked in on Seth.
He was dead.
Trish stopped whistling.

13

I ROCKED SLOWLY on the yellow curb with my head in my hands. I was in a suit, the only one I owned, but wearing silver Nikes. The Anderson Bradford Funeral Home loomed behind me. People were in there, but I couldn't bring myself to go in. I was numb, shell-shocked—sick to my stomach. I didn't have a pair of dress shoes to wear to my best friend's funeral. What was my problem?

I just sat there slowly rocking. The preceding three days had been a devastating blur.

In a mad scramble, Feral had cleaned all his drugs out of the house and driven away in his van before I was allowed to call the police, who in turn alerted the EMTs, who in turn alerted the coroner. You can't cut out the middleman. The cops insist on being involved whenever there is a dead body.

All of that was a dreadful, painful nightmare that left a massive hole in my heart where Seth used to live. I was just hoping, somehow, to get through Seth's viewing without breaking down in tears in front of everybody.

Finding a corpse of someone who OD'd is a lot different than it seems on TV, in a movie, in a dream.

I hadn't eaten since.

A car drove past me and honked lightly. After a few moments, I heard voices and looked up. It was Studio Mike. He had a blonde lady with him. I stood and held my hand out. He gave me a hug. He looked more heartbroken than me. I looked curiously at his head. He wasn't wearing his Gilligan hat.

"I don't always wear that hat," he said.

"Oh."

"You alright?" Nervous for my answer, he slipped in, "This thing starts at 6:30, right?"

"Yeah," I confirmed, "6:30."

He walked away with the blonde, not thinking to introduce me, as he said, "We're gonna go get a seat," as if it was a concert. I wished with all my heart that it was.

"Come sit with us," he hollered back to me.

I nodded.

I wondered if it was his wife—returning from the abyss where ex-wives go until they sometimes come back. My mom had done the same thing once. Cars were coming in the lot. I looked nervously at my wristwatch. It was dead too. I shook it even though it was digital.

Feral and Trish shuffled over. Feral looked like he was there to accept an award. He'd shaved. He had on shiny shoes. He was wearing his best Jerry Garcia tie—a gift from Trish the previous Christmas.

I looked away. Otherwise, I was gonna kill that motherfucker. It'd been his coke. His pills. Both.

An older gentleman I didn't recognize walked past with two elderly woman. They all had canes. It looked to me like they were entering the funeral home to case it out, to prepare for their own swiftly approaching funerals.

Then I saw somebody I'd forgotten all about.

Shannon, Seth's ex, was weeping openly as she stepped towards me. My head began to spin. I sat down on the curb again. I said to myself, "Please don't come over here. Please don't come over here…"

The weeping grew in intensity. Shannon sat down next to me on the yellow curb. Her clutch purse fell into a puddle.

She didn't notice.

One strap of her spaghetti string dress slipped off her shoulder. Her make-up was over applied. Mascara ran down her cheek, making her look like a punk rocker.

Nothing farther from the truth.

"We were gonna get married," Shannon said, bawling against my shoulder.

She hugged me. I hugged back, limply, without any emotion.

"We were gonna move to L.A.," she said.

I thought, "Oh fuck," as I looked up and saw Denise Santalucia walking through the parking lot. She saw me and started coming closer but was intercepted by Feral and Trish at the side of Trish's station wagon.

I watched Trish wrap up Denise with a big hug. Feral looked up at the clouds, through the clouds, from behind his aviator sunglasses.

"I got a tattoo," Shannon said to me.

It was on her right shoulder blade. A cartoonish snare drum with two crossed drumsticks. It said, "SETH" on the face of the kick drum. The tattoo was crusty. Enflamed. Brand new. She'd just gotten it the day before.

"That's nice," I said, not meaning it, knowing that was horrible. Her tears dried up. She stood.

"Gotta stay strong," she said to herself.

"I'll see you inside."

She walked up the creaky wooden steps into the funeral parlor. A guy was standing on the porch smoking a cigarette. He was in a very nice suit. I figured he was one of two people: the guy running the funeral parlor or Seth's brother Mark. Before I could say anything to him, he flicked his half-lit cigarette onto the bricks and walked into the funeral parlor.

The service was just beginning.

I followed.

I was surprised to see so many people come out. Not that I should've been. Seth was really loved. I was afraid to walk into the main chamber. I didn't want to see him there, lying in his casket, because I didn't want to say goodbye to my friend. I wanted it all to be a mistake or, even better, a joke. Yes, I wanted Seth to be faking his own death.

But if that was really happening, he'd have to have faked all the way through his own joke ... and that was impossible. There was nothing Seth found funnier than his own jokes. The laughs would have slipped from those now-tight lips, and, well, they were not holding back laughs. They were blue painted pink by professionals. The smile seen on the corner of the mouth was put there by a mortician, not an inside joke—those were over.

I stood in the foyer and milled around while people filed in from the porch. There was Aldo and Gail. Aldo had on a leather cap and a button up shirt with small starbursts all over it. Gail was in a long, green dress. They both looked frazzled, like they'd just lost their dog and had been out hanging up flyers on every single telephone pole in the world. That dog was gone forever.

Aldo grabbed my shoulders and asked gruffly, "You gonna be alright?"

"I don't think so," I said.

"Awwww," Gail said, pushing away Aldo's thick hands and hugging me ... hard. "I'll take care of you sweetie," she cooed.

When she let go, a part of me never wanted that hug to end. She was warm, the opposite of death. She smelled like cherries.

Others arrived: Seth's friends from Catholic school (I'd gone to public), girlfriends of the ancient past, neighbors, his high school track coach, music store coworkers, people he'd played in various bands with. The place was packed. Sold out show.

Another guy in a suit appeared, but this one was cheesy and un-tailored. He came up, touched my back lightly, and said, "The service is about to begin if you would like to step inside."

I walked in shell-shocked. All of the seats were taken. I stood along the back wall, just looking at the casket from afar.

To my dismay, Seth's drum kit was set up in the corner beside the casket. I thought this was something he wouldn't have wanted. That's what happens when you die though: people latch onto the thing you were best at, and that becomes the summary of who you were to them.

An old man started to talk. A priest. He wasn't dressed up like a priest, but he still had on his little white clerical collar. He said a lot of nice things about my friend. The emphasis was on what a great drummer he was. Apparently, the priest had a son who used to play with Seth in a Christian rock band back when they went to high school. It was a short service, but a lot of nice, heartfelt things were said. Afterwards, a line formed. People were going up to the casket to pay their respects. I got in the line with weak knees to say goodbye to my friend one last time.

The person in front of me turned back and half smiled. I recognized him as one of Seth's Catholic school friends, we'd spoken at various parties, but I could never remember his name. Some people are just like that. The kid said hello and asked me where Ethan was. I said, "Fuck Ethan."

He turned and didn't say another word to me.

The line inched up. There was a poster board packed solid with photos of Seth. That was the saddest part: having to look at that. It was sweet, and the memories were bright, but boy was it ever a kick in my gut. There he was, an innocent little kid: just a toddler, naked in a bath tub; playing catch on a lawn somewhere, with a baseball glove almost as big as him; riding a red BMX; just a beanpole skinny adolescent sitting behind his first drum set; fishing on a boat with some guys I didn't know; at prom with Shannon; on stage with me, playing a show at Spider bar. All that life ... gone.

The line inched up, and I looked down briefly at his face. I silently hoped he'd sit up and say something funny—one last funny thing, a dirty joke or something to break the tension. But no, he just lay there in a very nice suit. I wondered if he had on pants. He probably wanted to be buried in his corduroys and Converse All-stars. I'm not sure anybody gets a choice.

The lid on the inside of the casket had a drum set embroidered onto it. I felt so bad about that.

I looked around at all the people at the viewing and got so angry at them. They thought they knew Seth. I wasn't sure many of them knew anything about him.

I wanted to leave something in his casket. I searched my pockets, but they were empty. All I found was a little scrap of paper—a gas station receipt. I didn't have a pen. I shoved the receipt back in my pocket.

I had to get out of there. The walls of the funeral home were collapsing. Still, I almost cracked up laughing when I thought about the sound that the cymbal made when it smashed into Ethan. That. I wanted to do that—to all those people—but I didn't.

I went out to the parking lot for some air. Seth's brother was standing there, smoking another cigarette.

"I'm no good at these things," he said.

"Your brother's dead," I said. It was so stupid, it just came out.

Mark said he recognized me from the photographs. "Seth said good things about you when we were together upstate."

"Oh?"

"The lake house. That funeral."

"Yeah, I'm sorry about all of it," I said.

He looked down at his shiny shoes. A stupid thing occurred to me. Another reason to be mad at somebody else over what had happened. Mark had given Seth the tip on that horse at the Kentucky Derby. Smartie Jones. If Seth hadn't won all that money, he'd probably still be alive.

"You were recording an album?"

"Yeah, we were," I muttered.

"I just wanted you to know that if you needed anything for it, I'd help."

I nodded. Sure. It was a good gesture, but Seth was dead. What was I going to do with Mark's money? I politely declined his offer.

"That's alright, it's over."

"It's over, yeah. It is, right?"

The doors opened, and people started to stream out. Of course, knowing that crowd, a good lot of them wanted to go over to the bar. It was walking distance. We crossed the street and went a block up to Spider Bar. The lights were off (as usual). Everywhere I looked, someone was smoking a cigarette. Walking in off the street was like breaking some heavy fog that'd crawled into the mouth of a cave and stayed to live. Your eyes slowly adjusted. Then the rest of the world was too right, even under splintered moonlight.

I could drink now. I could drink everything. I didn't give a fuck anymore. I wanted to get so drunk I'd walk out on the railroad tracks and fall over and lie there until I got crushed. Cut in half. All of the above.

We gathered across the whole bar, filling it up. Gail's stand-in bartender, a kid with long-ass sideburns and a nose ring, couldn't keep up. Whiskey shots for everyone. Beers. Beers. More beers. But somehow the sorrowful mood rapidly slipped away. The sadness attempted to lift, because it couldn't battle against the alcohol. The jukebox helped too.

I was talking to Mark for a while; he had a lot of questions. He wanted to know what was gonna happen to my living situation now that Seth was gone. Would I be able to make up his slot of the rent? I explained that our rental situation was … weird.

"In what way?"

"We haven't paid rent in four months."

Aldo leaned in, "In life everybody needs an escape plan."

"True."

Mark told me that his grandfather was in a prison camp as a child.

"The family got out. When he got old, he built a stone house on a lake. First he built the escape tunnel, then he built the house."

"That's what I'm talking about," said Aldo. "Where is it? Where does it go?"

"It's in the master bedroom and goes into the wine cellar and out to the river."

"American dream," Aldo said, "escape."

Feral bought more shots. Aldo bought more shots. Gail kept giving me quarters for the jukebox.

"Pick some songs, hon. You always pick the best songs."

Everyone kept knocking drinks back. It was not fun. It was not jubilant. It was drinking to survive.

I looked down the bar. Denise Santalucia was standing behind Shannon. They hadn't been acquainted yet. Shannon was drunk. Denise looked on edge. Shannon started to lightly sob. "I miss my love," I heard her say.

Denise stiffened. "Who?"

"Seth," Shannon said. "My Seth."

Denise stepped up, "Seth was my guy. Who are you?" Shannon pointed to the tattoo on her shoulder blade, all raw and swollen. Denise reached back and slapped that raw tattoo as hard as she could. With her next motion, Denise kicked the barstool out from underneath Shannon, who went down to the floor—hard.

The bar got shook up. By the time I could even think to react, Gail was pulling Denise out of the bar into the streetlights and the rain. It looked just like one of those old G.L.O.W. matches. She had that little girl up in her arms in a bear hold, with her legs kicking, elbows being thrown, and lots of squirming. After Denise was carried out by Gail, who had to push the door open with one of her feet as she came to it, someone helped Shannon off the carpet. She wasn't hurt, but she was in shock. What'd just happened?

We kept drinking, but it wasn't the same in there. Death kept seeping in.

Aldo said, "That little girl has some fire in her."

When we all separated, it felt, in a way, like the last time any of us would ever see each other again—as if Seth had been the only thing that could ever link us together.

The Blue Samurai

I DROVE BACK TO LAGOON HOUSE. Most of my things were already in cardboard boxes. I'd been packing. I was moving out. I didn't want to be there any longer. When I walked in the door, Feral was at the kitchen table. He'd been eating a peanut butter sandwich.

"We've got a problem," is what he said, but I couldn't understand a word of it on account of the peanut butter sandwich.

"What?"

He gulped down a glass of water, frowning.

"I'll show you," he said, wiping his chin. "I fucked up, and I didn't know how to break the news to you."

He stood up from the table, and we walked back outside. At the A-Team van, he opened up the back doors and pulled back the gray painter's tarp. Beneath was something … troubling. It was the original Andy Warhol print that had been hanging in K Neon's ocean house. The Blue Samurai.

"You fucking stole that?!"

"I know, right?! Crazy."

"CRAZY?! ARE YOU KIDDING ME?!"

"What do I do?"

"Bring it back," I said.

"You're outta your mind."

"Well," I said, "what was your plan? To sell it at English-town flea market?"

Feral shrugged. His eyes went wide. "I have no idea what

my plan was. I dunno ... find some bigwig-connected black market arts dealer."

"And that didn't work?"

"No!" he shouted. "No, that didn't work." Then he whispered, "Bro, I don't wanna go to prison."

"I'll talk to K."

Feral yanked the painting out of the van and carried it to the backyard, where the deck used to be.

"Not happening," he said, setting the canvas down on the sharp red stones. "Just gonna have to take matters into my own hands."

From the collapsed shed, he pulled out a metal jug of gasoline left over from when he'd had the boat. I watched, shell-shocked, as he began to douse the painting. Then he tossed his electric blue bic lighter on the canvas. In the wind, we watched it burn. The smoke—thick, black, and doomed—uncoiled like a bad luck snake.

When it was over, I went into the house and started to drag my boxes out into the F-250. Feral watched me do it for a while. Finally, he helped.

"I'm gonna miss having you around."

I wanted to break his ribs, every single one of them. Instead, I just climbed in the truck and drove away.

Haircut

I SMASHED THE ACOUSTIC GUITAR against the wall. Fragments scattered everywhere. It was Studio Mike's house, so I shouldn't have done that. I was sleeping on the couch downstairs, even though Aldo had threatened me with, "If you don't come and stay here, I'll..."

"You'll what?"

"I'll think of something."

He couldn't even think of a good threat, so I didn't take him seriously.

Mike's downstairs couch pulled out and became a comfortable bed, with springs that sang out like shrieking angels. The room was private. The TV worked. I'd have to vacuum up all the pieces of the guitar before Mike returned home from his train job. There was only the faintest dent in the wood paneling.

Drinking. Everything was drinking—poison poured perfectly from fountains that burned all the way down. I lay sideways on the couch, sweating. Windows shut. Lights out.

There was a knock on the window.

June was looking in. I opened the window.

"You look like death," she said sorrowfully.

"I feel worse than that."

"Heard about your friend. I'm sorry."

"Sure. Yeah. You didn't do it though."

I got up and let her in the back door. I hadn't seen her in over a week. I led her back to my nest, the couch.

"What happened to Seth?"

"He did too much."

"Too much…. I lost a friend that way. Rory. It hurts still."

A fly buzzed around our heads. I didn't swat it. June opened the window. It left. We sank into the couch.

"He'd won a bunch of money," I said. "That was that. He got lucky. Imagine that."

I just sat, unresponsive. She sighed and put her hand on my shoulder. "I was trying to figure out how to get in touch with you. A lot of things happened," she said. "Me and K broke up. I got on a bus on a whim … but I didn't make it very far."

"How far?"

"Atlantic City. Blinking lights and nothing for me."

"Not your kind of town at all," I said. "Why'd you break up?"

"We had a fight. Kinda about you. But not your fault. I consider you an innocent party."

"What a waste of a fight. But you're back."

"It was a good fight, I guess. Things came out."

"Like what?"

"You don't want to hear about this now …"

"Believe me, I do."

"I used to lie too much," she said. "Decided I'm not going to do that anymore."

"Where'd you decide this?"

"Room 32 of a Holiday Inn. Just the other night. Didn't sleep. Played all my records till someone knocked on the door and asked me to stop."

"What kind of lies?"

"I've been with boys. I told Karen I hadn't … ever. I was trying to impress her. I shouldn't have said that."

"Karen, ha, that's great."

"Yes, Karen. K. Anyway, one of the boys I'd like to forget about forever … for bad reasons. The other was Rory. I'd like to forget him for other reasons. Good reasons. You can want to forget people for good reasons too."

"I'd like my mind erased completely, please."

"You know I'm stuck on her. I'd do almost anything for her. Maybe that sounds pathetic. You ever like someone that much?"

"No, I guess I haven't."

"What's the nicest thing you ever did for a girl?"

"I drove a girl from Brooklyn to Philadelphia because she

didn't have money for the bus."

"To get laid."

"No, not to get laid. But that happened."

"I told K I'd do something for her, and maybe I want to do it too."

"Go with your gut."

She hugged me. I was sweaty and on another planet. I didn't think to hug back until she'd pulled away. The room was spinning.

"Lee, you look in the mirror anytime lately?"

"There're no mirrors in that bathroom," I said, "and I don't go upstairs anymore. I will dwell in this basement forever."

"Saw Trish last night at the boardwalk. She said you were here and could use cheering up. I can tell it's true. So I'm gonna … cut your hair.»

"What logic," I said.

She opened her purse. This wasn't a negotiation.

"It'll be good for both of us," she reassured me.

In one hand she held a sharp pair of scissors. There was no light, but they were glowing. Then she put a straight razor on the glass table.

"You'll slit my throat," I said, 'cause that's what people are supposed to say whenever someone is giving an amateur straight razor shave. But I added, "and I don't care."

"Fine," she said. I sat in a chair as she hovered over me with the scissors. Snip. Snip. I felt the scissors close at my ear. Snip. "Do you love K?" she asked.

"Not in the slightest," I said.

"Then you get to live, fucker." She laughed. "Take your shirt off."

I took the shirt off. The hair fell off with it. She sat facing me, trimming my beard with the scissors. It was the oddest thing. She was just hacking it off. No care or concern. Like clipping a hedge that'd be ripped out with a pickup truck afterwards.

"You know what you're doing?»

"I used to cut my mom's hair. My dad's too. They're gone."

"Gone. I'm sorry."

"It's sad when someone dies, of course. But it confirms what love is."

"Never knew my dad. And I'm terrified of my mom being dead. I mean, she might be. I don't know."

"Why don't you know. If she is, you'd know."

"She left me."

"Left you where?"

"With Aldo, when I was twelve."

"With Aldo? Why?"

"They were serious. Probably gonna get married. They had no business taking care of a kid. One night I got sick and had to go to the hospital. They took me but were too high to be in a hospital. You know what I mean. After that, he got clean … for me. She didn't like it. She left. Florida. I went looking for her a couple years ago. I had a letter that she sent, eventually, from rehab … handwritten. I kept it in my wallet for a long time."

"Where is it now?"

"It got destroyed by the ocean. The day I first saw K. I went swimming with it in my pocket. That's not important. Letters get destroyed."

"So then Aldo's like a dad. Your dad."

"I got through high school somehow, living with him above the bar. That was hard. We ate a lot of cereal together. Ha. Then I drove. First place I drove was to see her. South. South. South. Penis tip of the USA. To the place where the letter came from. But the rehab was gone. It was a strip mall. The rehab place was a place that sold tires. The tire people didn't have an address for my mom. It'd been over three years since she'd been there. No-one had an address. I didn't have the balls to contact the state. I mean, where would I start? What state?"

"I'm so sorry."

"Please stop saying that."

"Okay, but is it any help if I tell you that it's not any easier knowing where your parents are buried? We could get on a bus or hop in your truck and go look my parents' graves. I don't want to do that. I could never go and look. Is that a help? I'm rotten. I'm afraid. It embarrasses me how terrified I am of going to that cemetery. That's a help, right?"

"It is."

Before I was aware of it, I was sitting on the lid of the toilet. She was rubbing shaving cream all over my off-kilter beard, which was all different lengths now. Her hands felt soft and alien. They were gentle.

"Let's talk about something else," I said.

"Like what? Ice cream? Fireworks? New Jersey?"

"K."

"It's weird with me and K," she said.

"Sounds about right," I said. "It's always weird. Girl and girl. Boy and girl. Boy and boy. Man and kangaroo. Girl and horse…"

"Girl and horse!" The shaving cream on her hands got all over her own face as she touched it inadvertently.

"Boy and sock."

"I took philosophy 101 last semester. And just so you know, the universe is always about wanting somebody more than they want you. That's what the whole universe is about."

"Been there, done that," I said.

She put the straight razor against my cheek and said, "She's never loved anybody. But I don't blame her." June drew the blade down, taking away the beard, taking away the shaving cream, taking away my hiding spot. "Probably nobody's ever loved her."

"But you," I said.

She stopped.

"I keep trying. Somebody decapitate me, please."

14

THE GIRLS WERE LAUGHING, taking slugs, explaining college life to us.

"My art professors are scary people," June said.

K explained, "I'm attending Brown to get on the path of world domination."

Mike sat on the edge of his computer chair, hypnotized by K and June. Where had they materialized from?

They'd been chased out of their little cave, the house on the ocean occupied once again by true blue honest to God adults. The horror.

No-one noticed the missing painting yet. That was the least of my worries.

I'd been paid; my pockets were full of money. It was temporary, and it would go away, but I couldn't resist the urge. I decided to take the girls out into the wilds of New Jersey. Dinners. Drinks. Amusements. We packed into my truck and braved the back roads till my gas tank was only fumes. We looked at weird shit on the side of random weird shit roads. West. Then north. Then back home. I took them away from the ocean, through the pines, into the farmlands. "Holy shit! There really are farms!"

"The Garden State," I said. "We call people down in South Jersey, tomato pickers."

"Ha! what do they call you?"

"Clam diggers," I said.

It was drag racing day out at the speedway. Sunday! Sunday!

Sunday! at R-R-Raceway Park! We sat in the bright aluminum stands as we ate sausage and pepper sandwiches and sipped orange sodas spiked with June's signature gin dumped in as cars exploded down the track below. The pleasant stink of exhaust. The sweet smell of fuel. Tires squealing. June sat beneath a yellow umbrella.

"I'm a Victorian era vampire, it'll vaporize me."

We shrugged.

At the swap meet, we walked around aimlessly, pointing at the strange mechanical guts of automobiles disassembled in the dust.

"What's that?" June asked.

"Its heart," I said.

"That's a carburetor for a 1973 Dodge Charger," K Neon said.

"Oh, go fuck yourself, K," I said.

We stumbled off, laughing. And she was probably right about the carburetor, but who the hell cares? I bought the last cherry slushy from a kid packing up his cart. The three of us shared it as we walked through the blazing sun back towards the truck.

I worked the pedal. June shifted. K Neon laughed at the cassette deck devouring reels of thin magnetic tape—mixtapes of the love songs of all our nectar-soaked youths. I kept looking down at June's leg, instinctively wanting to put my hand on her thigh, but I fought the urge. We were strangers still. She was distant and secretive. I was wayward and run-down.

The sun was going away like a flashlight with a dying battery.

Coming back, round trip. Last leg. We wanted hamburgers and just one beer each. Little sips. There was a row of red wine bottles beside the pullout couch back 'home'. Mike would be done with his recording session at about 10 p.m.: some girl with a violin making a Christmas album. We had a few hours to kill. So I pulled into a random strip mall with a new bar inside. New bars gotta be inspected.

Inside, I was greeted by more darkness: a dimly lit cave with Lou Reed singing low and wounded on the jukebox, "Linger on your pale blue eyes ..." I took a spot at the bar, and K dug her hand in my pocket looking for quarters to put into the jukebox. Her bleached hair was down, straight and long. Her eyes seemed to glow in there, small coals hovering as she left.

June Doom said, "I know from experience that you should

have sent me to that jukebox. K cannot be trusted with a juke-box."

I nearly thought that June said, "K Neon cannot be trusted at all."

It wasn't 30 seconds before I felt a clasp on my left shoulder. It was Costa. I had no idea that the bar was his. He was an old, wealthy Greek. I'd built a waterfall for him a while back.

"My friend! I've been looking for you," he exclaimed. "I have a job. I want you to make waterfall for my partner."

"I'm retired," I said.

"Retired! What are you, 22?"

"I was supposed to go out west," I said. "Maybe I still will."

"Out west? What, like Clint Eastwood and horses? Tumbleweeds?"

He asked me again to do the waterfall job for his partner. I said I would.

"Um-fahh!"

Well, after that, Costa kept bringing us free beers. The food never came, just beer after beer after beer. We raised glasses! He was just so happy to see us in his brand new place. I stumbled into the bathroom then pissed for forty-five minutes, laughing at nothing. It felt good to feel wanted.

Sideways. Blurry. Things were spinning. I materialized in a booth with the girls in the farthest shadow of the bar.

Our beers were almost gone.

K Neon spoke, "So, me and June have been talking."

June looked down into her beer, hiding in there. She wouldn't look up.

"We wanted to ask you a question," K continued.

I already knew the question. This was political posturing for June Doom.

"Ask away," I said, knowing in my gut what was coming.

"So … would you be into a three way?"

I knocked back the rest of my beer, stood up.

"Yeah, let's go."

They looked at me like I was from another planet.

We left ripped. We couldn't make sense of life underneath the streetlights. We stumbled into my pickup truck. June and K held hands while singing two different songs—all the wrong lyrics anyway. I turned the key. Things rumbled. K whispered something in June's ear. June laughed low and nervous. I shouldn't have been driving, but I was. I pulled out onto route 70, very much aware of how bad the cops were on that quiet two-lane stretch of highway.

It was the kind of town where they drink your blood, gulp after gulp. No sympathy. It wasn't a minute before I saw the red and blue lights flashing behind me. Whoop Whoop. I pulled over onto the grass.

The storm trooper came lumbering out of his squad car. He was a young guy. Baby faced. I was done for. K Neon rolled down her window and started really talking it up with the officer. Lovey Dovey. Almost pillow talk.

"Hello officer," she said seductively, "I like your hat, that's trés sexy. Can I wear it?"

She was a saint, but he wasn't distracted. The cop leaned in the window and glared at me.

"License and registration," he demanded sharply.

Jesus—I started digging around but couldn't find any of that stuff. I mean, I dug in the glove box. K had her legs spread on either side of it as I dug around, but my paperwork just wasn't there.

"I have it somewhere, but I can't find it now, pal."

"Step out of the vehicle," he said darkly.

Now he had me out on the side of the road. All the tests. Follow this penlight. Touch your nose. Walk the line. All the tests. I was done. This was it. They had me. The police had me right where they wanted me.

I silently prayed for some kind of inspiration from the great line of lucky losers who'd come before me, the spirits that haunt the destitute roadside night. Back where I was facing, I watched the neon sign of Costa's bar flick out.

"Alright, I know somebody's been drinking tonight. I smelled it when I came to the window."

"Officer, she's wasted," I said.

He just glared at me. "Which one?"

"Both of them," I said. "I go to the bar at the end of the night to pick up the drunk girls to bring them home. It's easier that way."

The cop started laughing. His bottom lip bobbed up and down as it hung open as he just laughed and laughed. It was like he hadn't laughed in twenty years.

"I'm gonna try that one," he said. "You know why I pulled you over?"

"No."

"I saw a bunch of garbage come streaming out of the passenger-side window."

"She's a drunk and a litterbug," I said as if me and the cop were friends.

That littering bitch. I'd have to kill her. I glared at K Neon's head in the rear window. Before the cop could handcuff me and drag me to the station, I'd have to slip away and quickly butcher her in the truck. She had a pretty head. Too bad I'd have to take it off with my bare hands.

The cop laughed, "Get your paperwork in order, okay? And get the hell outta here. Right now."

Then he let me go. No insurance card. No registration. In a town infamous for evil, blood-drinking cops, with nothing better to do on a Saturday night then be evil and drink my blood, he just let me leave.

I drove us home in silence.

But when we got in the driveway, I pushed the cassette tape back in. It started to howl and pop. Made all kinds of distorted noise. June leaned over and put her whole body onto me. For the first time, she kissed me deeply. All the world and silly shit it insinuated was of importance was completely obscured.

The Dark

THE LIGHTS WERE OFF. A small stream of street light came through the venetian blinds beside the pullout couch. There was no moon. We'd sipped all the poison of the world and somehow survived.

Clothes in a pile. A ceiling fan wobbled, uneven and ineffectual. There was no music. No words. An anxious, unnerving buzz throbbed through the pitch black. We were wrecked.

June and K, topless, lay warm and volcanic across me— lips colliding, tongues deep, hair falling onto my belly. Nails dug into my shoulder. I tried to imagine if June had nails. I couldn't remember. Little coos. Excited birds.

I was flat on my back, they were meeting in the middle over my chest. A hand ran up my right thigh and lingered slowly. I wasn't sure who it was. I felt around, trying to identify who was who, but it felt pointless.

My hand was on someone's ass. I felt down lower. The legs moved up. A knee came to rest on my hip. I felt the space between the thighs—soaking wet. I rubbed slowly. Wet panties. Both girls felt similar in that darkness. Lithe. Smooth. Hairless below their eyebrows.

Someone's hand touched the side of my face delicately. A kiss on the lips, biting the lower one … hard. Our teeth clicked together. She smelled like wild cherry soda and cloves. Another set of lips went down my chest, sucking the flesh over my heart, pecking down my stomach. Another hand rubbed me through my boxer shorts.

"Oh, you're so hard."

A mouth kissed my thigh then licked its way up.

"Come here. Come help me with something."

My boxer shorts were pulled down, taken off completely, and thrown into the deeper darkness beyond. I felt a tongue running on me like electricity. So good. I closed my eyes and saw more darkness. One mouth wrapped around me. More kissing on my leg.

"You try."

"Oh, I dunno."

"Come on."

There was a pause, a tension. Then I felt another mouth wrap around my dick. Slow, tentative.

"Keep going."

A hand pushed down on the back of the head. The slight scrape of teeth. A small gag. Gasps from coming up for air. They were taking turns kissing and sucking, and I had my hands on the back of both of their heads—just held there, forcing nothing. It seemed like they were having fun. I could have died right there. That would have been the highlight of my adult life up to that point. I shuddered.

Someone stopped, came back up, and started kissing my mouth. I thought it was K. I kissed down her neck. A sharp collarbone. I started sucking on a nipple. A small moan. Surprising. I reached down carefully and slipped a finger inside.

"Go slow, please. Slow."

I was surprised.

She guided my hand out and said, "No, just kiss me. Go slow."

The mouth sucking my cock went deeper and deeper and then stopped. I felt the lips kissing my hand between restless legs. A girl was going down on her girl. I kissed a mouth. She hummed back at me. I heard a noise—the front door opening, footsteps on the creaky stairs. We froze, as if we'd be exposed.

The lights flicked on, appearing underneath the crack of the door and shining through the keyhole—might as well have been a fire hose turned on us.

"Shhhhhhh," I said.

"Shhhhh," they each joked in return. "Shhhhhh, be very quiet. Don't make a sound. We're hunting rabbits."

One of the girls climbed on top of me and rubbed my dick back and forth across her pussy. It was wet and slick. She put me inside. She began to slowly move, grinding me inside.

Upstairs, the refrigerator door opened. Glass bottles rattled around.

More kisses on my neck. I felt around, rubbed someone between the legs. Whoever was on me stopped, and I rolled onto the other one.

"This alright?" I asked. There was no response.

The legs spread, and a pair of hands rubbed my shoulders. I slipped my dick inside, and there were hands that pushed against my chest.

"No, stop."

I went along with it. Stopped.

"I can't do this."

Someone sprang up from the bed and walked out of the room in a huff of embarrassment. The door opened. Bright light flooded in from the hallway. There was a pile of laundry next to the washing machine. The door shut. Dark again. The mouth returned to me, continued to suck. The room was slowly spinning. I wondered if I was gonna get sick. Too drunk. Far too drunk. At the same time, I was gonna cum. I felt it rising. Getting close. A tongue licked the head of my cock, and then I felt a hand rubbing me off—faster and faster.

"You're gonna make me cum."

A deep sigh of pleasure from the darkness, "Go ahead."

Whoever she was closed her lips around my dick. I came. A pulse. Another. Then it was over. She rose from the pullout couch, and the springs sang out. I breathed a heavy sigh.

The light was on in the hallway. I heard someone crying, softly. Someone else spat into the trashcan.

"That wasn't fair."

"What is?"

I fell asleep. Too far gone. Upstairs, the TV switched on. Top volume. The Conan O'Brien show. Triumph the Insult comic dog. The world was spinning in a slow orbit around the sun, which was very far away and a part of no-one's life I knew.

15

WE WERE AT A MCMANSION off the highway. A job Steph got for me through the quarry. She's too kind. I had to build a waterfall into an in-ground swimming pool.

The swimming pool looked perfect, and not just because K Neon was swimming slow laps in it for exercise.

Feral, mouth breather that he is, leaned on his shovel and stared down at K in the pool.

"I could be a champion swimmer if I gave a fuck," Feral said.

"You're the worst swimmer and person that I know."

The water was crystal clear. A coral reef-patterned tile, wavering below the surface, was barely disturbed by K's perfect strokes. She told me she'd been a lifeguard at the college pool, that she'd been the captain of her high school swim team.

"I'm diabolical in the water," said K.

We all can't be that way, but watch us try.

Also: watch us drown trying.

The house had a bamboo shoot tiki hut with a kegerator in it. That made the job all the better. "Must be 5 o'clock somewhere" sign. Jimmy Buffett concert tickets in a frame. Corona beer souvenirs galore. All of us had red solo cups full of beer. The sun was just getting hot. It was 11 a.m. The cicadas were screaming in the trees. The flowers were fat and heavy. A boombox so loud, it was distorted and ugly. But the lemon sun was out and made everything beautiful.

I felt a little speck of happiness returning. My recent bruises were lightening, slowly, but at least it was something.

I had my shirt off and was getting a deep tan while I worked. Over on the deck, June was reading a paperback book in her red bikini that matched her dyed head. Beside her, on another chair, was Trish, who was leafing through a magazine. She was in a one-piece swimsuit with a dress bottom and resembled one of those hippos from Fantasia, which I only really realized because she kept saying it. She's cool. She knows how to make fun of herself. We can all get better at that and become more beloved as a result.

Trish would yell out to Feral, "I'm reading about aphrodisiacs. Did you know that an Italian sub can be a turn on? Especially for a fat ass like me?"

"No, I didn't know that, babe," Feral said. "What's your point?" He passed me another shovel full of cement.

"My point is, if you go and get me a sandwich from the deli, I'll be, like, mad turned on, and maybe I'll take you in the tiki hut and rock your world."

Feral looked at his wrist, but he wasn't wearing a watch. He hadn't had a watch on in many years. "It's not lunchtime, yet."

"I could go for a sandwich, too," June said.

"Not me," K Neon chimed in. But that was no surprise. She had never been hungry, not once in her entire life.

I was distracted but tried to get some work done. I'd taken down a section of white PVC stockade fence. It was easier that way; I could back the F-250 right up to the edge of the pool and drive across the lush lawn.

I finished stacking concrete blocks about two feet away from the bullnose paver edge of the pool, setting the blocks on a base of concrete "mud" with re-bar running up the middle to strengthen the whole thing. Feral was helping by filling up the space between the blocks with cement. It wasn't quick work, but it was enjoyable work. That's all you can hope for in life sometimes.

We were just emerging from our devastation. We were making efforts to return back to the land of the living. The birds chirped about sex and food and war, so we focused in on that.

I even felt bad for K and June, who seemed to be waiting around for me to come back to life. They just kept kissing me and bringing me more beers, more wine. They took turns listening to my heart.

"It sounds like you're alive, but your eyes look so dead."

"It's a magic trick," I said. "I'm operating this body remotely."

"From where?"

"A secret chamber where the air is hyper-charged and vivid."

"Rad."

"Come outside. Let's lay in the grass, darling."

The sun felt good. I was in it. Needed it. It was treating me well.

When I built waterfalls into swimming pools, I liked to have people there with me. It made the job feel less like work. A party: that's what I wanted. I liked them there, swimming in the pool, drinking, listening to the stereo. It felt good. Back then, I used to bid kegs of beer into the price of the job.

As per usual, I'd done the same at this mansion. It was one of those cookie cutter houses: big, boxy, and looming but lacking character. Beige vinyl siding. The streets lacked character. Not one chimney pushing back at the sky. No winter wood smoke in the air. A development of identical houses, not homes—crackerjack mansions occupied by investment bankers and low-level attorneys.

I hopped up in the bed of the pickup truck and shoveled yellow dirt against the back of the concrete wall. Feral jumped up and helped too. Little by little, we got all of the dirt out and relieved the springs. The body raised. That was over two and a half tons of dirt.

"That's that," Feral said, hopping down. He went and filled two red solo cups up in the tiki hut. When he came out, they were foaming over. We sat drinking with the girls for a while, letting the cement set.

"What's next?" K asked as she came to the edge of the pool and looked up at me.

"Well, the world is your oyster, K Neon. Really … whatever you want."

She laughed. "I know that," she said. "I mean with the job."

"Stone," I muttered, grinning.

I kicked off my sneakers and lowered myself into the swimming pool.

"Now the work gets enjoyable," I said.

Feral began to pass me flagstone from outside.

"No, man," I said, "I need a boulder."

"Oh, you gotta be kidding me."

"No joke," I said.

Feral went over to the pile of moss rock next to the tiki hut. He made me proud. He hefted a boulder, weighing at least 100 pounds, while grunting and turning red. He set it down on the ledge. I filled the gap with wet concrete mud, my fingertips already burning from the limestone.

Feral brought over two more boulders and set them down on the edge of the pool between the concrete block wall and the water. Feral must have felt bad for me. He was working too hard for it to be anything else. He felt bad for me. He passed me more flagstone. More scoops of cement from the wheelbarrow. He felt bad for me.

I doggie paddled into the cool, inviting water. The girls drank on the deck. It went like that for a while, with me just bobbing in the water, building the waterfall from inside the pool, and Feral helping as much as he could. A little while later, June Doom and K Neon drove my pickup truck across the grass and went to the deli down the street.

Trish sat forward in her chair, put her tabloid magazine down, and said, "I called Denise a few times. She doesn't answer her phone."

"She's probably the most heartbroken out of anybody," I said.

"She really liked Seth," Trish said. "I was talking to her a lot. We were getting pretty close pretty quick. I thought she needed a friend. She'd call me at night, and we'd talk for hours."

"That girl especially," Feral said. "She liked the way coke smells just a little too much."

Trish didn't say anything.

"Look who's talking," I thought.

Feral said the concrete was done in the barrel. I hopped out of the pool. That was it till after lunch.

"I think she might be in rehab," Trish said. "Or maybe that's just wishful thinking."

I lay down on the grass, starting to feel fuzzy drunk. I looked up at the blue sky. The clouds were all there, suspended, not moving a single millimeter. Time was frozen. We were all trapped in amber. Or purgatory. Or worse.

I almost dozed off. When I opened my eyes, the girls were coming back in the pickup. They had two large, brown paper bags loaded with sandwiches and chips. Italian special: cappicola, ham, salami, and provolone with extra vinegar, a little oil, salt, pepper, and oregano.

June sat down next to me on the lawn.

"You alright?" she asked, looking at me.

"Not at all," I said.

She gently ran her hand through my hair.

"The sun is making it light—looks like you have highlights. Oh, what's this?"

She pulled back a loose section of the lawn next to us and revealed a small burrow with tiny rabbits.

Everyone came over. June picked one up and held it.

"It's so small!"

"You shouldn't have touched it," K remarked. "Now its mother will abandon it."

June put the rabbit back in the burrow and patted the grass down.

"I don't know if I believe that," June said.

None of us knew the truth.

We ate slow and silently on the concrete apron. I sucked down beer as quick as I could. Being drunk was the only way I could deal with any of it back then.

I went back in the pool. Feral continued to work with me.

I said, "I think I'm ready for a wheelbarrow full of pebbles." I liked to put them in the concrete so that the face of the waterfall showed a lot of stone rather than concrete.

He took the barrel around to the pile, filled it, and came back. He was walking all wobbly. Just as I said, "Hey man, be careful," the barrel tipped out of his hands, and the entire contents went into the swimming pool.

Thousands and thousands of little river stone pebbles sunk down and came to rest point at the bottom on the fake coral pattern.

My jaw dropped.

"Alright, well, you can guess what's next," I said.

We all started diving down into the pool, almost making a little game of it. Who could carry up the most pebbles—handful after handful were tossed back into the wheelbarrow. All of us diving down for pebbles and coming up for air reminded me of playing with Seth when I was a kid.

We used to throw pennies into his aunt's swimming pool and scoop them off the bottom. The person who came up with the most won. The loser had to vacuum the pool.

I wondered how many things were gonna remind me of

my friend … and for how long?

We were catching our breath. A slew of guys showed up in the yard. It was a regular hit squad: two wielded weed whackers and wore long-sleeved shirts, gray jeans, and wide-brimmed hats, while a funny-looking white guy with a big beard and wrap-around rainbow sunglasses pushed a large commercial lawn mower. I watched in wonder.

It seemed so weird, having people come to your house and do all this stuff for you. Couldn't this investment banker guy do anything for himself? I wondered if he had to hire somebody to come and fuck his wife for him.

Just then, June surfaced and threw another handful of pebbles in the wheelbarrow. Trish and Feral and K and I looked at the yard workers. June screamed, "NO!!"

She jumped out of the swimming pool and ran out onto the lawn. "STOP," she screamed, waving her arms frantically.

The guy on the riding lawn mower was forced to hit the brakes. He killed the engine. The weed whackers kept going in the distance.

"What? What is it?"

"Babbits!" she yelled, meaning bunnies but (mostly) saying rabbits. She pointed at the lawn at the base of the blades. "There! Stop!"

She opened up the burrow and scooped the terrified animals out. They curled into tight balls in her wet hands. She held them close to her heart for protection, while they trembled at the sound of a leaf blower being fired up just beyond the remaining white stockade fence.

16

AFTER WE GOT ALL THE PEBBLES OUT of the pool, we went back to work. It wasn't half an hour until Feral dumped an entire wheelbarrow of cement into the swimming pool. I put my head in my hands and just shook my head. The clear pool was now a gray cloud of filth. There was no remedy for that either. It happened. I just had to roll with the punches, as if life was just one long series of sucker punches delivered accidentally by an idiot who hadn't meant to hurt you in the first place.

"I think we're done for the day," I said, to everyone.

They folded up the chairs and dried off. The night was getting chilly anyway—almost too cold for swimming. When I looked up at the moon, I saw two of them. It was time to sober up. Dry out.

The A-Team van wouldn't start. None of us knew what the hell the problem was. We all looked under the hood only to scratch our heads and say, "Yeah, that looks like an engine."

June was in the driver's seat, cranking the ignition and pumping the pedal. Not much was happening, just a sickly wheeze.

"Kick the tires," I told K Neon.

She laughed and booted the tires. Nothing happened except that she hurt her foot a little bit.

We were far too drunk to solve any of the complex problems of the universe, let alone something as astronomical as a Chevy Econoline that wouldn't start.

It was near dusk, and the work was about halfway complete. The day had taken a turn for the worse after the accident with the thousands of small pebbles falling into the pool.

June and K rode in the truck with me, clutching the rabbits. Feral and Trish lay flat on their backs in the bed of the pickup, like corpses, praying that I wouldn't get into a car accident. What a thing to pray about.

I took the girls to Studio Mike's with the rabbits. Then I drove Feral and Trish back to Lagoon House. They were quiet in the cab of the truck. It'd been a long day. I wasn't looking forward to going back to that house, but I decided, "One last visit."

The marshes were thick with reek. Low water. The smell of death rolled off the bay.

"I won't miss that smell," I said, "as long as I live."

Feral just made a guttural noise. I looked over. He was as white as a ghost.

"Are you gonna get sick?" Trish asked.

He leaned over her, rolled down the window, and heaved out the side. Vomit sprayed all down the side of my truck. I didn't comment. I just pulled over and idled. He continued to heave into the cattails.

"You done?" Trish asked after a while.

Feral laughed and then wiped the gruel from his chin.

"Yeah, for now!"

Trish pointed into the marsh.

"Lee, remember when you crashed this truck in there?"

"Oh god, how could I forget it?" I said.

"I'm surprised you still have a license."

Coming from the other direction, making the marsh grass sway, was a pretty serious-looking line of trucks: two massive dump trucks and a flat bed with a large bulldozer chained to it. I wouldn't have given the convoy much thought, but I saw something sticking out of the top of one of the dump trucks, Captain Cock—our rooster weather vane.

I pulled the F-250 up alongside of the house where I used to live and couldn't believe what I saw.

Half of it was gone. Torn down.

The living room, the kitchen, and the dining room. Gone. Demolished and removed down to the concrete foundation.

"What the fuck," Feral hollered.

The front door was gone too, but there was a note hanging on a nail in some of the remaining vinyl siding beneath the window that used to be mine.

"GUYS, HEY, WE MOVED YER STUFF INTO THE OTHER ROOMS. I'M SORRY U DIDN'T TAKE ME SERIOUSLY. THE DAY AFTER TOMORROW, THE REST OF THIS DUMP COMES DOWN. PLEASE HAVE ALL YER STUFF OUT BY THEN. THIS HOUSE'S BEEN SOLD FOR THE LOT ONLY. GET OUT, FOR REAL.—J DISANTO"

Feral ripped the note down and crumpled it up as if all of this was a surprise.

"I didn't think that joker was serious," Feral said.

Trish said, "Yup. Apparently."

The electric and the water for the house were cut. Cords terminated. Line plugged. We walked into the open shell of the small house. We were stunned but shouldn't have been. We'd been warned, right?

Feral opened up my old room. It was packed solid with boxes. You really couldn't get in there. A wall of cardboard boxes filled to the gills. Records. Tapes. Posters. Figurines. Trinkets. "Everything there?" Trish asked.

"EVERYTHING HERE? HOW THE HELL AM I SUPPOSED TO KNOW FROM LOOKING IN THE DOORWAY?"

"What an asshole you are," Trish said. She walked into their bedroom. "I found the TV, so that accounts for all of our valuables."

I went to sit down at the dining room table (force of habit), but it was gone. So I just stood there, uncomfortably, in front of the invisible dining room table. No dining room either. The wind blew a plastic bag off the street and into the house.

I heard the house phone ring. It was unmistakable. Quacking. Trish answered and then yelled my name.

"For me?"

I took the duck and put its ass to my ear.

"Hello?"

"Lee?"

"Who's this?" I asked.

"Mark," the voice said, "Seth's brother."

He was wondering how I was doing, what was going on in New Jersey. I looked around at the house that was half leveled to the ground. Right beyond my feet was the concrete foundation. Twisted electrical wires with plastic wire nuts were poking out.

"Things are good," I said.

"I'm glad. Look … this is awkward, but you're a stone ma-son? My brother said that. He said you do great work."

"He was just being polite," I said.

"Seth wasn't polite."

"So, what, you want me to make a headstone?"

"Was thinking."

"Sorry, Mark, I sold my saw."

"I understand that you feel weird being asked."

"Yeah."

Silence.

"When we were kids, we used to go to my grandfather's cabin in the mountains and sail on his boat up there. Seth was always happy there."

Seth had talked about that place. I knew it from his description. Golden lake. Dirt roads. Swans, ducks, and turtles. Old wood. Sailboat with mildewed ropes. A tire that swung over the water. Squeaky floorboards. Wine cellar. River rushing through the stone. His grandfather's grave.

"It's all our idea to be buried there together."

"Oh."

"As a family," he said. "It's important to me that it gets done right. By someone who loved my brother."

So, then, that was it. No matter what, I had to do it.

Mark said he wanted to build Seth a tomb up in the mountains at Aunt Kathy's house, "To house my brother's ashes." He said it'd been Seth's favorite place in the world. He wanted me to have the job. A stone tomb to house his brother's ashes.

"Will you do it?"

Feral was still yelling. He was arguing with Trish about their prospects, about having to go and live with Trish's off-the-boat, Irish mother. Where else would they go?

"I'll do it."

"Oh, good. That makes me happy," he said.

We talked about money, he wanted to know where to send the check.

"I'm kinda in-between residences right now."

"I've had enough of you. I'm outta here," Trish screamed at Feral.

"Everything okay?" Mark asked.

"Oh, just some wild animals," I said. "I live amongst them—thrashing."

"Super. Then I'll mail the money to the mountain house. It'll be in the mailbox when you get there."

The whole thing happened so quickly, I didn't know what

to say. Life is like that sometimes though, isn't it? I hung up the phone and walked out of the room. Feral was still spazzing out, pretty much rightfully so I supposed. After all, his house was gone.

"Can you believe Trish? She wants me to go live with her mother. Her mother is a nasty woman. A total bitch."

I said, "Really? She seemed alright to me."

"In what way?"

"Well," I said, "I crashed into her. Totaled the back of her LeSabre. When I got to her house, she'd made me dinner. She had a place set for me and everything."

"Made you dinner after a wreck? Well, whatever. I'm still not excited about the idea."

I helped him load the F-250 with all his cardboard boxes. We drove away from the house, out of the marshes. Trish was at the Wawa smoking a cigarette next to the pay phone.

"Come on," Feral said. "Let's go to your mom's."

17

THE ROAD OPENED UP. We drove in a caravan towards Mount Mercy. Tull Lake. Everyone was excited in their own way. Leaving. We were all leaving. That's what we all wanted from our lives, what the whole world wanted. Feral and Trish were leaving the mother's house. Myself, June, and K were getting away from Studio Mike's pullout couch.

June said she very much wanted to help me with my work. K seemed indifferent to the entire thing. What else was new?

I was sitting by the passenger window with my hand on K's knee. K had her hand on June's knee. The windows were down, and we were cruising along. The summer air poured into us as the mile-markers flashed by. June drove the truck. Ten and two—her hands at all times. She was nervous, because she hadn't done any real driving before.

"I'm great as a bus passenger."

"It's easier in a big truck like this," K said. "Don't worry."

"Why's it easier?"

"Everything will get out of your way," K said, kissing June's cheek.

"Within reason, everything will get out of your way," I offered. "Don't hit a mountain or anything."

June smiled, but the smile faded quick. Each approaching road sign, fork in the highway, car in her rearview, and cop on the side of the road made her nervous.

We'd crossed the New York State Line many hours before. New Jersey peeled away. The ocean went first. Then the industrial wastelands disappeared as we crossed through the Meadowlands and past Giants Stadium, Elizabeth, Newark airport. We saw the urban sprawl of New York City. Once we were over the George Washington Bridge, we'd officially entered NY. Then, the suburbs of Westchester. River town after river town. After that, railroad lines cut through the center.

"Just keep pointing north," I said. "Keep pointing north. Aim for those mountains."

"What mountains?"

"They're there. You just can't see them yet."

June was so serious when she drove. I think that's when I first really started to develop a major thing for her. K was fooling around. She'd reach down and play with my dick and give me little bites on my ear, but my attention was locked in one hundred and fifteen percent on June Doom—the way she sat with her chest up close, into the steering wheel, while biting her lip. I kept stealing glances of her while K threw herself at me.

Feral and Trish followed behind in the van. He'd agreed to help me do the work without much prodding.

"This house is a secluded paradise in the mountains near a little river and a clear lake."

"Can't wait."

I said, "I even think there's a little pier to fish off. Maybe, if I remember right, there's also a rowboat."

We barreled up the highway, closing the gap to this place of seclusion. My pulse quickened, and it wasn't because K was practically jerking me off. She started to play with my fly like she was gonna unzip me and start to make me feel really good. I kept looking over at June. There was something about her. I didn't get the same feeling from K. She just wasn't all there for me.

June took her eyes off the road for a moment, looked at me. The truck was just gliding forward. June Doom and me stared at each other as if we were saving each other from some unstoppable force. K kept kissing my neck. June let out a sigh and looked back at the road.

"You two have fucked … alone. I know it. And that's terrible."

"No," K said very seriously. "No we haven't."

I didn't say a word. There was a problem developing. It was, as all problems are, based off of a lie. Lies, plural, really. K told June that she didn't sleep with me, that she wanted to sleep with me, that she wanted us all to sleep together. June was reluctant, but K kept pressing the issue. It didn't quite go off the way K wanted. She was still trying to get the atmosphere right.

K took her hands off of me.

I said, "This is the exit here."

June left the highway. I relayed directions from a hand-written note on a slip of paper. After a few turns off of the main drag, we were rising up into the mountain on a winding road flanked by tall Douglas firs.

I pointed at a small dirt road up ahead, "That's it, there."

The lake appeared before us. It was beautiful and expansive. The road became gravel that led up to a small stone house. It was a good-looking place.

We parked in the dirt driveway. Feral pulled next to us.

"This place is the shit," he exclaimed.

I immediately went to the mailbox. There was an envelope in there addressed from Chicago. I opened it up. A small note written by Mark was included with the cash. It was all there. I could just tell it was. I didn't bother to count it out or anything. I just put it back in the envelope and put the envelope in my back pocket.

I tossed the key to the house to K, who insisted on going in right away. I walked along the edge of the lake and looked across.

On the other side of the water, there were a few massive houses. That surprised me. Seth said that the house was isolated and that there weren't any neighbors. Looking out, I counted five homes towering on the other side of Tull Lake.

One of them was very modern. The place, which looked like something out of the Hollywood Hills, had a sick-looking yellow speedboat docked on its pier. This place wasn't how Seth said it was at all. It'd changed a lot in the fifteen years since he'd been here.

"It looks really developed over there," Trish said.

"Yeah, huh."

"Look at that goddamn cigarette boat," Feral said, excited.

"What?"

"I don't think that's what it's called," Trish said. "It's a speedboat."

"Specifically, a cigarette boat," Feral said. "Thing probably goes a hundred miles an hour."

We walked inside the house. K and June were standing in the living room, slowly looking at all the taxidermy victims: six deer, bucks with antlers. A squirrel. A raccoon. A few large trout. Some ducks.

"Seth's grandpa was a big hunter," I said.

"Yeah, you can say that," K said.

The place was nice but dated. The decor was left over from the early seventies. Feral sat down on the brown and orange couch, and dust exploded everywhere. I opened some windows.

K and June went their separate ways, leaving the house to go off and argue it all out. The relationship was disintegrating, again, right before my eyes. The problem was and always would be that June loved K but that K didn't have an ounce of love for anything. To K, everything was just some kind of off-handed fun. It was beginning to hurt my heart just thinking about it: the way June looked at K, while K was looking at anything else.

I took a slow walk around the immediate property, looking for where I would build Seth's tomb. What a thought. Where on the earth would I dig the foundation? Where would I place the blocks that I'd cover in stone face that would hold my friend's ashes for as long as it takes rocks to get broken down and destroyed by the elements of this Earth? Later, walking back to the house, I found K sitting alone on the back steps. She looked different, she was wearing cat-frame glasses.

"Ripped my last contact," she said. "Glasses from here on out."

I nodded, "You still look good."

"Listen, I don't think we should be alone anymore. No more fooling around. I don't see what the big deal is. But June is hurt."

"Sure," I said, looking beyond her, into the house, after the ghost of June's presence.

Everything and everyone seemed like a ghost back then.

"We'll all stay together. We won't go off alone. It's only right," I said.

"Thank you."

18

JUNE DOOM HUNG DRIED FLOWERS from her mother's long-ago funeral over the sheer curtains in the mountain house guest room. Outside, everything flickered like the world was film being fed through an 8mm grindhouse projector. Splatters of light struck everywhere reflective, creating a slowly rotating light show—glass and high-sheen metallics caught the last rays of the falling sun. Reality was exaggerated. Colors were over-saturated: thick green, gold, plum.

I admired her silently from the doorway. Unaware of my presence, she nursed her last clove cigarette as if she could make it last forever. The last of the sunlight streamed in, making June glow otherworldly. Obsidian rock necklace, rings, opals, and turquoise. Legs crossed high. War-torn stockings. A few of her toes were exposed, and her nails were painted random, haphazard neons. K did that on the beach the day before we left. My blood moved.

"You look like punk rock Emily Dickinson," I said.

"Thanks, I think," she said, southern-drawled, as she faced me doe-eyed.

"Where'd the flowers come from?"

She pointed to her rabbit pelt suitcase, locked on the bed.

"You travel with flowers?"

"Everywhere! ... And a gem collection, and a travel record player, some important albums, books, and one other outfit. The rest is a secret. Isn't it nice that way?"

June, pointing at the window, said the dead flowers caused

"negative energy" to bottle up, and that it fucked with "the flow of the room."

"'Cause you like negative energy?"

Her clove cigarette sizzled and popped.

"When the time is right, it's useful. I think it's dumb to try and stop it," she said deadpan. She wouldn't look at me. I made her nervous, which made me nervous. We kept ping-ponging that feeling for hours.

I scanned the room, running my eyes across June's unpacked belongings.

She came with just that rabbit pelt suitcase, but she'd already found a lot of pretty, weird, artistic things to place all around the guest room like talismans. She was a scavenger. She could find beauty anywhere: the pine needle forest, dilapidated tool sheds, demonic attics, odd trails leading up into the haunted mountainside beside the cold rushing river. Interesting objects were everywhere: colored glass; old paintings, warped and yellowed by time; a crate of sheet-music for organ hymns; black and white showgirls with fresh faces from beyond the grave.

"Here comes trouble," I said as I stepped over the threshold into her room.

"Come on. You know the deal. We can't be in the same room alone."

Direct orders from her girl, K Neon. There was too much tension. Too much had happened already. The three of us were welcome to do whatever we wanted with each other when we were together, but it was wrong and off limits for us to wander off alone, to pair up—however that broke down. Mathematics. A whole lot of sinister mathematics that no-one understood.

But K Neon was gone. She took my F-250 down the mountain with Feral and Trish. Supplies: groceries, beer. They were rumored to be searching out a hidden waterfall. I opted out of going because I heard June tell K, "I have a migraine headache."

But she didn't.

"You've never had a migraine in your entire life," I said.

"How the hell would you know?" June smiled, full teeth. "Come no closer! I'll have to kill you."

"Is that what's in your secret suitcase? Guns?"

"Rare earth minerals, Jupiter sea shells, dragon tears, stardust, and guns."

"I won't leave, but I will put on a record," I offered as a compromise. "Then we won't be alone. We'll have the whole band with us."

She sighed painfully and tried to make a sour face at me, but it wouldn't hold. I walked straight to her record collection and held up a vinyl sleeve: Rolling Stones, Hot Rocks 1964-1971.

"There's a chunk missing. Hazards of travel, my dear," she warned.

I shrugged and put the vinyl on the tiny turntable, ignoring the ripped away section of the disc and what it meant for our future.

In blissful surrender, she said, "We'll have to flip it before Wild Horses. The hole…"

I shut the door behind me and locked it. She looked up, exposing her throat. Didn't show any fear even while wearing a disguise. There was a magnetic understanding that could not be undone now that our nuclear reactions had been initiated.

She kissed my neck. I ran my hand through her bright red hair, wondering what color it could really be beneath all the chemicals.

The arm of the record player dropped. "You Can't Always Get What You Want" crackled into life. A chorus of English voices began as June pulled her shirt over her head, showing me where her heart was.

Then my jeans came down. I struggled to kick my sneakers off. She just kept pushing my pants, but I couldn't get my shoes off. Her skirt hiked. The fishnets tore away.

We fell like maniacs onto the sharp-spring bed.

When the needle took a nosedive into the abyss following the opening four bars of Wild Horses, June and I were already past the point of no return.

We were panting and sweaty. She bit my earlobe so hard it began to bleed. She had one sharp tooth that she didn't realize. She'd never bit a man's ear before, because she'd never been with one the way she was while the record player went into hysterics—the arm falling off the edge of the earth and into the netherworld.

Afterwards, she said, "I feel better now," with her head on my chest.

"We'll have to tell K."

"Yes, we will."

Apocalyptic fireworks were being loaded into cannons, prepared to explode all around us.

June stood from the bed, naked; took the dead flowers

down from the window; opened up the suitcase; and delicately put them away ... for a time.

Tunnel

J UNE WAS ON TOP when the front door opened. We were startled from our dream by K's voice.

"Lucy, I'm home!"

We weren't so brave anymore. June put the rest of her clothes on. I pulled my shirt over my head.

"You've got to get out of here," she said. "Out the window."

I shook my head, pointing at the floor. "Let me show you something."

I moved the bed. Underneath, was a small door.

"Escape hatch," I said.

"Helllllllo," sang K Neon out in the living room.

We climbed down through the trap door just as K began to lightly knock on the locked bedroom door.

"June?"

The cellar was cool. Vintage vino was stacked on dusty racks.

"A lot of nice wine down here," I said.

"A little birdie told me that you can open one with a shoe-lace," June said. "We're trapped now. Show me."

"We're not trapped," I said. "See that over there? That's a door."

"To where?"

"Let's find out."

We walked down a long passageway made of stone and just barely illuminated by the sun on the other end. We came out, undetected, in the rocks beside the house.

I walked one way—down to the river. June walked the other way—back to her love.

19

I WENT OFF ALONE, HUNTING ROCKS ... again. The mountains seemed like they were meant for that type of thing anyway. As I drove, massive stretches of jagged rock uncurled through dark forests, piles of leaves, broken limbs, puddles of standing water opaque with rotting debris. The animals watched from their perches in the shadows as I passed in the machine. They didn't know what to make of me, and I wasn't sure what to make of them.

It was another Saturday morning. I was just trying to find some sort of person to ask for directions. I was lost up there, trying to build a tomb.

At the foot of the steep dirt road, there was a paved, two-lane road that ran east and west. I headed west, farther away from the highway. I knew there was nothing back in that direction. When June drove us in, there'd been nothing. Now, I was eyeing my gas gauge with a small bit of concern. What was around here?

The change in altitude completely screwed up my hearing. I kept opening my jaw as far as it would go to try and make my ears pop. No luck.

The paved road was desolate and seemed to lead nowhere. I drove for ten minutes, thinking, "Is this really a road to nowhere? Does it end in a goddamn dead end? There's probably one house on it, ten miles up. One lone house with a crooked mailbox; a sign on a dead elm tree at the foot of the gravel driveway that says, 'DO NOT ENTER, I GOT A SHOT-

GUN—chicken wire, and a barking, gray dog."

Then, up ahead, I saw a fork in the road. I headed to the right, and within another five minutes, I saw civilization appear before me. Small houses. Porches. A woman pulling weeds out of a flower bed in jeans and a green shirt. I stopped the truck, and the woman looked over at me.

"Yeah," she said, "what is it? Don't gawk too hard at me. My husband'll show up. That's no good for any of us."

"I'm looking for…"

"For what," she interrupted, wiping the dirt of her hands on a smock. "What are you looking for?"

I noticed a cat sitting on the wooden deck. It was eyeing me suspiciously too.

"A quarry," I said. "For rocks."

"For rocks?" She shook her head. "Nothing like that around here."

She looked at my license plate.

"Jersey. Doesn't surprise me. I went to Wildwood once. They charged me to go on the beach. Everywhere else in the world, beaches are free. Nothing free in Jersey, huh?"

She told me to just go and take the rocks. They were right there. Right there on the mountain for the taking. I felt so stupid. I'm from the ocean. There's no mountains where I'm from. You have to buy them by the pound. I thanked her and drove off towards town.

"Town" was nothing but a tiny gas station, a general store, and a hardware store that looked like it was closed. I went to the door and knocked. Nobody was inside.

Finally, a guy walking by said, "What're you doing?"

"Need to buy something."

"It's Saturday," he said.

I got back into the truck, did a U-turn, and pulled into the gas station. The same guy was walking back the other way with his dog. He shook his head at me and my New Jersey license plates.

"Still Saturday, smartie."

When I got back to the house, Feral was out on the rowboat, casting a line on the still water.

I said, "You catch anything?"

"Just boredom."

"Try harder," I said.

"You're scaring the fish away," he said. "Thought you said this was a sailboat?"

"Mast fell off. Now you gotta row."

"This boat sucks."

"Just don't sink it, please."

I went into the house. There was music coming from June Doom's room. There was a light under K Neon's door.

I stood in the hallway, trying to figure out which door I would choose.

20

K NEON CAME INTO MY ROOM and woke me with kisses down my neck. The springs in the bed sighed.

"I thought you said we shouldn't do this," I said, not exactly stopping her.

"I'm all alone," she cooed. "I need someone. I don't care who it is." Her voice was playful, but I couldn't tell how much of it was true. I guess anything you say is true. Jokes don't hide anything.

"Can't decide whether that sounds really free or really sad," I said.

"Sad," she said, breathing in my ear, "so sad. She won't talk to me. If she won't talk to me, the good times don't come gushing. I wanna go out on a date right now."

"This side of the world is closed until further notice."

She took my hand and pulled me up out of the bed. We walked through the shadowy house. On the couch, I could hear Feral snoring underneath the amputated heads of the animals mounted on the walls. The wood paneling caused every sound and inference to be amplified. I thought I heard a noise in June's room, but I hoped it was just the wind. There was no wind though.

Outside, we walked barefoot across the wet grass and the slimy leaves. She tried to hold my hand, but I wasn't gonna go that far with it. I took it for two steps and nonchalantly released it. K is too smart to not notice, but she didn't say anything.

She wanted to go out on the rowboat. I didn't put up a

fight. The stars were out, and there was a heavy mist on the lake. It seemed otherworldly, something that would only happen once in a person's lifetime. It didn't matter what the circumstances were.

The air was warm. The water was cool. A mist rose out of the lake and made a shroud for us at lake level. It hovered there around us, but we could still see the stars, magnificent and bright. We pushed out from the pier and paddled into the mist, vanishing from anyone looking from the house.

The bright moon reflected off K's cat-frame glasses, making it look like she had the moon in both of her eyes. She looked smarter, more dangerous, with the glasses on. I liked that.

At the center of Tull lake, I stopped rowing. We drifted. K sat, with hands gripping both edges of the boat. Her mouth was open, and she was looking up at the stars.

"Which one's do you know?" she asked.

"Oh, Jesus. None. The Big Dipper ... the Little Dipper. I dunno. Orion, I guess. I know that." I pointed, "That's his belt."

She began to name all the constellations. She knew each and every one of them.

"You know the story of Orion?"

"No."

"There's many. Myths. My favorite is that Orion, the hunter, fell in love with seven sisters. They were called the Pleiades: the beautiful daughters of Atlas and Pleione. Orion could have had any one of them, but he wanted all of them. So Atlas took his daughters and put them up into the sky."

"Sounds rational."

"To protect them from the irrational Orion, the seven sisters were hidden in a cluster of stars inside the belly of a bull, Taurus. You see it there?"

K pointed up. I could see it clearly. I nodded.

"It's the death of Orion. Those girls. That bull. Orion went up into the heavens after them, and now he fights in the sky with his bronze club every night—mauled by Taurus, who tries to put out Orion's eyes with his horns."

"That's where we're at, yes."

We drifted in a slow circle.

"Did June talk to you? About us."

K laughed coldly. "She mentioned something. I didn't believe it."

"What?"

"She said she loves you," K said, unbuttoning her shirt and pulling it over her head.

"Loves me... No shit?"

I felt good hearing that. K kicked off her cutoff jean shorts. She was in her bra and panties again. It never felt far away for her to be in that state of undress. She undressed as quick as a superhero can put on their costume.

"I don't care. Go ahead, love each other," K said. "I'm fine with that."

She ran her hand up my thigh and pulled at the button on my pants.

"I'm all brain and pussy, there's no blood for my heart."

She sat down in the base of the boat and started undoing my belt. I told her, "Come on, knock it off."

She looked up at me, grinning darkly. The moon reflected off of her glasses.

"Ten thousand dollars says you won't make me stop as soon as I put you in my mouth."

"Do you have ten thousand dollars?"

"Of course I have it," she said, "Do you have it, poor boy?"

"Poor boy. Hilarious." I pushed her away from my belt. "Be cool, K. I'm not gonna fuck around anymore on June. That's over."

There was a horrible sound from across the lake: the engine of the speed boat as it came to life. It was the worst sound I'd ever heard in my entire life. K Neon looked like she was in a slasher film wilderness and just heard a chainsaw.

The speedboat started to move away from the dock. We could see it in the moonlight, like a predator that was coming straight for us. We were sitting ducks. My heart slipped from its meaty cage and smacked its way down into the pit of my stomach.

"GO! GO! GO!" K frantically beat against my chest with the hammers of her fists.

I started to row, and she continued to pummel me. I snapped at her, "Calm the fuck down!"

The canary yellow cigarette boat started to rip around in the moonlight, but we were obscured in the fog—unseen in the mist. The boat began to pick up speed around the outside edge of the lake, as if it was using the entire body of water as a small track. I thought about the cars drag racing at Raceway Park as I watched in terror the speedboat pass by us some hundred and fifty feet away at high speed. The engine dug in, rumbled. I heard a voice from the boat scream out in glee. It was a man's voice, hollering at the moon above, having fun, oblivious to our presence.

The first waves from the wake of the boat smacked into the side of our rowboat. We rocked diabolically.

K Neon said, "We're gonna die out here."

I tried to row, but the waves were coming from every direction. The throttle of the boat dropped to max at that point. I could hear the exhaust screaming out. Water sprayed into the moonlight. It was certain death. The speedboat opened up. The waves rose. One more lap around, and the boat started to move away from the outside edge of the lake. It cut across the open water of the center.

Well, not quite "open," because we were there—occupying the bull's-eye like a solid red dot.

The boat headed straight towards us. It was going to crush us completely. At the last second, it veered slightly away. Our rowboat flipped. I went into the water and swam one way. K swam the other way. She was like a bullet tearing through the water, but she was going the wrong way across the lake—away from our house. I called her name and got a mouthful of water.

As the sound of the speedboat got louder again, I had to worry about myself. I had to think about how to keep my body from getting cut up in the blades of the propeller. I had to think about keeping my skull from getting smashed in by the bow. Horror. Absolute horror.

K Neon could take care of herself, couldn't she? She was a natural swimmer. I'd seen her in action, like a little goddamned Scandinavian mermaid. I gulped down more of that murky water, kicked my feet, and doggie paddled like an idiot through the moonlit water, while the waves whacked into me.

All the while the engine of the speedboat got closer. I felt hot death breathing onto the back of my neck. I took a deep breath of air and swam down as far as I could into the water. To this day, whether it really happened or not, I swear I felt the rush of the boat and the spinning of the propeller pass over my head.

I stayed down there and swam as hard as I could beneath the surface. It felt like Jaws was on my heels. When I came back up, I treaded water in the middle of the lake. The speedboat died. Its throttle lessened. I continued to bob in the dark water, as the yellow monster slid through the waves, back towards its own dock, unaware of the melee it'd caused.

I thanked the stars above for my life. I thought about K Neon, who was most likely dead, and swam towards the dock. There, a man hopped off the speedboat and whistled as he went into a nearby house.

I pulled myself up on his dock and walked to his door. I was about to knock when the door opened up. A fat man with a buzz cut came out in a huge hurry.

"Yo! Hey! What are you doing?!"

I froze. He had a head like a Rottweiler. Thick arms. He was wearing cargo shorts and sandals. I could hear the Grateful Dead playing from inside the house. It was "Sugar Magnolia."

"I'm your neighbor," I said.

"Why you all wet?"

I pointed at the lake.

"Okay," he shrugged, glaring at me. I took note that his gray t-shirt said "Hakuna Mattata—It Means No Worries."

"I'm from across the lake," I said, pointing at our little stone cabin across the water. It looked so peaceful and innocent over there.

"Oh! My neighbor," he said. "Right on! Right on! The way you said it, it was like you were a creature of the lake. Why'd you swim over here? Next time, yell. I'll pick you up in my truck."

Any sense of present danger evaporated.

"You gotta excuse me, bro. I am so super stoned."

He invited me into his house. I didn't hesitate to go inside. I was looking for a way to politely mention the homicide that'd happened on the water.

"Ron," he said, introducing himself. I gave a fake name for some reason. I wasn't thinking clearly.

"Doug," I said.

"Doug, you wanna smoke a bong with me?"

He didn't wait for an answer. He left the room and came back with a three foot-tall bong.

He said, "I get some real good shit, so be careful."

I nodded dumbly while he packed the bowl.

I said, "That your speedboat out there?"

"God is it ever! My pride and joy," he said. "Being a medical sales rep has its plusses, lemme tell you. Speedboat ownership is just one perk."

"Sure."

"I know, I know, the lake is a little small for it. Used to

live on the ocean in Virginia Beach, but that fell through." He scowled, rubbing his fingers together as if signifying "too much money." "Now I'm lucky if I get to rip around on my speedboat twice a year. Gotta wait till my bitch-ass wife is out of town with the kids."

I looked all around. There were pictures of his kids everywhere. Everywhere. All the walls. All the tables.

He took a massive hit from the bong, sucking in all the smoke. A world record. He exhaled it all and, without missing a beat, said, "JESUS! I didn't bother you with the boat, did I?! I'm so stupid! I must have woken you up in the middle of the night, and you came over to rag me out! I'M SO OBLIVIOUS!"

"Kinda," I admitted.

"Dude, I am so frickin' sorry! I feel like such an inconsiderate neighbor! What the hell is my problem? Seriously, I want you to kick me in the head as hard as you can."

"That's alright."

"No! Kick my head like a football!"

I politely declined again. He said it was a wise choice. He said his head was equipped with the most serious and sinister metal plate that money could buy. He knew. He was in the medical rep business after all.

"I was in a very serious accident," Ron said, "a couple years ago. Never been the same since. A riding lawn mower crashed down on my head in a Home Depot."

"Oh, wow—hey, so, I want to talk to you about something kinda important."

"Shoot, what is it, amigo?"

He lit the bong again, taking another colossal rip. It hurt my lungs to watch.

"I was just out on the lake in my rowboat..." I began.

"Beautiful night. Love that mist! And above, the stars out in full regalia," he said, nodding. "Go on."

"So, you were zooming around and you kinda hit my rowboat and..."

"What! Are you fucking with me?!" He was wide-eyed. "I hit your boat! How inconsiderate of me! Dude, I apologize! I was so smashed, man. You gotta understand: my wife keeps me on a very tight leash. She thinks I got brain damage or something and..."

"Yeah, that's not the worst part," I said.

"Listen, I'm gonna make this better," he said, putting the

bong away. "I'm gonna get you a new rowboat. Fuck that! A regular boat. Little outboard engine. You'll love it. You'll thank me one day."

"I think you killed my friend…"

He didn't say a word. He just stared at me. Then he looked over his shoulder, like maybe I said that to someone who was sitting behind him. There was just a wall behind him … with some photos of little, blonde, angelic children.

"We were in the boat when you hit it."

"Holy shit," he said. "Holy shit. Holy shit. Holy shit."

That's all he kept saying. When I suggested that we call the cops and get some divers out here to look for the body before the fish ate too much of it, he just kept muttering, "Holy shit. Holy shit. I should have listened to Harpie," he said. He was nearly catatonic. "The speedboat was a bad idea."

He went to the window and looked out at Tull lake. The mist was just clearing off the water. Little pieces of the rowboat floated on the surface.

"There's your boat," he said, punching the sliding glass door lightly. Thud. "Your friend ... was with you?"

"She swam one way. I swam the other. You were doing laps at top speed, almost killed me. I went way under."

"Oh." He started to squint. "Your friend … is she a hot blonde in a thong with all kinds of leaves and stuff stuck in her hair?"

"What?"

I went to the window. K had just stood up about a hundred feet away on the banks of the lake.

I went out onto the deck and yelled.

"Help," she said weakly.

Ron got a towel to wrap around her. I ran down, hugged her, and started pulling leaves out of her hair.

"My glasses," she said.

They were gone, thrown into the lake. They sank.

"You've been sitting here like this? Didn't you hear me calling your name?"

"Yeah," she muttered. She was disorientated, shivering slightly. Her skin was all goose bumps.

"Did you get hit?" I asked, feeling the back of her head for a lump, dried blood, any signs of damage.

"I hit my head on something. I couldn't see where I was going," she said.

She really was blind without her glasses. She'd gotten to the shore after the mad swim, narrowly dodging the boat herself, and didn't know which way to go. There'd been no lights, and even if there had been, the world was a blur to K without her glasses. She'd passed out in a pile of leaves, too proud to yell for help. This annoyed me.

"I was right over there. I could have come and found you if you'd yelled."

"I was…"

"What?"

"Embarrassed."

"Oh, Christ." I hugged her. "Next time, yell for help. Everybody needs help sometimes, K."

Ron took her into the house. She drank a cup of hot tea. We sat in silence in the kitchen for a long time. Eventually, Ron put on the TV in the other room for some noise. It was cartoons. Then K went and took a long hot shower.

"She seems really weird," Ron said. "She gonna be okay?"

"I think so."

When K came out of the shower, Ron gave her a strange emerald dress to wear.

"Everything my wife has is like that," he explained apologetically. "She loves emeralds."

We were both just ecstatic for our own reasons that K wasn't dead at the bottom of the lake.

"Eat some Honey Nut Cheerios or something," Ron said.

K sat at the table, staring at the table cloth, finally looked up, and said, "Let's go."

Speedboat

SPEEDBOAT HAD A SOFT BRAIN. The longer I was around him, the clearer that became. One eye would drift when he talked to you. A slight dribble of drool was always on the cusp of rolling over his bottom lip.

He insisted on taking us back to the stone cabin after we'd found K.

"Come on. Hop in Blondie, and I'll zoom you over there, 'cross the lake."

K looked horrified at the idea of getting into that speed-boat. Maybe she'd never get in a boat again. I didn't blame her. The boat was named Blondie for two reasons.

"I think Debra Harry in 1977 was the hottest chick ever in the history of Earth," Ron said, "and my favorite movie is Fist-ful of Dollars. That's Clint Eastwood's name in that: Blondie."

"You named it after two different people?" K asked.

He nodded like a drunken child—all grins while drumming his fingers across his globe shaped belly.

Seeing K's fear, he said, "Let's take my truck."

He had a brand new, black, 2004 Ford F-350 Super Duty with dually tires and massive chrome pipes.

"Look at this truck," I said, impressed. "It could easily crush my F-250."

We climbed inside his monster truck with much effort.

"What do you use this for?" I asked.

"Just driving," he shrugged.

He was a man of many toys. He was an overgrown child

surrounded by playthings that served no real purpose other than entertainment.

After Ron cranked the engine, it rumbled and music exploded out of the speakers at top volume. Ozzy Osbourne. "Crazy Train."

"THIS IS MY FAVORITE SONG," he shouted.

K yelled in the back seat for him to shut it off.

He hit the advance button on the CD player, lowering the volume slightly. The next song was also "Crazy Train."

"My friend Terry made me this CD. It's all 'Crazy Train,' man! My favorite song!"

Just to test it, I hit the advance button. The next track really was "Crazy Train".

"Randy Rhodes invented that," he said, "that finger tap shredding method."

I looked at K in the rearview mirror. She looked seasick: white as a ghost.

Ron grinned wider after his offering of insight but sensed our unease and turned the CD player down lower. Now, it was just the sound of the engine rumbling. Ron eased us down a little dirt road at the base of his driveway.

"We'll have to go all the way around the mountain," Ron said. He was high, and then he was low. I began to sense a deep sadness in him. I put my head against the headrest and tried to close my eyes.

"You own that cabin now?"

"No," I said, "I'm just here for a couple weeks doing some work."

"Like what?"

"Stone work. I'm building a crypt."

"A crypt? Whoa." He was visibly interested. "I'm fat as hell," he said as he grabbed his gut. "I gotta do something to get rid of this lard. You need any help?"

"Help? Really? It won't be much money."

"For free. I'll work for free."

I didn't say anything. I just let it sit. Sure. If he wanted to come over and mix cement and lug around stones, that was completely up to him.

We went down the mountain. Twisty, winding roads. At the main drag, he made a left. At the fork in the road, he hung right. I recognized where we were then.

He turned onto our dirt road, went back up the mountain, and pulled up to the stone cabin.

"Man, that road is way outta the way," I noted.
"That's why I wanted to use the speedboat," he said.
K got out of the truck and practically ran into the house.

21

I DOVE DOWN ENDLESSLY into the lake looking for K's glasses. It was hopeless. I dove down all afternoon. It seemed like the thing I had to do.

There I was again, diving for pennies in the neighborhood pool with Seth—whoever gets the most pocket change wins. (Except he was dead now.) There I was again, picking up pebbles off the bottom of the coral reef swimming pool at the crackerjack waterfall mansion, while the girls rescuing rabbits out of the lawn. (The bunnies were at the animal shelter.) There I was, kicking my feet as I descended down into the darkness of Tull lake, looking for something on the bottom— glimmering just for me.

The lake was piss warm, but as I went down, it got immediately cooler. I swam down with eyes wide and unblinking.

K was going back down the mountain soon. She was taking June with her. Things hadn't worked out between the three of us. June decided she didn't know what she wanted, who she wanted. She was jealous. She didn't want me to kiss K. She wanted me to herself. She wanted K to herself. K just sat there dumbly, her head in her girlfriend's lap, squinting blindly, as she said, "I want Trish to drive me to the nearest bus station."

"Us," June said.

So I swam down, again, near the center of the lake. It had to be close to where we were when the rowboat flipped us out. The closest I'd come was a Coca-Cola bottle stuck in the mud.

I went back up and floated again. The blue sky ripped by. I

noticed the lack of a water tower, the lack of power lines, the lack of planes zipping by overhead. I floated on my stomach, being very still, as I waited for the water to become clear.

Finally, I could almost see the bottom. It was meditative. Every once in a while, a fish would float by without a care in the world. I thought about how it would feel to be a fish and be scooped up by human hands, beaten on a rock, and then eaten.

I thought I saw something down there in the mud. So I swam down and groped around with my hands.

Her glasses.

I swam to the pier holding them. Feral and Trish had just pulled up in the van. I could see June, standing on the porch as she talked to Feral. I saw him nodding. I watched June point at the van. He was telling her it was no problem. He'd give them a ride to the bus station. That was the end of it.

I ran, dripping wet, across the pier. When I got to the porch, K was coming outside with her bag.

"Hey," I said.

"What," K sighed icily.

"I have something for you."

"Well, I don't want it."

"You sure?" I asked, holding up her glasses. She squinted. June came walking out too.

"You found them?!" June was surprised.

I handed them to K, and she stuck them on her face. I watched the tension and misery leave her body as her vision returned.

"At the bottom of the lake?" June inquired.

"At the bottom of the lake," I said.

June looked thoroughly impressed.

"Like magic," she said. And like magic, they decided to stay with me there.

22

S PEEDBOAT WORKED HARD FOR HALF AN HOUR lugging boulders for Seth's tomb. Then he said, "I could really go for some Gatorade." He tapped Feral on the shoulder. "Come on, let's go on a Gatorade run."

The two of them walked to the dock, conspiring. They hopped in Blondie and zoomed across the still face of the pink water, sending a small tidal wave into our meager dock.

I sat down in the pine needles, looking at the base of the wall. It was a ten by ten foundation. Seth's ashes would sit in there one day. I wanted the work to come out perfect, but I'd never done anything perfect in my life.

June walked out of the house and sat down next to me in the pine needles.

"I think it was real nice what you did for K."

"I like her. I don't want her to leave. She'd take you with her."

June put her hand over mine.

"I'm not going back to Rhode Island," she said, "I'm transferring to Austin."

"Texas, huh?"

"Yeah, I don't really feel so good on the East Coast. Not that it's bad here…"

"It's all just temporary anyway," I said as I threw a rock. It bounced off the crypt and back at us, landing in the pine needles at our feet.

"Where'd your helpers go?"

"They went across the water. Needed something from the house."

"Coke?" she asked, as if channeling Madame Woo-the Dead.

"Probably."

"Feral's been talking about it a lot. How it was a mistake to come up here, 'cause there was nobody holding."

"What am I gonna do, right," I said. "People live their own lives."

"You think that still, even after your friend died?"

"I can barely live my own life," I said. "Who am I to tell people what they can't do?"

"I don't believe you when you say that."

"Who knows what anybody really means."

"You should be in college. You're smart."

"I've never been inside one ... for any reason."

"Why does it bother you?"

"It doesn't."

"Then you should go."

"I don't have the money, and I don't know what it's even good for."

"I'm gonna be sixty thousand dollars in debt," June said. "Then what?"

"I'll rob a bank. Do you wanna be my getaway driver?"

"What's it pay?" I joked.

"I'll pay your college tuition. That's the deal. Come with me to Austin. You can be my roommate."

"We're not allowed to share a room..."

"Karen's orders." June got quiet. "We just broke up. It was for the best. One of us loved too much. One of us loved too little."

I didn't say anything.

"She didn't seem to care," June said. "That made it worse."

"Many of the things floating in the ether just seem to make it worse."

"No matter."

The speedboat started to come across the lake. Feral was driving and laying on the horn. Ron was swinging his orange t-shirt over his head.

"God help us all," I said.

The boat came in at breakneck speed. As they got closer, Feral appeared to be panicking at the controls.

"He doesn't know what he's doing," I said.

The boat got closer. Ron pushed Feral out of the way, but it was too late. The speedboat hit the pier.

We jumped to our feet. K and Trish came out of the house. We all stood around, looking at the wreck. The pier was mangled but hung on.

"You alright?" Trish yelled.

Ron jumped on the dock. It tilted but didn't collapse.

"We're fine," he said, laughing.

The two of them came walking towards us. They looked like they were on their way back from a concert. Feral had a Pepsi in his hand.

"This is a RonBomb!"

"What is?"

"This!" Feral passed me the soda. "It's Pepsi and vodka," he said.

I passed it right back.

"Pepsi and vodka," Trish said. "What the fuck?!"

"Sorry about your dock!" Ron punched Feral on the shoulder. "Hey, you said you knew how to drive a boat."

"He sunk his boat," Trish shouted.

"Your driving privileges are hereby revoked, bro," Ron said sternly. "This is a seventy five thousand dollar cruiser."

I went back to work. That's how the afternoon was. They all watched me work. June helped out a little bit, passing me flagstone and tools as I needed them, but I mostly worked alone while they watched.

The evening descended.

Ron kept trying to persuade us to come back to his place.

"Let's party," he said desperately, like he would die if the evening ended. "Let's party, please."

I said, "I'm not feeling it."

The girls all looked tired.

"Come on. I've got the biggest hot tub any of you guys have ever seen."

Then he elbowed me in the ribs.

"I've got some sick tequila too."

Reluctantly, I agreed. June and K insisted on riding over in the F-250. Feral and Trish took the boat back across to the lit up house, which was glowing like heaven.

"Automatic timers," Ron said as he walked to the mangled dock. "So I know exactly when it's time to party."

23

I T WAS THE FOURTH OF JULY. NO-ONE HAD FIREWORKS.
The girls were bored. That wasn't a good thing. Bored
girls will kill you.

It was the first hot night in the mountains. We sat on the
concrete apron looking at Ron's pool, which was still closed
for the season. Beers were sweating in our fists.

"It's too bad," June said. "I'd like to swim."

"I know," I said. "Me too."

Ron had been vague. He didn't mention his swimming
pool wouldn't be open. Now didn't we look like assholes in our
bathing suits? Drove all the way over here, and the pool's still
closed, and his beer was skunked.

"You want to get out of here?" I asked K and June. "You
two want to go find the river? A stream?"

They shrugged.

"A polluted toxic river that will melt your flesh off? I know
where that is."

"Stop trying to take us back to Jersey," K said.

"So, we'll just sit here frowning. Looking at that tarp covering the pool," said June. "What a nice tarp."

"Fourth of July. Here ... a goddamned light-year away
from the boardwalk," I said darkly.

Headlights flooded the driveway. Feral and Trish were back.

"I got the charcoal, and I got cold beer," Feral shouted as
he barreled through Speedboat's fence. Trish labored with the
ice, some hot dog rolls, and a king size bottle of mustard.

"We were all gonna die out here, weren't we," I said.

"How can you ever hope to survive this far away from the Atlantic Ocean?" K Neon mocked. "Poor thing."

"Goners. Absolute goners," June said.

I gave us all the sign of the cross.

K Neon jammed her knuckles in my ribcage.

Everyone else descended on the coolers and the barbecue grill, telling stories from town. I went in to talk to Ron, who was leaning slack-jawed against his own countertop.

"I'm sorry about the pool," he said.

"What about it?" As if it was a nonissue.

He pointed at my striped swim shorts, "Go take a dip in the lake, maing…"

"K Neon will have to be institutionalized if we start night swimming."

"I'll make it up to you," he said as he began pouring us all shots of medicine in shallow glasses. He was trying to be a good host. Quicker than I expected, he leaned over, whacked me on the wrist, and said, "Hey, I know what would make this better."

Ron took out another shot glass. Filled it up. Now there were six shots on the counter.

"I'm gonna get my neighbor over here. He's a complete and total train wreck. You'll love him. He's got nine confirmed kills in this decade alone."

As much of a train wreck as Ron was, it was dangerous for him to think that way about somebody else.

He went out on the deck and started to yell into the woods behind his house.

"YO TERRY! HEY TERRY! COME OVER HERE!"

A light came on through the woods.

"WHAT??!?!"

Then, just like that, there he was: another big, drunk idiot with a dented head floundering through the door … obliterated.

"What's up, guys," Terry said sideways, enveloped in camouflage pants and a cutoff Van Halen T-shirt that was too big for his scrawny frame.

"Just trying to get drunk," we said as if one life force.

"Trying?" He looked at his watch. His long, scraggly hair fell across the band. "Guys, it's nine o' clock at night. I've already been drunk, sobered up … got drunk again, sobered up, and now I'm working on my third drunk of the day."

Ron looked at me, dead serious.

"Terry here was Special Ops."

"Oh?"

"Is Special Ops," Terry said. "Once you're Ops, you never become not Ops."

He just looked like another crazy, backwoods maniac.

"This guy could kill somebody with a blueberry pancake," Ron said.

Terry nodded.

"Did you say something about a blueberry pancake?" Feral said, walking in the kitchen.

Terry leaned into the stove with his elbow on a burner. It wasn't a joke. He really could kill somebody with a blueberry pancake.

"I can knock you unconscious with one finger," Terry said.

"Sure. I can knock myself unconscious with drugs and alcohol though, so I'm good," I offered.

That eased the tension. Terry wasn't gonna have to kill anybody. Thank God.

We forgot the girls and went to quick work on the shots.

"Where's Harpie?" Terry asked.

"Mother's house."

"Oh? A bachelor, you are?"

"Another night or so," Ron said.

"Offer still stands."

Ron busted out laughing.

"What offer?" Feral demanded.

"He wants to kill my wife for three thousand dollars."

"Oh! I don't wanna," Terry said, "but I will…"

"With a Belgium waffle?" I asked half-jokingly.

"Fuck you man," Terry said, snickering. "But I could FYI."

"Hot tub," Ron offered, peeking out the window at the bored girls.

"Hot tub," Terry nodded.

"It's the only way," Feral said, shrugging.

"I'll warm that motherfucker up. Your girls will be happy," Ron said as he went out the door.

He crossed the lawn, swinging his arms like Quasimodo by the shed, and flipped on all of the flood lights. We shielded our eyes.

"This is a goddamn big house," I said to Feral.

"What the hell does this guy do?" Feral asked.

"Not much," Terry offered. "He's got brain damage from

getting hurt inside a Home Depot. One of those riding lawn mowers fell on him and clobbered his head open. Aisle ten."

"Brain damage paid for this place? I gotta get me some."

The stereo fired up. It sounded like the Huey Lewis and the News were set up on his back patio.

"He's got some great brain damage-funded stuff."

Ron walked back over and said to the girls, "Come on over here, to the other side, I want to show you girls my deck. Don't you want to see my deck? It's big and beautiful."

I encouraged them to ignore this.

The hot tub was good. In quick order, the girls were all dunking in, while we were all drinking and drinking and drinking—like our throats were full of sand. Then I went in, sunk to the bottom, held my breath, and passed like a turtle under all the beautiful feet of these summertime girls.

When I came to the surface, Ron and Terry were off somewhere smoking. I was fucking around with the stereo, singing along—all the wrong words to the wrong song.

"You wanna see my deck?" I said to the girls mockingly.

"Man, he's a creep," June said.

"He is," K said. "You see the way he's looking at me? Pennsyltucky trash."

"We're in New York," I say.

"Same difference."

When Ron came back, he was practically carrying Terry. Ron's brain damage-strength weed was no match for Terry's normal brain weakness. Before too long, Terry was off in the stones vomiting up hamburgers and hot dogs.

Terry opted to walk himself through the woods to his house.

I had no idea where Feral and Trish were.

Then it was just myself, June, K Neon, and Speedboat, who was all cross-eyed and insistent that the girls make room for him in the bubbling water. This was cause enough for them to flee the tub. They'd had enough. They toweled off and walked, bare feet in the green grass, to the F-250.

I tossed June Doom the keys and said, "Don't crash."

As I stood there with Ron, I wasn't sure what to say. Jesus Christ, it was some house. Where was I gonna live? I had nowhere to go. I was out on my ass.

Ron said desperately, "Let's do a shot. You like tequila?"

"Sure."

"Come inside my house, dude, I got the best tequila you've

ever had."

We went in the house. The lights were all out. He stumbled around in the darkness, crashing into things like a two hundred and seventy five pound pinball. I went in the kitchen and leaned against the counter. He was screwing around with the stereo again in the living room.

A song I didn't know was on.

Then he came into the kitchen with a bottle and poured us both a really big slug. We knocked them back. It was really nasty shit. I know good tequila. This wasn't it.

"What the hell was that?"

He held up the bottle.

It wasn't even tequila. It was a plastic jug of mescal. Whatever. I thanked him anyway.

Then something really strange happened. Over the stereo came the opening strains of "Thunder Road" by Bruce Springsteen.

"THIS IS MY FAVORITE SONG." Speedboat said as he stomped around the kitchen.

"Mine too," I said honestly. And then it was official: I was sentimental drunk.

"Screen door slammed. Mary's dress waved. Like a vision she danced across the porch while the radio played..."

Here I was, in a big empty house funded with brain damage money in the heart of Mount Mercy. I was so far away from where I should have been.

Not here. Not at this house or any other on the lake. I should have been East—the ocean and the boardwalk all lit in a wild dream while fireworks popped above them like flowers on fire burning themselves apart while the Ferris wheel rolled forever end over end over end...

Speedboat sang out of key and in another world, but he knew all the words. He swayed back and forth, looking at me with pained, heavy eyes that said, "Do you really have to leave?"

So I said to him, "Hey, you got any more of that good tequila?"

"YEAH," he shouted, happy as they come.

"Alright, let's have another," I said.

We knew all the words. We sang them all. Then we put the song on again, just as it should be done.

Then the door opened, and three small children ran into the house. Ron's kids. The lights switched on. A woman in an emerald green dress stood there holding a silver harp.

"Hey babe," Ron said.

"Hey…" she said like an angry prison guard.

"You're back early."

"Nice to see you too," she said.

"Harpie, this is my friend…"

"Hi, Harpie," I said. She drew her fingers across the silver harp, making an angelic string of notes.

Harpie

I SLEPT IN JUNE DOOM'S ROOM—held on tight to her while I listened to the darkness outside fall onto the mountain. As I held June, her breath sounded like a song that I was familiar with but couldn't explain the meaning to.

I couldn't help but think about Seth, how he said he'd spent so many nights lying next to Shannon, pretending to be asleep, while wired on coke.

With the gray daybreak, I came out in my boxer shorts. Feral was in the living room, as if he was just another piece of the furniture that needed to be dusted. He was gazing out the back deck's bay window, scratching his face. "This is amazing," he whispered. "Come over here."

"What?"

"Don't ask 'what' like a schmuck. Just fucking look."

Across the lake, Harpie was sitting on the dock in a large, white, wicker chair. She was in another emerald green dress, and her wild and curly red hair was blowing around in the breeze. Mist was coming off of the lake as she played her large silver harp. We could see her fingers moving but couldn't hear the music.

The wind was blowing away the music and the mist off the cool lake as if it was all the same.

"Who's that?" Feral asked with wonder in his voice. "I keep thinking there'll be a ripple in the middle of the lake. I keep expecting a hand to come up with a sword."

"Excalibur."

"Excalibur, right on. That's what I need."

I thought about the hundreds of thousands of lottery tickets crumpled up on the floor of his van.

"Who is that enchantress?"

"I think it's Speedboat's wife."

"Ssssh," he said. "Let me just have this moment, where I just pretend she's some mythological creature that's slipped out of some weird dimension and come here to change my entire life."

I looked at Feral. Felt bad for him in a way. He was always fucking up. The things he touched fell apart.

He'd burnt down our town's only video store. He was always getting shit on by seagulls. I've never seen a person get crapped on by so many birds. One time, we had a big party and these jugs of crappy vodka. We dumped an entire jug into this watermelon, and it sat in the fridge. Nobody ate the watermelon. It just sat in there and rotted for three weeks. One night, there was nothing else to drink, and the liquor store was closed. I watched in disgust as Feral ate the rotten watermelon just to get drunk.

He opened the window very slowly as not to disturb her, as if she was a bird that would just fly away.

"I wish she would sing," he said, spellbound.

"What song you wanna hear, man?"

"Anything but KISS," Feral said.

He looked at me so heartbroken. He killed Seth. He knew it. I knew it. It was inescapable; he was the most responsible. It was his coke. It was always his. He was the vein of that kind of thing with the group. I had to get away from him.

"We won the Kentucky Derby," I said.

"What does that mean?"

"Well, he won the fucking Kentucky Derby. That's where all that money came from."

"Oh."

"Good luck killed Seth."

"You should break my teeth out, man," he said. "That's what I deserve."

"Would that make you feel better?"

"It was an investment, ya know. He was gonna sell it for a profit."

"Nobody's responsible for anybody else's life."

"You don't believe that. I can hear it in your voice."

As he turned his face back towards the window, I wanted

to slam his face into the glass, push it right through. The blood would come right away. The glass would get stuck in his hair. He'd hold the cut with his hands while muttering curses then slump off to the bathroom while he bled all over the hardwood floor.

Instead, we watched Harpie on the pier. She'd stopped playing her harp and was looking at the house, but I knew she couldn't see us in the window.

We were invisible.

"Tried to do something good for you," he said.

"What good could you do, man?"

"Come look."

He led me down the hall. Trish was gone from the room or sleeping separate from him now.

"Look."

My guitar was leaning in the corner.

The broken neck was clamped, sandwiched between two pieces of wood. He said, "I know you said not to mess with it, but I did anyways. Sue me."

He set the guitar down in front of me on the shag carpet. "Well," he insisted, motioning to it.

I didn't understand.

"Unclamp the damn thing. Let's see if the glue held."

I twisted the knob. The clamp popped off. The wood fell away. The neck stayed in position.

"It worked," I said, surprised as he was.

"The real test will be tuning that thing up," he said.

We both looked at it down there, sitting flat on the carpet as if it was a thing of wonder that would, any second now, float up, start spinning in the air, and solve all the world's problems. I picked up the phone. Listening to the dial-tone, I started to tune the bottom string.

"What are you doing?"

"Dial tone is an f note."

I put my finger on the first fret, hit the string with my thumb, matched the dial-tone with the note, and hung up.

"An F note? Holy smokes," he said. "Never would have guessed."

Tomb

THAT MORNING, I DRAGGED THE LAST STONES up from the banks of the river and broke them apart with a heavy hammer. Everyone must have been awake, must have been twiddling thumbs, but they were very far away. Only whispers. Only guesses. I stacked stones. I mixed cement. There was no noise. Whoever was talking, was singing, was stirring coffee cups with metal spoons, was doing it beyond the walls of my invisible bubble.

Moss on boulders. Sticks and mud. Bare feet. Small cuts on ankles, on wrists. Fingers burnt from limestone. Water from a galvanized bucket dipped in the rushing river and dumped into a wheelbarrow with a hole. Shovel moved through and through. But I didn't squint when the sun came through the canopy of the trees. I didn't worry when I tied in the wall of my friend's crypt to the wall where his grandfather's ashes were. I barely noticed either. When the sun ducked behind a renegade cloud, the sweat on my body became a chill across my skin.

I smashed apart a stone on the back of a harder stone and gathered all the chips. I scattered those chips between the inner walls and covered the floor with sharp points to keep away unwelcome animals. Unwelcome others. Unwelcome dreams. I crawled into the crypt and lay down on the chips of stone. Not sharp to me.

I closed my eyes but didn't sleep. No-one would have stopped me if I did. Low ceiling. There was less and less light with each breath I took. My heart slowed. My lungs were an accordion of heavy breath.

Thinking about things. Pictures in the dark. A football thrown down a dead-end street where we had broken all the street lights. Fireworks shot out of a bottle of Jim Beam. A map of Los Angeles underneath crossed pupils, slacked mouth, words like a roller derby at 3 a.m. Swimming at night in August rain. Racing in the Nissan on a dirt road through darkened pines. Graveyards not like this—rows and rows of crumbled stones. Death, just an inside joke on a Saturday night.

When I did crawl out, all elbows and knees, there were noises in the trees again. Things began to move. Life was returning.

Midday. Cement curing. Job complete ... or as close I could complete it. Beside the gap, the door, the entry, I stacked the last of the stone so that Seth's brother could close off the space after the ashes were placed inside.

Knew I couldn't bring myself to finish.

24

HARPIE WANTED TO THROW A PARTY. No-one objected. She invited all of the neighbors from the surrounding lake houses, which weren't many, and encouraged us to call people up from Jersey.

"This area is like a vacation paradise," she said. "Tell your friends. Plenty of room, here. Saturday night."

The look in her eye recalled sharks at feeding time. Animals in the zoo, looking at the zookeepers. What you got next?

Harpie leaned against me, her big breasts pushing together. She'd been into the red wine. Her teeth were gray and purple.

"Who wouldn't wanna get up into these mountains?"

Ron, sat there dimly, drunk, with his dented head. He ignored his wife falling all over everyone as if it was her art. She had a way of talking too close. She had a way of touching a person too much when she spoke. Desperation. I could see it on her. Ron had a way of yawning when she spoke.

For some reason, I was feeling nostalgic. I wanted to be around everyone I knew. I kept picking up the phone and dialing numbers, drinking more beer, dialing more numbers. I called everyone I knew ... everyone I could remember a phone number for.

Studio Mike answered on the eleventh ring. I'd been bugging him to come up here for a couple days. Even emailed him our address. "Sorry, bro. I was asleep."

I said, "Come upstate. Get up here." I was drunk. "Just come, man."

I imagined I could hear, inside the soundproof walls of his home studio, his Gilligan hat flopping around over the wires.

"I can't," he said. "There's a band coming in."

"Alright," I said.

"Hey," he said, "Ethan was looking for you."

"For me?"

"He said he owes you money. I told him where you were."

"Ah fuck it, whatever. He doesn't owe me money though."

"Well, have fun up there."

I said goodbye.

K Neon came and sat down on the other side of the kitchen counter.

"You alright?" she asked.

"Probably not," I said.

She leaned across the counter and kissed me on the mouth. I kissed back. June walked into the kitchen, saw us, and said, "You're both pathetic people."

"Pathetic?" K Neon seemed offended. "I don't think so."

"Really, you both are," June said, walking back out onto Ron's back deck.

The night slipped away after that. I kept drinking. Ron and Feral were all about it. The stereo went to maximum capacity, and the beer kept flowing.

I woke up on the couch. My lips were split from dehydration, and crusted drool ran down to my chin. The sun was in my eyes. The clock said that it was two in the afternoon.

Harpie cornered me in the kitchen.

"Let's go for a ride," she said.

I didn't protest. She led me outside and said, "You drive."

"That's fine."

As we went down the mountain, animals scattered at the sight of the truck. Out on the road, we headed farther—towards the highway. She wanted to go to the grocery store and the liquor store. We headed east on the highway.

"You're friend died?"

"Yes, he did."

"Ron tried to kill himself, you know."

"How did he try?"

"Once with pills. Once, I found him asleep on the back deck with a rope tied in a noose, just hanging over the limb of a big tree we used to have."

"Used to have…"

"'Cause I had a tree service come and cut it down."

"I don't know what to say."
"Who would? People die. People are dying."
"Yes," I agreed, turning down the gravel hill towards town.
"You want some advice?"
"Yeah," I said.
"Don't try to figure anything out."

25

THE WHITE BMW SKIDDED UP, blocking the driveway. I was standing on the crabgrass talking to June in the shade of the elm tree. I turned my head and couldn't believe what I saw: this sudden materialization, like a bad dream. I blinked, but the car was still there.

Ethan got out. His hair got shaggier. He had a beard. He turned to face me but didn't look the same. Something was wrong with his eyes.

"What's he doing here?" June asked.

"Best question I ever heard in my life."

Denise Santalucia was in the passenger seat, looking straight ahead. Her makeup was running. Her eyes were puffy and wounded.

In the backyard, horseshoes clanked on metal pins, hitting the dirt, ricocheting up into the sky. People were yelling. Classic rock blared on the radio. All of that was a million miles away at that point.

"There you are, you fuck," Ethan yelled.

"What's the problem?" I asked, setting my beer can down at my feet in the nest of roots under the elm tree.

"I've been looking for you."

"For what?"

"You know for what," he said while walking towards me. "She's pregnant," he said. "It's your kid."

"No, man," I said.

"Well, it's not mine. She's your problem. I brought her here for you to take care of. It's your kid. You can take her to the clinic. I'm not."

"Get in your fruity little car, turn around, and go the fuck back to mommy and daddy," I said.

The crazy sonofabitch really did want to fight. I didn't think he had it in him, but I realized it too late. He lowered his shoulder and slammed into me, knocking me on the ground. He was fighting like a wild animal. His arms flailed all around. His knees drove up into me. We rolled around in the dirt. His soft, pink hands closed around my throat.

I could hear June yelling out. Then ... I didn't hear much of anything. Ethan's fist caught me in the side of the head and made my ears ring. When I swung my hand around, it connected with the side of his face, and we fell over the other way.

I hit him again—punched him in the throat. His foot came up and hit me in the gut. This drove him back. I followed him down to the earth, smacking his head into the nest of roots underneath the elm tree. He groaned.

I stumbled to my feet.

Ethan was still on the ground. Blood oozed from his brow. Sloppy.

June stood there, frozen.

Denise yelled, "STOP!"

She'd come out of the car at some point and was standing there by speedboat's mailbox. Stop? Sure. Yeah, we were stopped. My whole head was swimming with noise.

I looked back at Ethan. His mouth was all bloody. He was still on the ground but started to move. After digging in his pants pocket, he pulled out a small silver gun. It was his father's gun.

"Stay back," he yelled at me.

I had no interest in getting any closer. Not with him pointing that thing at my nuts.

Denise yelled, "STOP!"

Ethan got up on his feet.

"SHE WAS MY GIRL!"

"I didn't sleep with her," I said. "Seth did, and he's already dead."

His lip trembled. It was a mistake he regretted right away. I could tell. Well, regret or not, I lunged at him. Punched him square in the nose. It popped. Blood bloomed all down his white shirt. He collapsed onto the crabgrass, writhing. I put my foot on his stomach and pushed down. The gun lay in the grass.

I was seeing red. I stomped down on that little chickenshit's belly. The air rushed out of him. I took the gun and stormed off to his BMW. Denise jumped out of my way. In one smooth motion, I smashed out the passenger side window with the butt of the gun. Then I started smashing out the windshield.

I must have thought I was a real hard-ass, like this was a mob movie. I just kept slamming the butt of the gun down on the windshield. It cracked worse and worse. It was safety glass. The windshield wouldn't fall in. What I was doing was a fool's errand. I hurled the gun down the hill towards the lake. Sploosh.

The car was still running. I bent in and dropped it in neutral. It started to roll forward a little.

I walked over to the F-250, jumped inside, and rolled right up to the smashed-out shitbox's rear fender. Then I hit the gas and pushed that fucking BMW right into the lake. It didn't get as far as I would have liked. The nose of the car sunk down into the mud. The engine flooded out.

When I backed the truck up, Ethan was standing under the elm tree.

"I'll kill you," he said, but the fight was gone from him.

It was gone from me too.

Denise, who was standing next to him, looked at him like she wanted to kick him in the balls.

"A gun? You pulled a fucking gun?"

Ethan didn't say anything. He just stood there. His eyes glazed over. The blood came down his nose.

"It wasn't loaded," he finally said.

I looked at Denise's belly, the small pout of it. Seth's kid was in there.

People started to come streaming out of the backyard. Terry. Feral. Trish. June. They were all there, looking at us.

"What happened?" I heard Feral exclaim.

"There was an accident," I said.

Ethan didn't say a word.

"Stupid fuck crashed his car right into the lake."

Terry started laughing. No-one else laughed. He was the drunkest ... or the highest.

Ethan called the wrecker himself. The tow truck came, hooked the back of the BMW, pulled it out of the lake, and yanked it up onto the flatbed.

Denise was in the house with Trish. Ethan climbed up into

the wrecker. I watched from the lawn as the truck pulled away. The muck and filth leaking out of the 5 Series left a wet trail on the road as it rolled away for good.

It wasn't until later I realized my wrist was broken. My hand was cracked. I'd done it hitting him. Or I'd done it with the gun while breaking out the windshield of his silly white car.

26

I DROVE K BACK TO COLLEGE. Providence, Rhode Island. We had one last conversation three hours after the drop off. The phone in my motel room rang.

"You want to come hang out tonight?"

"And do what?" I asked.

"Friend of mine, Jackie, she wants to meet you. It'd be fun. We could come over there."

"Another time," I said, hanging up.

Motel

I WAS OUTSIDE A DIMLY LIT BAR. IT WAS RAINING. In this time of the world, there were still pay phones, and it was often raining. I dialed Studio Mike's number. It sounded like I'd woke him. That didn't surprise me.

"Been trying to get a hold of you," he said.

"I've been around."

Mike laughed, "Been around? I'm sure you have been."

"I took that girl back to college."

"Which one?"

"The one I don't like as much as the other one," I said.

"Oh, what a problem to have."

"Gone," I said. "The one I liked took a jumbo jet off into the impossible distance. Texas."

"Hey, listen," Mike said, his voice low and gruff, "this is important. I've been getting phone calls from that label."

My heart stopped.

"I mailed those demos out. Well, they've been calling. A woman. Cheryl."

Ethan's sister.

"Been twice now, dude," Mike said. "I've been trying to get a hold of you. You gotta get a cell. It's 2005, get with it."

"Alright, alright. What do they want?"

"You gotta talk to them. I'm not sure, but they seem interested in Ottermeat."

"Did you tell them the drummer's dead?"

"Absolutely not," he said. "I didn't say a word about that."

I paced around in the booth. The operator's recording came on, "Please deposit seventy-five cents for each additional minute." I scrambled in my pockets but didn't have any change.

"Hey, give me that number!"

"What, the label?"

"The number that keeps calling you."

"Oh, fuck. Hold on…"

There were shuffling papers. I waited for the line to go dead.

"Here you go, write this down…"

I wrote the phone number on my arm with a BIC pen. It was a Seattle area code … not that I knew that off the top of my head back then. Mike and I didn't get a chance to say anything else to each other. The line went dead. The rain came down harder.

I didn't wanna leave the phone booth. There were a million reasons not to leave it. The rain didn't help things either. It kept coming down harder and harder. The wind sent it sideways.

I smiled like a madman, but my biggest fear was that I was too late. I'd call the label and they wouldn't know who I was or what I wanted.

I opened up the door and ran out into the rain and down the street. I was parked two blocks away on a side street. I drove like a maniac through Providence, back towards the little ratty motel where I was staying in Warwick.

There, I got on the phone in my room and called the number in Seattle. A woman answered. After I explained who I was and why I was calling, she said, "I have no idea who you are."

"Well, I have no idea who you are, either, so that makes two of us."

"OK, I'm gonna hang up on you, now."

I mentioned Ethan's sister, their lawyer. That meant nothing to her. She said, "Yeah, I know our lawyer's name too. I also know our janitor's name … it's Paul."

"You were trying to get a hold of me," I said.

"Me? I was trying to get you? No, you have the wrong person…"

"I'm looking for Cheryl!"

"Oh … shit." I heard the girl yell for Cheryl. She came to the phone.

"Hey," Cheryl said, out of breath. "Who's this?"

I told her. She seemed excited to talk.

"I was trying to get in contact with you."

"Yeah."

She said she was impressed by the tape we'd sent. Not the one with Ethan, the weirder one. The one with all the noise.

"You play guitar?"

"That's me."

"Okay. Can you bring the band out here?"

"Yeah," I said, "I certainly can."

She gave me an address. "Come to that address and ask for me, alright?"

"Sure thing," I said.

"Cool. I'm so glad that you're interested. That makes my night."

I put the phone down.

Holy fuck. Come out to Seattle and meet with a record label about a deal? That's what was happening here? I couldn't believe it. I sat there on the edge of the bed in the rotting motel room, looking at the wall and all of the brown spots from people that'd smoked in there for an eternity.

I didn't have any money. Barely had enough to pay for the motel room itself.

The next morning, I stuck a For Sale sign on the back of the F-250. Within two days, I sold it to a guy who had a lawn cutting service. He was going to use the truck to haul around lawn mowers. Good for him. I took his cash to the airport, bought my plane ticket, and flew west with my guitar and my tube amp that was still dusty and full of concrete powder.

27

I'D LOST CONTACT with everyone. They drifted in and out of my life. I blinked for a second, and those people were gone—replaced by new ones. I found myself in a new city, sitting out on a shaky fire escape and looking down on a new street—brick paved and frost-lined.

Fog in the mornings. Green plants hanging in all the windows. Pretty girls on bicycles with scarves flowing behind them as they rolled downhill. Some wave at you. Some don't even notice. It's hard to keep track of all the humanity and what it really means as it comes, as it leaves, as it settles in.

Seattle. I was there … again. I'd just come back from a three-week tour of the west coast. I was playing guitar in a band that the label hooked me up with. Things were good but not smooth. The guys in the band were cold, distant, strange. They played nervy new wave music and had a violin player. Not my first choice.

It was all because of Cheryl, the lady at the label. She felt bad for me, and how could you blame her? I showed up at her office with a backpack of clothes, a broken guitar, and a busted amp. When I broke the news to her that the drummer of the band she wanted to sign was dead, she just sat there with her mouth open.

"Like dead dead?"

"Built his tomb with my own hands."

I sat down on the couch in the lobby. The bitchy receptionist I'd spoken to earlier brought me back a cup of coffee. The morning was slow and weird. I was jet-lagged. My broken hand was almost useable. I never had it looked at. I still could barely make a fist.

Cheryl took me out to brunch. I'd never been to brunch.

"It's just what stupid white people call breakfast after 9 a.m.," she said.

She bought me mimosas and bacon, eggs Florentine, fresh bread baked right there. I ate the garnish, not understanding. She ate it too so as to not make me feel bad.

"Tastes minty," she said.

She probably just felt bad for me, but she said that she had some session work with a band if I was interested. I jumped on the opportunity. Their lead guitarist had wound up in rehab. Pills.

"Interested? Yeah."

One thing led to another. Another session. Another session after that. Before long, I was living above a little coffee and donut shop, Top Pot, on Summit Ave.

I was hooked on Nick Drake, Pink Moon. I used to play it on a never ending loop. It's hard for me to think about that time and that neighborhood without internalizing a Nick Drake song.

It was a cramped apartment, and I really didn't have anybody. I used to go and sit down in Top Pot. I was lonely. I still carried around a photo booth snapshot from that night in Seaside when the Ferris wheel jammed and we played Mrs. Pac-Man and Frog Bog. June and K would forever sit there, in black and white, grinning like devils. The picture was right before we went to see Madame Woo-the Dead.

One afternoon, I took a black Sharpie and colored K Neon out of the photos. She disappeared into the black void of my forgotten pleasures; June Doom became brighter.

She hadn't left my head at all really. That's how it was. I thought about her too much. Where she was. What she was doing. I carried the snap shot around with me everywhere. And if I felt especially alone, I'd take it out. Then she was there. June … a whole row of her, grinning—each cell only slightly different than the one above it, and all of them with a blacked-out apparition.

Our nervy new wave band with the violin player started the tour at the Crocodile in Seattle. Shows followed at the Northern in Olympia, Washington. Then we slowly made our way south—the Doug Fir Lounge in Portland, the Chapel in San

Francisco, the Fulton 55 in Fresno, the Constellation Room in Santa Ana, Muddy Waters in Santa Barbara, Echo and The Smell in Los Angeles—before finishing up at the Til-Two Club in San Diego.

Los Angeles. That was the worst. The whole time I was there, I felt like my blood was glue. My teeth were packed solid with grits of sand. I drank way too much and didn't sleep. I thought about Seth the whole time and his big plan to get us out to Los Angeles. Here I was, doing what he wanted to do. He was dead. I was alive. But there was no joy in it at all.

The whole tour, I kept looking out at the crowd of people and hoping to see June. I never did. We weren't in communication. She had no idea how I felt about her. I'd just figured it out myself. She didn't have a crystal ball. …well, maybe she did. That wouldn't surprise me.

When the tour was over, we went back to Seattle. I figured the band was probably done with me and that I'd go back to doing session work for the label, but their manager liked me and asked if I'd like to fly out to Idaho, where there they were from, to work on some new material. I agreed.

In the meantime, I was back in the apartment. I missed a lot of things about New Jersey. Mostly the weirdos I left behind. My place was small and cramped but clean. Where were all of Feral's boxes? Where were his VHS tapes and records?

I took out the photo strip.

I stared at June.

I grabbed my bag that I never unpacked.

I went back out onto the street.

28

TEXAS SUN. SWEAT. I waited outside the entrance to the lecture hall building, pretending to read the campus newspaper. I'd never read a newspaper in my life. I could see in through the glass door. The security guard at his desk was splitting time between watching a basketball game and checking the IDs of kids walking in. I wondered if the security guard was gonna hurt me as bad as Boyd had that night at the boardwalk.

The second he stood up to use the bathroom, I slipped inside and past his desk.

There were two lecture halls. One was empty. The other one was crammed solid with kids. I opened up the door and walked inside.

I'd seen this kind of thing in movies, a college lecture hall, but was never in one myself. It could easily hold three hundred kids. I looked up at them as they sat amphitheater style: legs crossed, slouched in their flip-up plastic chairs, but "Where's June Doom" was all I thought.

I scanned the rows. There were too many faces. I kept thinking I saw other people that I knew, but they had no purpose being in Texas (or in some cases alive). Maybe all the dead were here in Texas.

I was standing in the aisle far too long. The door opened again, and the man who must have been the professor walked in. He carried a leather briefcase. He wore a corduroy blazer. His hair was long, gray, and slicked back. He was running this show. He whisked past me as he made his way to the podium in the center of the lecture hall.

I was running out of time, or it felt like I was running out of time, so I took the stairs two at a time. I passed rows of oblivious kids, who were focused on the professor … not me. I needed to find June. I was going crazy. I really was.

Why did I have to find her right that minute? Was something bad gonna happen to my brain? I had no real idea. I couldn't really explain it. The thought had just been growing and growing. It sent me away from Seattle in a dizzying circle.

I took a flight to Austin-Bergstrom International Airport. I hadn't slept the night before. Nervous energy. So much nervous energy—a steamroller crushing my spine. On the flight, I downed Jack and Coke after Jack and Coke, but they didn't have any effect on me. I couldn't get drunk, so I just stopped. Completely.

That was that. The last drink I ever took.

Our jet skidded into a wall of heat and dust and still-air. Then, after a cab from the airport to the university, I just kept asking, asking around on campus, till I found a girl who knew exactly who June was.

"Red haired chick with the Joy Division shirt? She's in my Classicism vs. Neo-Classicism course."

I bounded to the top of the lecture hall. The professor started to talk on the microphone. He welcomed everyone and made a comment about what a nice day it was outside, about how all the birds were going crazy for it and would probably shit all over his Jaguar.

"That's all they seem to enjoy. Who am I to stop them?"

There were some laughs. I took a seat and looked down at him. He told another joke.

"I'd like to save all that bird shit for a year and dump it on their tree from above in a hot air balloon. Wonder how that would make them feel."

Everyone laughed at that. I settled into my seat, still scanning the backs of all the kids' heads.

Where was June?

The lights began to dim. I realized the professor was going to have an audio-visual accompaniment with his lecture. I sank down into my seat, relaxed, became comfortable with the idea. I wasn't gonna find her right now, but somehow I'd weaseled my way into a college lecture.

The professor began to show slides. He began to talk

about them. It was done in such a way … a way I'd never even considered before. I found myself surprisingly enthralled. I got sucked into his lecture, entranced by everything he was saying. I almost had to slap myself.

Jesus Christ! Here I was, finally, in a fucking college lecture. I wanted to shake the kid sitting next to me and ask, "What took me so long to get here? Why did I hold out tooth and nail against this?"

About ten minutes went by. The light changed below; the door had opened. I watched a figure walk into the lecture hall. A girl.

It was her.

I couldn't see her. She was cast in shadow. But I knew it was her. No doubt in my mind. She sat about six rows below me and two seats in.

Instantly, I stood up and started making my way down the aisle like a lunatic. I climbed over the back of the empty seat beside her and tapped her on the shoulder as I sat down.

"June," I said.

She flinched away from my touch.

"June," I said, "it's me."

"What the fuck," she uttered as if drenched in cold water. "What are you doing here?"

"I'm here for the lecture."

"Lecture? Are you insane?"

"You were late," I said a little too loudly.

The professor stopped talking into his microphone and looked up into the seats. He couldn't see us because of the lights shining on him, but he was conscious of our noise.

"Seriously, why are you in Texas?"

"You," I said. "For you!"

"Don't be crazy," June said.

"Hey, I got off an airplane and came here to find you."

The professor spoke into the microphone, "Is there a problem out there? Am I interrupting something important?"

"Let's get outta here," June said.

She stood up, and I followed her through the lecture hall, down the hallway, and into the brightness.

I kissed her.

We fell against the block wall. The security guard at his little desk leered at us. We were high entertainment to him. June kissed me deeper. I was looking for all the answers to my life in her mouth.

I found most of them.

Ace

THAT CHRISTMAS, JUNE CAME BACK to New Jersey. We'd been seeing each other a lot. I took whatever excuse I could to go see her in Texas. She came and stayed with me in Seattle on all her breaks.

We both missed snow. There were many feet of it in my hometown, where all my friends were. We met in Denver and hopped on a flight together to Newark. Feral picked us up at the airport in Seth's old car. The Altima.

"Why are you driving this?"

"Van was hit by a train. Cut in half. Probably for the best."

"Oh," June said.

Feral said, "How's your hot blonde girlfriend?"

"I wouldn't know. She's a bitch. I haven't talked to her in a year," June said.

"I stole a fancy painting from her. Burnt it in my backyard."

June Doom stared straight ahead and said, "Just as well."

Feral didn't live with Trish any longer. They were still seeing each other, but I got the impression that things were on the rocks. That it was just a matter of time. They were both incomplete. They were both still on search and destroy missions.

But it was the holidays.

Denise and Trish had an apartment together. It was a nice place—a condo that'd sprung up on the same vacant lot where Commando Video had once been: an acre and a half of woods between the road and Food Universe.

I looked out the window in awe of the beauty of the snow

falling on the industrial slums of Newark/Elizabeth/Linden—New Jersey. The armpit of America. You have to be from here to think it's beautiful. Even then, there's something wrong with you.

Feral turned his head.

"You alright?" he asked me.

"Ahh, it's a lot of things," I said, pointing all around the interior of Seth's car. (I'd never been in it comfortably like this. I was always stretched around the drum set, fighting for survival.) "It's the snow, I think."

"Snow? Doesn't it snow, like, every day in Seattle?"

"It doesn't snow at all in Seattle."

"Get the fuck outta here," he said.

"For real."

Feral looked in the rearview.

"June, tell me this bad man is lying, playing me for a rube."

"He's not, Feral. People think he's fucking around, but he's never lying."

Jesus Christ, that almost brought a tear to my eye. June had somehow gotten to know me better than anybody else had ever gotten to know me in my entire life.

I decided right then—in the Nissan, as we drove past the Bayway oil refinery with all its sick smoke and toxic waste bellowing into the sky—that I wouldn't let June get away.

"Actually got a job," Feral said.

"Who, you? No fucking way."

The ride was good. We spent it with the radio on low and just shot the shit, told jokes, recounted things that seemed like a decade away ... though it'd only been a year.

When we pulled off the highway onto route 9, Feral said, "They're at Mary Beth's house. You guys mind going there?"

"Not at all," I said. Trish's mom... I wondered if she'd ever gotten that LeSabre fixed.

"Tomorrow, I've got to get over to the Mayweather," I said out loud to no-one in particular. "Aldo is being Santa Claus again and passing out gifts."

"He lost a lot of weight," said Feral.

I was honestly surprised.

"He's skinny now. Looks good for an old fuck. He'll have to stuff pillows under his shirt to play Santa Claus now."

"You see him around?"

"Aldo? Damn right. Trish says he's doing good as fuck. She knows better. She takes his blood ... I don't know why.

But I see him almost every other day at my job. I'm a big shot orderly at that place now. You should see me, man. I mop the hell out of the Mayweather. I'm a mopping maniac."

"An honest job … holy smokes."

"Yeah. Ha! Tell me about it. It sucks in its own special way, but then that's alright too I guess. Your boy Aldo reads to this… Well, I'm not sure what's wrong with the guy, but Aldo reads to him a lot."

"Sounds about right," I said.

"I'll take you over there," Feral said. "Tomorrow. Just say when. Nothing else going on."

He pulled into the development behind Food Universe. The sun fell. Christmas lights blinked on. That's the good thing about the development back there. It didn't seem like the people had any money, but Christmas lights didn't suffer in the least. I guess when you have less, you've got to have spirit to survive.

Feral pulled up to the front of the house. There was the LeSabre. It looked beautiful with the lights blinking around it. Good as new. Some things can be fixed.

"Looks good."

"Bro, it's an old-ass LeSabre. Get a life."

Feral knocked so loud on the front door that he shook the wreath and bells.

Mary Beth shouted, "Come in!"

They were at the long, wooden table when we walked in. The house was warm. Willy Nelson was singing "Pretty Paper." I heard a baby softly cooing.

Denise, Trish, and the young boy Jackie, whose birthday party I crashed that time, were all playing Yahtzee. The dice rattled around in the plastic cup then tumbled across the table. Mary Beth met us in the doorway and gave us all hugs.

"I don't know you Belle," she said to June, "but I can tell right away that you're my favorite."

"Ma, I'm right here," Trish said. "Don't be telling strangers that they're your favorite with me right here."

"Well, you keep hitting Yahtzee. I can't help it."

We stepped into the kitchen. Trish gave me a kiss hello. Denise waved awkwardly. Things had ended strangely between the two of us.

I walked right to the baby and peeked down.

"What's this little guy's name?"

"Ace," she said.

"Ace?"

I wanted to cry. I really did. I looked down into the baby's eyes—the same eyes as Seth. The baby also had the same hair, and would probably grow up with that same gap between his front teeth.

"Pick him up," said Denise.

"Not yet," I said. "Give me a little while."

We sat down at the table. Mary Beth asked a score of questions. She wanted all the updates. She'd heard a lot from Trish about my band.

"I even got a CD player for my car now," she said, telling the story of when she met me … when I crashed into her down by the river.

Denise said, "I've seen an even better crash."

"When?"

"He hit my ex's car. Pushed it into a lake," she laughed.

"A lake!" Mary Beth seemed very amused. "So, I guess I got off lucky!"

The wine came out. Many bottles of red wine. Mary Beth passed the glasses out and said, "I got a little prayer for friends that I like to say during the holidays…"

Mary Beth stood up. Her over-sized gray sweater hung down on her scorecard. She raised her glass.

"It goes a little something like this: may all your silly or dire or imaginary troubles lessen and find all the holes in your pockets on your way to Heaven. Or if you get lost and stumble into Hell, save me a spot at the bar."

We all raised our glasses and took a sip, except for Denise, who just did a salute with her glass and set it back down. She was still breast-feeding.

"Here's to friends and family, those that are here, and those we wish were here," she concluded.

I took another sip. Willie started singing "Rudolph" in the other room. The record had a scratch in it; the needle kept jumping. Trish got up to fix it.

"What's that?" I asked, pointing out a small, framed picture on the wall.

"Oh! That picture's crazy," Trish said. "Remember that?"

"Damn right, I do."

It was a photo of Trish as a little girl dressed up as a witch. The photo had been taken at my old house long ago. There I was dressed as a werewolf with big, fake, hairy hands.

Mary Beth said, "Look how little you were!"

We all stood there looking at the picture. Then Mary Beth said, "Oh, I got an idea…" She looked at June Doom. "Will you put on Elvis?"

June Doom never looked happier in her whole life. Elvis on the record player on Christmas Eve.

I transported myself away from the table as a new game of Yahtzee started up. I stopped and peaked inside the cage of babbits that June saved from the lawn mowers. I tried to guess what their names would be.

"Whaddya guys want? Carrots? Fresh water?"

They blinked at me but looked content. I sat on the couch and watched the fire for a little bit. Then I went out into the living room. Trish followed.

"You look good," she said. "Happy."

"That's the rumor, and I believe it."

"Something came to my apartment for you a couple days ago. A letter."

She passed me the envelope.

"Oh boy, what's this?"

It was from Mark. He hadn't been able to get a hold of me, because I was always somewhere different in those days. So he sent the letter to one of my friends (my oldest friend, now that I think of it). Trish left me to read it.

Lee,

Wanted to write to you and let you know that Seth was lucky to have a friend like you. Sometimes the world can get pretty gray. It's not all sunshine. Today, I feel a hurt in my heart lessening because my brother's ashes are resting in a safe little spot here on our mountain. Everybody ought to have a tomb like this for themselves and their loved ones.

The lake is quiet. It barely moves. I like that. The water is, mostly, the way I remember it. We both loved it here as kids. We didn't have the easiest childhood, with our mom and dad ditching us the way that they did, but we used to look forward to the summers here.

Now, I think I've got no choice but to stay here. I'm leaving Chicago. This place is the right kind of quiet. There's a sentimentality here that I don't wanna be away from. I think everybody should cling onto that aspect of their lives.

I'm sitting at the kitchen table, looking out the window at the water now as I write this, remembering how my brother and me used to paddle out into the lake to fish. We never caught any fish, of course, but that's because there weren't any to begin with. And our outtings always ended the same way, with the rowboat flipping.

Put two brothers in rowboat, if it doesn't flip, something's wrong.

Really, what I wanted to say to you was thanks. Your friendship has meant a lot to me. You and Seth were like brothers, and anybody who is a brother to mine is a brother to me. Please try to stay in contact. It'd mean a lot to me. My address will always be here at Tull Lake, and you are welcome, whenever you'd like, to come and stay.

The neighbors seem friendly and ask about you often. The guy across the water, he came over yesterday and we had a talk. He said he'd hit the old rowboat with his speedboat and vaporized it. He's going to bring over a new one he says. That's probably for the best. New boat, new memories.

Maybe I'll even be able to catch a fish in it.

I hope things are easy. I hope you keep things light. I hope you enjoy it all deeply.

Be good at all costs,
Mark

P.S. About what we'd talked about. Florida and your missing person ... I did finally get in contact with your mom thanks to some big help around the office. She was hard to find. If you're ready and want to talk to her, I have an address and a telephone number. I hope that's some help. She sounded good, like she would like to talk. Pick up the phone.

Denise came into the living room holding baby Ace, who was so small and quiet. She sat down on the blue couch across from me.

"How are you these days? Okay?"

"I'm alright," I said. "Bombshell after bombshell."

"My parents still hate me."

"Give them time," I said.

I told her about living on the West Coast and flying back and forth to see June when I could. Denise told me about how she was terrified when she found out that she was pregnant, but that it was the best thing that had happened to her.

"I'd probably be dead if it wasn't for this little guy."

Denise pushed down the strap of her shirt and exposed her breast. The tattoo: Daddy's Little Angel. Ace sucked her nipple, and Denise looked down at him.

"Everybody wants something. It's nice to be able to give them what they need."

"Yeah."

"'Cause, life is weird and hard …"

"Certainly."

"But, I don't feel like how I used to feel."

"You never will."

"Things change, right?"

"Yes, they do," I said. She winced. The baby bit her. He was feeding a little too rough.

Elvis said something about angels and heaven and hope on the record player. It sounded spot on. In the kitchen, I could hear the cup shaking and then the roll of dice on the table.

BIG THANKS to Rae Buleri; the Idiom kids—Mark Brunetti, Keith Baird, Andrew "Ink" Feindt, and Chris McIntyre; the Uno Kudo crew—Aaron Dietz, Chuck Howe, Erin McParland; An extra big thanks to Ashley Perez, who was kind enough to give some close thoughts on F-250 when this novel was just a third draft; thanks to Christopher Allen for his close eye and attention to detail, Scott McClanahan, Brian Alan Ellis, Sara Lippman, Ben Loory, Amber Sparks, Ryder Collins, Alex Reed, Jason Neese; and the fine people at the Night Owl Cafe—Robert Vaughan, Meg Tuite and Michael Gillan Maxwell. You each helped make this book something a wee bit better. Thanks to my family, both sides, the Smith's and the Buleri's. Much love. MUCHAS GRACIAS.

Bud Smith is the author of the novel Tollbooth, the short story collection, Or Something Like That, and the poetry collection Everything Neon. He works heavy construction in New Jersey, and lives in New York City.

www.budsmithwrites.com

Piscataway House
Publications

Pisctaway House Publications is an independent
publishing company based out of New Jersey.

Our books range from the anthologized back
issues of The Idiom Magazine to a collection of
Haiku from Central Jersey Poets to the collected
writings from the MFA program at William
Paterson University.

You can learn more about PHP and The Idiom
Magazine at www.theidiommag.com